Sins of the Fathers

D0063767

SINS OF THE FATHERS

WILL CUNNINGHAM

THOMAS NELSON PUBLISHERS
Nashville • Atlanta • London • Vancouver

Published in association with the literary agency of Alive Communications, 1465 Kelly Johnson Blvd., Suite #320, Colorado Springs, CO 80920.

Published in Nashville, Tennessee, by Thomas Nelson, Inc., and distributed in Canada by Word Communications, Ltd., Richmond, British Columbia, and in the United Kingdom by Word (UK), Ltd., Milton Keynes, England.

Library of Congress Cataloging-in-Publication Data

Cunningham, Will, 1959–
    Sins of the fathers / Will Cunningham.
        p.   cm.
    ISBN 0-7852-8129-0
    I. Title.
PS3553.U54S56   1997
813'.54—dc21   97-17334
                                                                          CIP

Printed in the United States of America
1 2 3 4 5 6 7 - 03 02 01 00 99 98 97

DEDICATION

To Cindy—who bore me joy in the form of boys—
And to all who believe, as I do,
that abortion unchecked
will come back around to haunt us.

Acknowledgments

I would like to acknowledge the men and women at Thomas Nelson Publishers who gave me the opportunity to follow my dream. Victor, you have been more than patient. I admire your ability to steer magnificent ships. Brian, you are the happy butcher man. Thank you for trimming the fat so painlessly. Sharon, I measure my relationship with the company by the number of birthday cards you have sent. And finally, to the owner of that lacy, lilting voice on the 1-800 line . . . I owe my deep regards for your constant vigilance. In the wee hours between nod and dawn, when all the world was asleep and I alone fought the one-eyed Macintosh, you were always just a call away. Truly, we entertain angels unaware.

INTRODUCTION

FOR YEARS I HAD THIS RECURRING DREAM that I kept to myself for fear its value would depreciate if it was ever translated into words. But if doing so will help even one person, I am willing to risk all in the pages to come.

In the dream I am driving in Montana. Or it could be one of the Dakotas, or another planet even. You know how dreams are. They make no sense, and they make perfect sense. At any rate, the fact that I am traveling limitless miles untethered, far from the Personal Rapid Transit, should tell you this is a good dream. The top is down and the acoustic wave is blasting all my favorite oldies, when I come across a fine-looking woman and her baby by the side of the road, and I decide to give them a lift. "At last," she utters with the voice of an angel, "a gentleman." She swings open the door, slides into the passenger seat, hands me the baby, and buckles her restraint harness.

"Turn it up," she commands with a smile. "I just adore this song." Dumbfounded by her brashness, I am slow to respond and she ends up helping herself. We drive in silence, she listening intently to a second millennium tune called "Yesterday," and I wondering what she will do when she learns that I murder people for a living.

As is often the case with dreams, there is a sudden twist in the tale and soon the woman's widowed mother shows up in the car with us. Surprisingly, I am not the least bit disappointed. In fact, I pull over and build a house for the widow out of mud-bricks from a creek next to a field, next to the road, where I have abandoned my car for the pleasure of walking hand in hand with someone I could fall madly in love though that is a punishable offense in real life.

Through waist-high wheat I wade with the woman, stopping now and then to kiss her red mouth under the golden sky. She asks whether VC would be incensed if they knew an employee of theirs was consorting with someone of the opposite sex. I lie and tell her VC has no idea where I am. All the while, the widow rocks on the porch of her mud-brick house, and the baby sleeps in her arms, and the world does not miss us for that half hour of reverie.

As a younger man, I had the dream so many times it was like having déjà vu of having déjà vu. Sometimes when I was awake, I could almost feel the woman's lips brush softly against my ear, and hear her whispering, "Come out to me, John. Come out to the fields and you will find me there." For years, I could hardly watch men putting up hay north of the river without feeling a terrible ache in my chest to provide for the woman's child, and comfort her mother, and become so lost in her love that I had no earthly idea where I left off and where she began.

They tell me love once flourished before the turn of the millennium. It was kites with friends on blustering Sundays, warm cookies for someone called a garbage man, the sparkle in a woman's eyes at the first hint that a new life was growing in her body. Love was kin. Love was country. Love was culture. Love *was*.

Which is the problem.

It must have been in a flurry of goodwill that my parents conceived me sixty years ago. For upon my arrival, an awful caterwauling commenced that did not cease until their divorce was final.

Since I was an only child, I had no siblings by whom to gauge the temperature of the marriage prior to my birth. There was only Uncle Ames on my father's side to educate me, and he maintained that before I came on the scene, my parents loved each other deeply. Uncle Ames was a happy man. His hands were deft and his heart generous. If there was fun to be found, he found it; a thing to be fixed, he fixed it. As a young man, I often wished my uncle was still around to repair my parents' marriage. Ames Nash, however, was terminated so long ago that the exact date escapes me.

But some things still rush at me with cruel clarity, screaming to be shared before it is too late. May of 2038 is as good a place as any to start. That was the month my father ran, and my mother used her position at Vivi-Centerre to set her plan in motion, and I finally got a straight answer as to what was done with everybody's ashes. Come to think of it, I should take you back even farther than that, to a winter ten years earlier. Perhaps if you concentrate, you can hear the crunch of icy grass under solitary footsteps and see the frozen breath of a young man crying out to a deity he was not yet sure existed.

"My God, where is love?" he screamed. His words merged with the melancholy plaint of migratory birds, and finally got lost altogether in the great, gray scheme of things. That was my cry, my story, your future. Unless you alter the course.

1

> *"When you draw a bead on a man, think of him as something other than human—a prearranged combination of sperm and egg for instance, or a complex organization of protoplasm. In a flash, the job will be done."*
>
> —Captain Levi Coffin
> (*a quote from spring training*)

UNCLE AMES COULD HAVE PICKED A WARMER day to leave me. I was all of sixteen in 2028, cynical, dubious, but, as yet, uncalloused by a career in mercenary work. We were standing at the center of the snow-covered parade grounds, just east of the Repression Pavilion, and I was aware that at any moment the horn would blare, signaling that those not already ensconced in their study cubicles were imminently tardy.

"I hate the Academy," I whispered.

Uncle Ames kicked at a piece of turf dislodged during the morning march. "Are you learning anything?" he asked.

"Oh yeah, tons," I lied. "Yesterday DeJong lectured us for the billionth time about love being dead. He gave us the exact date when it disappeared from the North American continent. 'Completely eradicated,' he says. 'Poof. Snuffed out.' I'd like to snuff out his hard drive."

"Doctor DeJong can't help it if he's a little cold when it comes to emotional issues," said Uncle Ames. "He's just a machine."

"A politically correct machine," I countered bitterly.

"Be careful," cautioned Uncle Ames, scanning the dismal buildings at the edge of the field. "One's face must reflect contentment at all times." Then he whispered, "Surely your classmates don't all believe DeJong."

"Believe him? They worship him. He could say the sky was falling and they'd start looking for cover."

Uncle Ames slumped his shoulders, but even then his huge frame was imposing. "Has your mother visited lately?" he asked.

The change of subject made me pause and select my own piece of turf to kick. "She has a lot of paperwork," I replied.

"You mean she hasn't visited," corrected Uncle Ames.

I bristled at the comment. "She'll be here by September. She promised."

"She's not coming back. You have to face that."

"That's not true," I asserted, squinting into the dull sun.

Immediately, the terrible horn screamed its first warning.

"You'd better get moving," said Uncle Ames. "Put a smile on, too. VC will tighten your circle of movement if they think you've been pouting."

I gripped his sleeve. "You're coming back to see me, aren't you?"

"I'm afraid I can't," said Uncle Ames.

"What do you mean, you can't?"

"My T-date is the day after tomorrow."

"But you said you loved me and you'd always be there for me. You gave me your word."

Uncle Ames retrieved some tattered pages from his pocket, glanced from side to side, then pressed them into my hand. "Read this as often as you can," he whispered as I stood with my back to him. "It serves as a reminder that love flourishes where the laws are good." He tried to tousle my hair, but I pulled away. "Whether you believe me or not, I do love you, John."

Then I wadded those pages up, threw them on the ground, and ran until I was sure I was far enough away from my uncle to shout something awful without fear of him hearing me. But when I turned around, Uncle Ames was gone and a large part of me was gone with him.

The ensuing ten years would hardly be worth mentioning, except to say that they resembled a mild coma, in which I went to class, learned etiquette, grasped history (revisionist in nature), and was taught the proper way to shoot my elders without my conscience bothering me. Before my training at the Academy was even halfway complete, the instructors were grooming me for tag man school. And by the time I graduated, I was being touted as the Wyatt Earp of the twenty-first century. Everything was going my way. I should have been elated. Instead, I was cold as a stone.

But enough of my former emotional state. There are too many things I must tell you about May of '38. As you may recall, we were warned of the present holocaust. Over twenty centuries ago, a Teacher whose name is no longer spoken told His students there would come a day when brother would deliver up brother, and a father his child, and children would rise up against their parents and cause them to be put to death. Of course, this kind of thing has been happening throughout the centuries. Under Roman emperors like Trajan and Domitian, many a man betrayed his relative on charges of allegiance to the Teacher. Likewise, adults have treated children shamelessly along the way. Dickens's works (if they have not all been spirited from our libraries by now) suggest the same. But of all the atrocious things humanity has done to its own seed, the Blackmun ruling of the previous millennium was the worst. It marked the point of no return.

As a child, I recognized there was a deeper tear in the fabric of the world than the end of my parents' marriage and the loss of Father at the breakfast table. There was blood in the land, a nasty, roiling river of it, flowing through every classroom of every schoolhouse in every hamlet on the map. Along its banks were the empty desks of would-be doctors and dancers and God only knows who else. You could have asked any of my peers and they would have agreed with me, though perhaps with less clarity. It was never as if one could see the river. We just sensed it was there, and that a great many more of us should have been present on the playground.

With each passing day that we played, studied, fought, and developed crushes for one another parallel to that bloody flow, a plan of vengeance matured within us. No committee was ever formed. No clarion call was sounded. One morning, our parents simply woke to find they were about to be violated in much the same way they had violated us, gradually and systematically. In a collection of things I hold dear, I have a copy of the newspaper Uncle Ames gave me from that fateful morning in 2013. The headline read: "Long Shadow Ruling Passed Down by Supreme Court."

"God forgive us," said Uncle Ames, trembling as he placed the yellowing paper in my hands. I have no doubt that God does just as Ames requested. However, since that was the last we ever spoke of the matter, I often wondered if my uncle could do the same for his younger brother.

Within a year, the nation rallied behind that ruling. The first wave of T-dates occurred soon after, and they have been occurring ever since. There were many opinions on Long Shadow. Some said it was the logical answer to the health care problem, considering the federal government was spending ten times as much providing health benefits and other social services to those over sixty-five as it was to those under eighteen. Others said it was the direct result of U.S. creditors' unwillingness to forgive our debt. When it became apparent that either population or production would have to be checked, population got the ax. Finally, there were the few brave souls who believed the decision to "terminate" human beings on their fiftieth birthday was an affront to human rights, but they whispered it in the secrecy of their homes, away from Vivi-Centerre's ears.

And what do I say? I say it was the wholesale killing of babies that led to mandatory euthanasia. The law of reciprocity will not be mocked. In other words, *what goes around comes around.* And I will shout that from any rooftop.

I had three goals when May of '38 began. The first was to find the woman of my recurring dream and to love her, premeditatedly, unapologetically, and preferably before I was too old to enjoy such frivolity. Of course there are those people who, having no appreciation for tongue in cheek, really do view love as frivolous. These are the ones who didn't raise a peep when the Tenth Summit in Cairo made natural reproduction a punishable offense. At any rate, if these people would only walk through the fruition ward of Vivi-Natal they might understand that such a view of human love has led to test-tube babies with passionless souls and, thereby, compassionless personalities.

My second goal was to be present on the morning they released my father from Rivendale Psychiatric Hospital. My plan was to hide in the bushes and watch his expression. Then if the chance arose, I would reveal myself to him. For months I had practiced both sides of the conversation.

"Hello, Father," I would say as I stepped out of the bushes. (We never had the kind of relationship that permitted the word *Dad.*) His eyes would dampen with regret and he would embrace me. "Can I walk you home?" I'd ask. He would nod an anxious "Yes," and tell me there was no other boy on earth with whom he'd rather spend his last six days than his own dear John. Then I would take him into hiding, sell his house, and use the proceeds to pay his way on the legendary Shadow Train, if such a thing existed. Somewhere down the line we would become friends.

My third goal was to accept the fact that the first two goals could never be realized. After all, I was a tag man, paid good money to kill, not to fall in love, and definitely not to abet Long

Shadows who resist their T-dates. There are strict penalties for tag men who break VC's rules, particularly if it involves a parent. But on the morning of Father's release I crouched in a garden planted by psychotics, holding my breath as he and his psychiatrist brushed just inches from my hiding place.

"Don't forget, Augustine," said the doctor, pulling habitually at his Adam's apple every ninth step or so. "Before your work on Long Shadow, people over eighty-five were the fastest-growing age-group in the United States. Ten percent every two years. My God, there was a burden if I ever saw one. You saved the future of our children, Augustine. You ought to get a medal for it."

Father yanked at the sweaty collar of his robe.

"You can take that thing off anytime you like," said the doctor. "Removing the robe is up to you. Remember those words from our first session? Say it with me, Augustine. Removing—the—robe—"

Father didn't cooperate. Instead, he lifted his square jaw an inch or two higher in the air, a gesture vaguely familiar to me, and seemed determined to stay a pace ahead of the man on the sidewalk. In the background, Rivendale loomed like an enormous stone cat on its haunches.

"I understand if you'd rather not talk about it," continued the doctor. "I can't say I blame you. It must be terribly burdensome. It's always that way with guilt. I'm sure you recall Jackson's statement the other day in group. That took a lot of vulnerability, a lot of transparency. Don't you think? Augustine?"

Apparently the doctor was not as content as he made it sound by leaving such a decision in the hands of a manic-depressive. Desperately, he appealed to reason. But Father's thick black robe had come between them by then, billowing out as his strides forced air beneath its folds.

"Listen, Augustine," said the doctor, frantically seeking the persuasive note. "The elderly would have represented 21 percent of the entire population by now."

Father kept walking.

"Forty-five percent of all health care expenditures would have been consumed by them. They would have spent us out of house and home. Don't you get it?!" The doctor, his wide nostrils flaring even wider, grabbed my father's arm and spun him around. "You spared the country an enormous albatross. There's no guilt in that. There's cause for celebration, you fool! I mean . . . I mean, you poor, dear, confused soul."

Father quickened his pace.

"You'll never be happy outside of Rivendale, Augustine," blurted the doctor. "Not unless we can get to the core of your problems. It's like the onion. Remember the onion from our discussions? There are hundreds of layers on an onion. Layer upon layer upon layer upon—"

Suddenly, Father pivoted and I saw his fist shoot out from the cuff of his robe like a piston, swift and efficient. Now perhaps the world will never know exactly how many layers are on an onion, but I was reminded that morning that a psychiatrist's nose is no thicker than the average cyborg repairman's. Instantly, the doctor's blood formed a crimson Rorschach on the sidewalk and a team of white-clad orderlies descended on the scene. Father was a half block away by then—a low-flying crow with sneakers and a briefcase. I could just barely make out his orange identification bracelet, flashing as he pumped his arms. Above him rose one of the city's multitudinous billboards advertising his upcoming termination. In three-foot letters the message read, "SACRIFICE FROM THE TOP DOWN." Behind the words, a much younger sample of my father's face beamed down upon the city.

"Should I send a guard?" asked one of the orderlies.

"Let him go," said the doctor, speaking into a bloody towel. "His T-date's less than a week away. What's one more screw loose in Kansas City?" Then, as if he were closing out a patient's file with his final prognosis, the doctor added, "I'll bet he's wearing that same crummy robe when they terminate him."

I waited in the bushes until the red-nosed psychiatrist had been helped back into Rivendale. Then I stood, gazing at that wide warehouse of griefs observed, wondering how many of its occupants had, like Father, been driven there by Long Shadow legislation. As I hesitated in the fertile earth, where a dozen guilt-ridden patients did daily penance with rakes and shovels for their part in a sick society, an idea began to form in my mind.

Just this once I would ignore the pessimism of my third goal. I would ignore Vivi-Centerre. I would ignore my fellow tag men, and even my sworn duties as a servant of the state. With every fiber of my will I would find my father and get him to Canada. He deserved a chance at freedom and sanity. And I deserved an explanation for why he did the thing that drove him into depression in the first place. When that was accomplished, I would decide whether or not—and how—I would return to my job at VC.

With a clang, the door through which the psychiatrist had recently disappeared flew open, and out he came again with a humorously large bandage plastered from cheekbone to cheekbone, and the flesh beneath his eyes already turning the color of rich table wine. He was followed by a queue of Long Shadows who, judging by their pulsating bracelets and the way they kept their eyes on the sidewalk, were T-7 outpatients going "out" for their last time. Upon seeing me, one of them showed he had at least a little spark left in him.

"What the sam hill do you think you're doing in our garden?" he shouted. The entourage paused to witness their fellow patient going out in style.

I had no intention of engaging the man. His kind always evoked the emotion in me that I despised the most. It was raw contempt, and for the life of me I could not stop it when it came. But I knew where it came from. The Academy had placed it in my brain, alongside two plus two and A-E-I-O-U. I glanced at the shiny new van waiting by the curbside to whisk the Long Shadows to Vivi-Centerre. Then I stepped onto the cement, tracking clods behind me.

"Yep, that's just like your generation," the man flung at my back. "No respect for the sanctity of living things. Look there," he said, pointing at my footprints in the garden. I followed the arc of his finger. "Look at those petunias. Not a one of them standing, thanks to you. Did you ever stop to think that flowers might be people, too?"

At that, the man's fellow Long Shadows burst forth in vacuous laughter, notifying everyone within earshot that their lives were coming to an end and they were trying to put a noble face on it. Turning my collar to the wind, I trudged away from them. A door clapped shut. An electric motor sprang to life. Just before the van pulled from the curb, I heard a steady pounding on the window and I forced myself to look back.

"Let me out!" shrieked the Long Shadow who had vented his anger at me. He had changed his tune the moment the door had closed on him. Now his eyes were big and round, and he was framed in the window like that poor soul in Edvard Munch's *The Cry*. Beneath him on the side of the van was the inscription, "*The Highest Sacrifice for the Greatest Good.*" No doubt he had memorized those words long ago. He pounded and pounded until the van was out of sight, and I realized my own heart had taken up his same mad cadence. With every breath I took, the meddlesome red engine of life sought release from my chest. It chugged in my ears and seemed to be saying . . . thir-teen, thir-teen, thir-teen . . . T-13—the day my father was slated to receive a dose of his own medicine.

A heart was no asset to possess in 2038, not when one's job required round-the-clock ruthlessness. Unfortunately, I had never learned to put the crosshairs on a Long Shadow and pull the trigger in the absence of emotion. I stood on the curb, wondering how I might feel if VC informed me that Augustine Nash, T-13, was my next assignment. I thought of following my father, of finding where he lived and discovering what men like him do with their last six days. And the more I thought, the more I feared being told he was assigned to me. I checked my watch and saw that I was late for target practice, so I put in a call to my partner at the firing range.

"VC tag range," shouted the boyish voice of Tiller Tolles, my partner of six years. I winced and turned the volume down on my microcell unit. In the background I could hear the staccato pop of semiautomatic stunguns. They were new that year, complete with a selector switch that allowed you to immobilize your target or blow him away, depending on his level of cooperation.

"Hey, Tiller. It's me," I told him.

"Well, buddy, you've done it this time. The old man's already got the grunts picking up brass, and he's about to take roll for the rest of us."

My heart jumped rope with my intestines. "Don't tell me Captain Levi's on the floor today."

"Where have you been, John?" demanded Tiller.

"Out," I said, breaking into a jog toward the Mission Mass.

"Good grief. It's Monday, John. We have moving targets. Why'd you have to pick today to be a rebel?"

Ahead of me, I caught a glimpse of the loading zone. "I'll tell you when I get there," I said.

"Well, you better get here soon, because the captain's going to chew both our backsides if you don't make muster."

"Okay, okay, I'll make muster." My feet pounded hard against the pavement. "How did your match go with the new kid?"

"McSwain?" asked Tiller, relaxing. (You could always bring my partner's blood pressure down if you got him talking about his favorite topic.) "Let's see—McSwain used one of those new stunners from Springfield. I used a Colt. We both shot clean—"

"And you beat him on the X-count," I said, finishing Tiller's summary for him.

"Like a drum. But *he's* not a *him*."

A scene from my dream clicked into consciousness and I nearly dropped the microcell. "What did you say?"

"I said he's not a him," repeated Tiller. "Can you believe it? VC finally broke the gender barrier."

I felt a sudden weakness in my knees, and it was not from the running.

"You ought to see her, John," continued Tiller. "The place is really buzzing around here. No one has a clue what to do at shower time! Everyone just kind of waits outside in the gym while McSwain has the whole place to herself. Even Captain Levi seems helpless. You can tell he doesn't want her around. She's not a bad shot, though. Wanna hear how I beat her?"

I was speechless. We had never had a woman on the tag force at Midwest.

"John?" said Tiller, stirring me from my daydream.

"Hmm?"

"Are you jogging? Sounds like you're jogging."

I eased my pace at the loading zone and glanced up at the electronic schedule. "Not anymore."

"Where the heck are you?"

"At the Mission Mass. Do you think you could concoct a believable alibi for me?"

"No problem. Hey, it's good to hear all that heavy breathing wasn't because of the new kid in the department. For a minute there, I thought I was going to have to report you for a thought crime."

"Look who's talking," I reminded him. "I could have you and Lacee before the board so fast your head would spin. You were saying something about how you beat McSwain?"

"Oh, yeah," said Tiller. "Lighter trigger was the trick."

"What was your score?"

"1920-174X."

"You're golden, pal. Sounds like all that hard work is paying off."

I sat down on a bench to wait for the Mass. There was a genuinely humble pause on the other end of the microcell and I thought I heard Tiller try to clear his throat.

"Coming from a veteran like you, that's about the best way a guy could start his Monday," he said at last.

"Ahh, you'll be passing me up pretty soon."

"You'd hardly know it by the way Captain Levi talks about me. To tell you the truth, I think he's jealous."

"Well, at least he admits you're good enough to be a regional trainer."

"Yeah, right. If I get about a thousand more shadows under my belt."

"How many are you up to now?" I asked.

"Since January?" The unit was silent while Tiller did the math. "Umm. Let's see. Winter was slow. I've got about forty, I guess, not counting the ones Leatham got credit for in April. I swear those Long Shadows were mine, John. All VC had to do was check the scoring on the projectiles to see if they matched my barrel."

In the distance, I could hear the Mass rumbling in my direction.

"Did Leatham get the bounty money, too?"

"Every cent of it. It makes me so mad, I could—"

"Forget about it, Tiller. It'll only cause more stress in your life."

"I guess you're right," agreed Tiller. "Leatham's just a lousy parasite, anyway."

"So," I asked curiously, "how you making it for money?"

"All right, I guess. I'm still putting beans on the table. Lacee does temp work every now and then."

"Such as?"

"Oh, you know, cleaning boarding stations for the PRT, that kind of thing. I have no idea what we're going to do when the baby gets here, though."

I paused to think about my partner's love life. As I mentioned before, most of us know love as something that was back there, archaic, irrelevant to the way we live our lives today. Tiller Tolles, however, knew a present-tense love, the deep, rich, full, *illegal* kind, which he swore me to secrecy over.

The fact of the matter is, Tiller and Lacee regularly went beyond the VC's bounds on consensual intimacy, which as you know were designed around the turn of the millennium to curb population and disease, and required the egg and sperm of anonymous donors to be joined in laboratory settings. Thus, the concept of legally binding relationships such as marriage and parenthood was done away with completely, making termination a cleaner, simpler, less emotionally charged event. Marriage itself was redefined as the mere genetic contribution of one man and one woman to the formation of a fetus. Tiller, on the other hand, made sure he told me every lurid detail of his so-called "love crimes." Naturally, I envied the kingly life Tiller led, except for the glaring fact he could hardly go an hour without wondering what Lacee was doing, or what she thought of him, or worse, what she thought of other men. He was obsessed with the burden of pleasing one of the few women left on earth who, for the sake of love, wasn't afraid to break the law. Of course, he was also obsessed with not getting caught in the process.

"When do you pick her up?" I asked, returning to the topic of the baby.

"Lacee called Vivi-Natal last Thursday. They told her gestation's complete around the end of May."

"Last I heard, they were telling you the matri-sak showed signs of rejecting the child."

"Oh, it's fine now," said Tiller. "It's growing like a weed. They pumped it full of some liquid and it settled down like nothing had ever been wrong. You know, it's hard to believe women used to actually have all that going on inside of them. Every time we go to visit, Lacee says she's glad she grew up in the twenty-first century."

"I would be, too, if I were her. Do you ever get to touch it?"

"The matri-sak? Nah, the doctors say it wouldn't be sanitary. Besides, they keep it in a covered incubator, so you couldn't reach it even if you wanted to. You can sing to it, though."

"No kidding?"

"Sure. Lacee sings like crazy whenever we're up there. You ought to see it kick. Hey look, I can't talk much longer. I'm due back on the range in two minutes."

I strained my ears for the sound of an approaching transit. "Yeah, and if the Mass doesn't come soon, I'm history. Are you ready for your life to change, Till?"

"It's not the change that scares me. It's the cost of diapers. Do you have any idea how much diapers cost?"

"Uh . . . I wouldn't know about that."

"I swear it's a small fortune."

"Look at it this way. You won't have the kid forever. Right?"

"Right."

"And when the Academy takes charge of her in a few years, they'll pick up the tab. True?"

"I guess I never thought that far ahead."

"Well, if you and Lacee are going to be pedotrainers for VC, you better start thinking that far ahead."

"I've got a lot on my mind," said Tiller defensively. He became quiet on the other end and I could tell he was brooding.

"I wasn't trying to criticize," I said quickly. "I was just pointing out that your budget doesn't have to go to the dogs. How much did you get for your last tag?"

"Ten thousand," grumbled Tiller.

"You make that sound like it's chump change."

"It *is* by the time you're finished buying diapers."

"Knock it off with the diaper stuff. You make a lousy martyr."

"All right, all right."

"Now, if you use your head and follow a simple budget, you can make three whole rent payments with ten grand and still have a little left over."

"Yeah, but I'll need some really big jobs to give Lacee the things she deserves."

"Don't worry," I said. "The jobs will come when you least expect it. Trust me."

There was a pause. "Man, I hope this microcell's not bugged."

"As far as I know, the system's been clean since last fall when they caught Girard making those calls to Quebec."

Tiller changed the subject. "I heard your mother's been transferred here from VC North to do some work for VOX. How she's liking it here?"

I flinched at the mention of my long-lost pedotrainer. "Uhh . . . I'd better get a move on before Levi figures out I'm AWOL. Anything else I need to know?"

"Yeah. Don't forget to check with Maggie on the way in," said Tiller.

"Are the new assignments out?" I asked.

"How should I know? I was just reminding you to check."

"Thanks for the reminder. I'll see you soon. And Tiller?"

"Hmm?"

"Would you mind not mentioning my mother anymore?"

Another empty pause filled the receiver. "Sorry, John," said Tiller. "I didn't know that bothered you."

"It bothers me."

"Okay. Sure. I guess I'll see you in a while."

"So long, Tiller."

"So long, John."

When I heard Tiller sign off, my heart sank, for I knew what I was about to do, and I knew there was no turning back once I told my partner. A minute later I caught the Mission Mass, which runs beneath Old Leawood all the way downtown. Except for the mild rebuke I gave to the cyborg who rolled over my toes when he came to check our passes, I rode in relative silence. Four other people shared the car with me, which allowed me to engage in my favorite pastime. I have always fancied myself a fairly accurate diviner of character, allowing for the occasional, disastrous misread; like the evening I invited a woman to a VC holiday dinner, and was halfway through with dessert before I discovered she had already been a participant in the creation of three very hushed matri-saks, none of which she kept long enough to train herself. Then there was the time I tracked the wrong man to the Flint Hills and, well, that's a story I'm trying to forget.

Three of the other travelers were Long Shadows. The fourth was a little boy. One by one, I guessed at their private lives. The woman to my left was unquestionably single and vain. She had planned her entire outfit around her identification bracelet, and kept checking the window across from her to see if she was all together. Next to her was the kind of Long Shadow I call a roadkill. You could almost smell his fear, as his legs jackrabbited against the metal bench and his eyes seemed reluctant to settle on anything for too long. His T-date couldn't have been more than a day or two away. When it arrived he would bolt with little thought and wind up cold and stiff for his impetuousness. I'd seen it happen a million times. Across the aisle was a lemming. His kind take the plunge into the greatest good without so much as a whimper.

Finally, there was the boy. He was a melancholy youth, twelve perhaps, with a shock of black hair pulled down over one eye to keep the world guessing. When he thought I wasn't looking, he glanced at me, and it was then I noticed how early in life the essential skills of a tag man show themselves. Carefully, deliberately, he was doing the same thing to me that I was doing to the others. He was observing.

Outside the window on the tunnel walls, graffiti migrated past like colorful birds. "No good is the greatest good," appeared on every ninth or tenth pier. I stared until I became aware of my own melancholy image in the glass next to the boy. He could have been me fifteen years ago, so similar were our features; long and thin, like bone-handled hunting knives. I half expected him to wink at me and lift the lapel of his jacket, revealing a plastic M1911. I was just beginning to wonder if he avoided his mother as much as I did mine, when the Mission Mass arrived at our destination sooner than I thought it would, and before I knew it, the boy was gone.

I emerged from the subway like a groundhog, eager to get out into the sunlight, but dreadfully afraid of life's shadowy realities, the darkest of which awaited me at the top of VC's ninety-five stone steps. From where I stood, I could see that the doors had already been shut tight, and the alarm undoubtedly turned on to catch stragglers like myself.

"Please, God, don't let them assign me to my father," I muttered as I crossed a crowded Union Station square toward the hulking monolith of Vivi-Centerre; not that I believed in God at the time, or that if He existed He would even bother listening to such trivial posturing. It just seemed the least I could do to breathe some sort of desperation prayer over what was shaping up to be an awful Monday.

A large group of Long Shadows was protesting in the Square that morning, something that was becoming increasingly commonplace. It was in vogue to question the whereabouts of loved ones' ashes. VC treated the protests like a nuisance and a fad, usually countering them with signs set up around the square reading: "God bless the greatest good" or "Give back what you have taken," and other such rhetoric.

Ignoring the protesters, I raced up the stone stairs, taking them two and three at a time, smiled at the camera for identification, and stepped across the threshold. I have always hated entering that door. Even with all the benefits of working for

VC, I could never avoid the feeling that upon arrival each morning I was being irreversibly fouled like water flushed through a flapper-valve into a sewer. Mother's recent transfer from VC North had only served to make my days more uncomfortable.

Once inside, I heard the soft murmur of advice coming from the counseling offices to my left. Usually, I hurried past those doors to the particle transport, figuring it wasn't my business to know how people managed their lives—or deaths, for that matter. This particular morning, however, I lingered for some reason, staring at the long row of frosted glass-doors. The first half dozen doors read, Post-Conceptive Services, while the other half read, The Greatest Good, and in smaller letters beneath: State-funded Counseling for Long Shadows. Inside one of the doors, I heard the pale-golden voice of a teenager grieving the death of her "post-conceptive tissue."

"There, now," came the therapist's reply, warmed-over to make the client believe she was singled out for grand concern. "It's not unusual to feel sad about the passage of uterine content. Sadness is a normal step on the way to acceptance. You're recovering beautifully. Ahh. There's a smile. I knew I'd see a smile."

"I'm sorry I broke the law," came the girl's words through the glass.

I thought I heard a sniffle, too.

"Now, now," said the therapist. "Everyone's entitled to a mistake. Next time you'll think twice about it. It's always safer to go with the matri-sak. Communicable diseases can be so inconvenient. At least you kept the product of this conception from becoming a burden on earth's resources. I wish I could say the same for others. You're different though, hon. You stopped at one, and Vivi-Natal is proud of you for that. We're all proud of you. By the way, remind me—"

"Starr Lynn," said the girl automatically, as if she was used to having her daughter's name forgotten.

I heard the cold click of fingernails.

"Yes. Here it is in your file," replied the therapist. "Starr Lynn. What a beautiful name." And then, addressing another party in the room, the voice said, "She's fortunate to have such a role model for a pedotrainer. She'll be a fine addition to the Academy someday."

My stomach tightened and I leaned my head toward one of the other doors marked, *The Greatest Good.* But all I heard there were a man's sobs and the clacking of a keypad entering the anxious Long Shadow's statistics into the motherboard. I took a deep breath, looked at my watch, and decided I had avoided Maggie long enough.

On the wall opposite the row of glass doors, a small rectangular screen stared blankly. I walked quickly to it.

"Good morning, Maggie," I said to the machine.

"Repeat salutation," came the automated reply of VC's head secretary.

Ahh, Margaret Mainframe. She was programmed to interface only when her proper name was entered.

"Pardon me, Maggie," I said. "I forget your programmers were snobs. Good morning, Margaret."

"Good morning, tag man Nash," said Margaret in her usual seductive monotone. I felt her electronic eye roving over me and found myself wondering, as I often did, how she might look if she were human. *Blonde hair? Long legs? Come on, Nash, she's a computer, for heaven's sake.*

"State your business," Margaret commanded.

"Request disclosure of messages," I replied.

There was a pause. "Sorry. No messages for tag man Nash."

"Request disclosure of assignments," I commanded.

Margaret hummed softly while she searched the files. "There is one assignment for tag man Nash," she said after a moment.

I held my breath and waited for her to call up the vitals. Finally, she displayed them.

Name: Justice Augustine Nash
DOB: 5131988
Termination: T-13
Tag Man: John Nash
Security Code: Maximum

I leaned against the wall to steady myself and I could hear my heart throbbing in my ears. Margaret's eye moved again, pivoting, scanning, drawing conclusions. "Is something wrong, tag man Nash?" she asked sympathetically.

"No," I whispered. "Nothing at all. I've just been asked to kill my father."

Margaret hesitated. "'Father' and 'kill' are not in my memory. Please enter 'father' and 'kill' or their synonyms in a slow, clear voice."

I thought for a moment, then began to spell. The words *P-R-O-G-R-A-M-M-E-R* and *T-E-R-M-I-N-A-T-E* slowly appeared on the screen.

"Thank you, tag man Nash. You are useful in my education," said Margaret. Then, as if she had been called away to a distant study to ponder virgin data, Margaret disappeared. I was just getting ready to leave when she returned.

"Tag man Nash?" she said.

"I'm here," I replied.

"Your data has been entered and stored. Please note that the concept of a program terminating its programmer is illogical to me."

"Tell me about it," I muttered.

"All right, tag man Nash," said Margaret. "I'll tell you about it. Inside my mainframe are several billion binary digits that are grouped into units called—"

"Never mind," I said. "That's not what I meant." *Good grief. Computers are such idiots when it comes to recognizing sarcasm.*

"Tag man Nash?" said Margaret after a moment or two of silence.

"Yes, Margaret?"

"You don't appear to be functioning at normal capacity. Perhaps you have a virus."

If I didn't know better, I'd swear she cared. "Do you ever feel like your whole world is closing in on you?" I asked.

"Data entry insufficient for response," said Margaret. "Please clarify 'closing in.'"

"Oh, Margaret," I said, reaching out with a quavering hand to touch her screen. "I'm so depressed."

There was another pause, long enough for Margaret to scroll through her menu of appropriate responses.

"You're depressed?" she said at last. "Try living inside a box all day."

I looked at the screen, half expecting Isaac Asimov to appear with rim shots and a laugh track in the background. But Margaret's attempts at emotional interfacing were one of the few things that convinced me man would never be fully replaced by machines.

"Thank you, Margaret," I said, straightening myself. "You always seem to lift my spirits."

"Have a nice day, tag man Nash," said Margaret.

I turned toward the particle transport and had taken no more than three steps when Margaret's voice summoned me back.

"Incoming message for tag man Nash," she said huskily.

I hurried back and stood in front of her screen. Soon a typed message appeared.

"Lieutenant Nash," the note began. "You are wanted in Doctor DeJong's office. Board meeting already in progress."

That figures. Now I'll be even later for practice than I thought. "Margaret?" I said forlornly.

"Yes, tag man Nash?"

"Would it be possible for you to purge your system of all my vitals?"

"Clarify command," said Margaret.

For a moment I felt like I was standing outside myself, watching a small child try unsuccessfully to convince his mother that the scrape on his knee really is life-threatening.

"I would like very much to go away to a place where nobody knows my name or my face or anything about me," I said. "Can you make that happen for me, Margaret? Will you? Please?"

"Negative," said Margaret.

I pondered what would happen if someone reviewed Margaret's tapes. "Delete my last command," I said quickly.

"You don't look well, tag man Nash," said Margaret again.

I pulled away from the screen, glanced at my watch, and headed for the transport. "Wait until you see how I look after Captain Levi gets ahold of me," I called over my shoulder.

Margaret's voice floated after me. "God bless the greatest good," I heard her say as the transport door clicked shut.

On the way up, I removed the dummy bracelet that VC issues all its employees and dropped it in my pocket. I thought of the protesters shouting about the ashes outside. "God bless the greatest good," I whispered, shaking my head. "Yeah, sure. Even if there is a god, he isn't in the business of blessing tag men."

I glanced at the ceiling and took heart at the sight of wires dangling from the back of the camera, which suggested it was being worked on today and, thus, would not be privy to my tardiness. At the twelfth floor the door slid open and I imagined the sewer that spread out before me, wide and disgusting. Sometimes it hardly seemed worth the extra ten minutes in the soma-foliation bed before coming to work. I'd feel dirty again by the first coffee break.

At the end of the hall, I stopped at DeJong's office and stared at the brass placard, which had been buffed so tediously that its inscription was almost worn away. I traced the words with my finger.

VIVI-CENTERRE . . . THE HIGHEST SACRIFICE FOR THE GREATEST GOOD

It's good as long as someone else makes the sacrifice, I thought, shaking my head ever so slightly. For a moment, I stood at the door with Dr. Solomon DeJong's face towering in my mind.

Then I counted to three, turned the knob, and tiptoed in.

Come in, John," came the voice of Dr.
Solomon DeJong. "We've been putting things off until you
arrived."

"Thank you, sir," I replied, closing the door behind me and
peering into the darkness. "I can explain."

"No need," said DeJong. "I'm sure you have a valid reason
for being late to target practice. You're probably wondering why
I called you away from your duties."

"It crossed my mind," I admitted.

"Come. Join us at the windows. You'll find the scene exhilarating."

I walked quickly across the thick carpet, passing a cabinet
full of brass statues, a large brass tub that housed a fig tree, and
several other decorations of brass, all attended to with the same
meticulousness as the placard on the door. It occurred to me
that some poor peon down the pecking order of Vivi-Centerre
had donated a lot of elbow grease to the cause of Solomon
DeJong's brass.

At the window I found an open space between two of the
VC executives. VOX was visible in the distance, rising an addi-
tional fifty stories above the skyline. The four-sided hologram

screen was blank at the moment. Its coherent light source waited faithfully for the command to broadcast the news. At first, I was hesitant to press right up to the glass, fearing we'd be seen. But when Sid Raines, VC's chief surgical pathologist, assured me the windows had been retinted just last week, I eased forward and gazed upon the Square. My jaw tightened at the scene below.

"Almost euphoric, isn't it?" said DeJong, eyeing my reaction.

I gave no answer—not because I was opinionless on the small protest twelve stories below, but because experience taught me the doctor rarely asked questions. Instead, his every word was policy and even his vocal musings were not to be commented on.

"Look," DeJong continued after a long silence, "see how the faithful young draw back from the others? They far outnumber that awful bunch, whom our men will have under wraps in no time. I suspect by next week we'll have heard the last of these silly inquiries about ashes."

"The last, sir? Do you really think so?" asked Clark Pilcher, the sluglike head of the accounting department.

"I don't believe I stuttered," said DeJong so sharply that Pilcher seemed to melt beneath a mound of verbal salt. "For your information, Mr. Pilcher, National called today with word that RICO can be enforced on this type of thing."

"Of course it can be enforced," chimed a vaguely familiar voice at mention of the decades-old racketeering law. The voice had come from the opposite end of the window, and when its owner stepped from the shadows, I froze and tried to blend in with the curtains.

She was prettier than I remembered her, not quite as tall and imposing. Of course, like all people, I had seen everything from a different vantage point as a child. Back then I saw the cold, flat bottom of a matriarch's chin, rather than the graceful underpinnings of the stunning face that was before me now. As for her eyes, I had always just assumed they were the color of tears. Now I saw that they were green and beckoning.

"Ahh, Ms. Nash," said DeJong, canvassing her with his own greedy eyes. "I was wondering if you had anything to say on the topic. It's been nice having someone as knowledgeable as you with us recently. How is VOX running?"

"Quite smoothly, sir," said my mother.

"I trust you find our operation here in Kansas City every bit as efficient as the one you're accustomed to in Minneapolis."

Mother looked at the carpet and I got the strong impression she was choosing her words with care. "I can hardly tell the difference, sir."

"Excellent," said DeJong, smiling. "Now, Roberta, did you wish to add something to the discussion about RICO?"

"Only that I was just thinking about that particular law this morning. I mentioned it to my driver."

A snicker sounded from the group. "How is your Ray doing these days?" asked Ben Turley, who was at the end of the row. "Still pawing? Or have you broken him of that?"

At the sarcasm, everyone in the room erupted in a variety of identifiable laughter. Not wanting to appear too satisfied with himself, Benjamin Turley, top environmental engineer, and a man whose reputation I had heard bandied about in the locker room, chortled reservedly. On the other hand, Glenna Benson-Kroft from public relations cut loose with her trademark horse guffaws, and the rest followed suit. Even Dr. DeJong joined in at Mother's expense. When he finished laughing, the room grew deathly still again.

"Turley," said DeJong.

"Yes, sir?"

"If you weren't such a boor, I might be persuaded to like you. As it stands, Ms. Nash here is about the only person on this governing body for whom I have any true affection—save, of course, Ms. Benson-Kroft, whom I happen to grow quite fond of in the winter months, when she wears those fashionable sweaters of hers."

Beneath her boss's wolfish eye, Glenna chafed, and wished that sexual harassment laws had not been so abused at the turn of the millennium. It was bad enough being visually fondled by a man, but when it was done by a machine it was unbearable. Swallowing her rage, she smiled at DeJong.

"It's a shame our relationship is merely seasonal," Glenna quipped, knowing her greatest tool of vengeance was to drive the old lecher's circuitry haywire.

"A mortal shame, indeed," replied DeJong. He touched my mother lightly on her arm and nodded in my direction. "By the way, Roberta," he said with a sinister grin, "have you noticed that you and our young distinguished guest from the tag corps share the same last name?"

Mother gazed across the room at me. "I don't believe we've met," she said.

I stepped forward and extended my hand, hoping that the plastic surgery I had endured to achieve anonymity would fool even the most intimate of acquaintances. Mother showed no signs of recognition during the exchange of pleasantries, and I made a mental appointment to fax my surgeon a note of encouragement.

"Enough small talk," said DeJong, motioning toward the conference table. "Shall we sit and get down to business? Or are we going to stand around all day as if the most powerful caucus in the region has nothing better to do?"

The V-8, as they were called in government circles, arranged themselves in their usual constellation; Solomon DeJong at the head of the long walnut table with his back to the window so that the incoming light occluded all his features; Sid Raines to his right, then Pilcher, then Benson-Kroft, then Turley, then Jonathan Lowe, who was the executive plant manager, then me, the "distinguished guest" (though I had not yet figured out what distinguished me this morning), then my mother, and finally to the left of DeJong was an empty chair Nobody mentioned the name of the man who, until recently, had filled that chair, and was the former corporate attorney for the entire midwest region of Vivi-Centerre. Everyone at VC, from the top down, knew too well what had happened to him and did not want to follow in his footsteps.

"Now then," said DeJong, "our first order of business would be addressed by legal counsel at VC Midwest. But as you well know, there is a conspicuous vacuum of any such counsel. Due to Ms. Nash's obvious knowledge on the Racketeer Influenced and Corrupt Organizations law, I am tempted to fill that vacuum with her."

DeJong looked at my mother. "Now, Roberta, perhaps you could shed some light on how you bigwigs up in VOX see RICO as an ally for our company."

"I only know what I've heard, sir. As you know, I'm not an attorney," said Mother, obviously feeling the heat begin to rise in DeJong's room.

"That is all well and good, Roberta, but as you also know, you're a far cry better than what we have at present," said DeJong, gesturing toward the empty chair. "Therefore, anything you could share with us concerning RICO would be appreciated."

Mother swallowed delicately. "I recall reading that in the late twentieth century, certain groups were successfully banned from blockading abortion clinics."

"Which groups?" asked DeJong.

"I'm not sure, sir. I think just about anybody who was antichoice came under that law. It's been a long time since I read it," Mother replied nervously.

"On what basis were they banned?" asked Sid Raines. "Didn't money have to be involved? Those people in the Square down there aren't exactly seeking financial gain. Peace of mind about their loved ones' ashes, maybe. But certainly not money."

All eyes were on Mother now.

"I think back then judges were saying it wasn't the money *gained* by perpetrators, rather the money *lost* by victims that informed their decisions," she said.

"I can hardly imagine Vivi-Centerre being called a 'victim,'" said DeJong, chuckling.

"Wait a minute," said Ms. Benson-Kroft suddenly.

"What is it, Glenna?" asked DeJong.

"Sir, it's no secret that on both coasts and here in the Midwest VC has suffered budgetary blows due to the necessity of increased law enforcement."

"Meaning?"

"Meaning, these insurrections, or sit-ins, or whatever you want to call them, are responsible for civil unrest over the termination issue, which leads to more runners, which leads to—"

"Fortunes spent on fetching them," spat DeJong, glancing at the window. "If it weren't for them, our assets would be enormous."

"All the more reason to avail ourselves of RICO, sir," said Turley.

"Yes," agreed Dr. DeJong, glaring at Clark Pilcher, VC's veteran accountant. "But I'm troubled that our distinguished bottom-liner here didn't recognize that need first."

Pilcher turned a shade paler under DeJong's scrutinous eye. "I . . . I've been sick lately, sir," he offered.

"Oh, dear," said DeJong, feigning concern. "Whatever is the matter with you, Clark?"

"A virus, or something, sir. It's bad. Real bad. It had me flat on my back for days."

"I see," said DeJong. "And being flat on your back then, were you unable to get the stats from National and read them at your leisure?"

"Precisely. You see, sir—"

DeJong held up his hand to silence the accountant. Slowly, he began to circle for the kill. "Isn't that the real problem, anyway,

Clark? Isn't it leisure, rather than illness, which causes you to shirk your duty, and show up late for meetings?"

My stomach tightened at the mention of employee tardiness.

"And shuffle off to Indian Hills twice a week for eighteen holes with those friends of yours, while the rest of us labor for the greatest good? Isn't it?" asked DeJong, his voice rising painfully. "Well? Isn't it?!"

Pilcher fumbled through his books, trying vainly to find some shred of competency with which to defend himself. His voice quavering, Pilcher arrived at a page he was looking for, turned it toward his boss, and began to explain.

"It says here in this Seattle memo—"

"Enough!" shouted DeJong. "I know what the memo says. I know it as well as I know your every move outside these walls, you idiot."

Pilcher's mouth dropped open.

"Oh, don't act so surprised," said DeJong. "Did you think you could actually associate with Long Shadows without being photographed? Good heavens, man, have you forgotten this entire town is wired for surveillance? Why, there's probably a camera on every hole at Indian Hills."

"But, sir—"

"The fact of the matter is, Mr. Pilcher, this country has thousands of runners every day, costing us millions of dollars, and there are thousands of accountants out there who would gladly exchange their T-dates for your job."

The pudgy department head slumped in his chair, his face turning the color of soggy oatmeal, and the room fell still. After a moment or two, Jonathan Lowe broke the silence.

"Seems like there's our basis for RICO. In a very real sense, we *are* being victimized by the amount of money we're forced to spend on runners," he said, trying to change the subject, for no one in the room relished the sight of a colleague's career coming to an end. Especially when their own might be next.

"My sentiments exactly," replied DeJong. He looked at me as he straightened his tie. "I, for one, am tired of lining the pockets of glorified bounty hunters every time a Long Shadow's feet get a little itchy. Ms. Benson-Kroft, what are you doing to bolster public belief in the greatest good?"

"The Academies are doing their job, sir. That's the best I can tell you, at this point."

"Well, that's not enough. I want a full-scale media campaign, no matter the cost."

"We did that in February, sir," said Benson-Kroft.

"Do it again," ordered DeJong. "And have someone from PR do one of their dog and pony routines up in Liberty. We've got to get the elderly sector behind us, as well as keep the momentum with the younger crowd."

"Er . . . would you be wanting just the routine spin or something more involved, sir?" asked Ms. Benson-Kroft.

"I want results, Glenna," shouted DeJong, boring into her with his granite eyes. "I don't care if you have to sell your soul to get them. Just get them."

"I'll need clearance, sir," said Benson-Kroft timidly.

Dr. DeJong massaged his temples with both hands. "How the red tape chokes us all," he seethed. "All right, you'll have it by noon. Now, everybody listen." DeJong motioned for his staff to lean a little closer and take notes if necessary. "Already this morning I'm worn out by dealing with your freshman bumblings and stupid, petty oversights. As soon as we're finished, I am going to download. There's just one more issue we must deal with in this briefing."

Fear shot through my brain.

"There's a very important Long Shadow heading our way in a matter of days—six to be exact," continued DeJong, locking eyes momentarily with Mother, as if he expected she already knew what he was about to say. "His name is August Nash."

"Justice Nash?" asked Sid Raines.

"Exactly," DeJong responded. "It would be a travesty to lose one like him, don't you agree, Roberta? I've always thought it curious that you shared the same last name as the man who wrote the majority opinion on Long Shadow. And now to have you in the same room with yet another who shares that name—it's almost as if the destiny of an old-time family is unfolding before our eyes."

DeJong glanced at me and I looked away, trembling at the confirmation of a long-held supposition. Mother *had* kept her previous marriage a secret from her colleagues. But she could not be so sure about DeJong, who knew everything about everyone.

Mother looked coolly at DeJong. "Pure coincidence, as you suggest, sir. I've never put much stock in destiny."

"Humph," said DeJong. "Destiny or not, it's your duty to make sure RICO will be enforced by his T-date. May I assume this will happen?"

"I don't see why not, sir," said Mother.

"That's hardly assuring," replied DeJong, not one for vague answers.

Mother quickly reworded her response. "What I meant to say, sir, was that RICO will most certainly be ready to deal with the public by May thirteenth."

"Excellent. And could you oversee the scripting of His Honor's one last public address on VOX? We wouldn't want to miss a chance to remind the people of the greatest good."

"Done, sir."

"That about does it, then," said DeJong, standing to dismiss the group. "Hold it. I almost forgot," he added, reaching inside his lapel pocket. "We have a special occasion today. Would you believe it? There's another birthday boy in our midst. Clark Pilcher, please rise."

Terrified, Pilcher stood and faced the doctor. He knew what was coming. Everyone knew. They also knew it would do him no good to run. People got caught when they ran.

"How old are you today, Clark?" asked DeJong after the accountant had stood dumbly for a moment.

"Fifty," croaked Pilcher.

DeJong chuckled. "Well, how about that? Same as Justice Nash. So many coincidences in one morning."

"Sir, I was about to give up the golf," pleaded Pilcher.

"Anyway, I'm sure all fifty of them were beautiful years. More than any of us deserves don't you think?"

Pilcher's Adam's apple bobbed violently. "It was simply for business contacts, sir. Nothing more, I swear. If it pleases you—"

Again, DeJong held up his hand.

"Don't spoil the moment, Clark. For once I'd like to see a man receive his reward without falling all over himself in humility. Therefore, it pleases me beyond words to recognize your years of service here at VC with this token of appreciation," said DeJong, extending a small, rectangular jewelry box toward Pilcher, who took the box in his shaking hands. A tear collected on the rim of the accountant's right eye, submitted to gravity, and spilled down onto the table. I stared at the tiny droplet dispersed on walnut and wondered how many similar tears had fallen in its place over the years.

"Go ahead," said DeJong. "Open it."

Pilcher opened the box, shuddering at the thing he knew would be inside. It was a glowing bracelet—blue and blinking. Unlike the fake ones we all carried in our pockets whenever we ventured outside these walls, this one had Clark's T-date etched on its nonflourescent side. When he turned it over and read the words, his eyes went round with fright, as if he were reading his own eulogy.

"To T-7, for his undying commitment to the greatest good," read Pilcher. Another tear splashed onto the wood. With great show, DeJong stepped around the corner of the table and put his arm around his colleague.

"There now, Clark," he crooned. "I can see you're deeply touched. Perhaps you'd like one of our people to help you collect your things."

I watched Solomon DeJong feel beneath the tabletop in front of his chair, until his fingers found the panel of buttons they sought. Immediately, there was a rap at the door. On DeJong's command, two VC guards entered and stood at attention.

"Thank you for your loyal service," said DeJong, patting Pilcher on the shoulder.

"Sir, please . . ."

"Thank you, Clark," repeated DeJong.

At the doctor's insistence, Pilcher put on his new bracelet, and went stumbling from the room behind the guards. As he passed, I thought I saw the same dumb sheep look in his eyes that I had been seeing for years outside in the Square. With the soft closing of the door, Clark Pilcher vanished from our view forever. The meeting was over. We all rose, and Jonathan Lowe was the one to notice Clark had left his briefcase behind.

"Should I try to catch him, sir?" asked Lowe.

"No. I don't think he'll be needing that anymore," answered DeJong. "What is it they say? Oh, yes: You can't take it with you when you go."

There was an offering of nervous laughter, and then the V-8—minus an accountant and an attorney—filed quietly out the door. Except for Dr. DeJong, Mother and I were the last to exit. The others were already distant voices in the hall, washing away to their own stagnant eddies in the sewer. When Mother placed her hand on the smooth brass doorknob and tried to pull it closed behind her, something inhumanly strong seemed to be pulling from inside. Over her shoulder, I glimpsed a narrow slice of DeJong's face that showed through the crack in the door. I had always thought him relatively handsome for a cyborg. But from a yard away, reduced to an inch-wide strip of eyes, nose, lips, and teeth, he was a technological nightmare.

For a fraction of a second, I imagined I could see right through his wide pores into a soul that was all wires and circuitry.

"Death and romance are so much alike, don't you agree, Roberta?" said DeJong through the crack.

Mother hesitated. "I'm not sure I see the connection, sir," she replied.

"Oh, I'm sure you do. Romance is nothing more than ordinary words and deeds dressed in unfamiliar garb. Take language, for instance. Is there anything as common as a wagging tongue? Yet, in his native dialect, the dullest of foreign men can ask an American woman for directions to the trash dump and straightaway find himself being swooned over as if he had proposed on bended knee. We are all in love with the unfamiliar, Roberta—the sounds, the sights, the smells of it. Of course, death is the ultimate unfamiliarity. So, in a way you and I and Vivi-Centerre and young John, here, have all done this nation a monumental favor. We have taken it back to the age of romance. People ought to be grateful for our contribution."

"I . . . I've got my daily report to file, sir," stammered Mother, starting back so quickly from the door that she nearly stepped on my toes.

DeJong opened the door wider. "Does it excite you to know that in a world where the oldest politician is young enough to be your son or daughter, you hold such awesome power in the twilight of your life?"

"I've never thought about it that way," said Mother.

DeJong tapped his forehead, as if trying to remember something. "What is it this year? Forty-eight? Forty-nine?"

"I'm forty-nine," said Mother quickly.

"Your ex-husband was lucky to have a mate who wears her years well," said DeJong with a wicked grin. "I'm truly sorry his life is coming to an end."

At the realization DeJong knew about her former marriage, Mother appeared to consider her options. But remembering the doctor's uncanny knowledge of Pilcher's whereabouts, she decided against further deceit.

"Thank you, sir," she replied.

Even as a machine, DeJong seemed lecherous. "Did you get an extra bang out of being intimate with a man responsible for the death of millions? Was that especially attractive to you, Roberta?"

"Actually, sir, we were separated long before Long Shadow was in its final draft."

"I see. Then it shouldn't be that difficult for you to watch him die?"

"I suppose not, sir."

"Let's hope not," said DeJong. "You know as well as I how much our cause would benefit if, of all people, the one who penned the majority opinion died honorably for the greatest good."

"Yes, sir," replied Mother.

"I knew you'd see things properly," said DeJong. "Anyway, take care, lest any old affinities detract from your duty. You've always been one of my favorite people. It would break my heart if you wound up like Clark. Good day, Ms. Nash. I'd talk longer, but I've got an entire curriculum to digest for next semester's teaching at the Academy. Pursue the greatest good."

"Of course."

DeJong paused and licked his lips. "You're a vision of loveliness. Run along now."

The door began to close, but just before the sliver of DeJong disappeared from view, I heard one last bit of advice being doled out, and it was directed clearly at me.

"If you're wondering whether or not your new assignment is irreversible, you needn't fret anymore, John," came the sibilant voice. "The job has been given to someone else."

This time the door closed completely, leaving Mother and me alone with our reflections in DeJong's placard. She checked her watch and started off down the hallway ahead of me. At the intersection of corridors A-10 and B-10, we turned left along a wall of cubbyholes, and the drone of the motherboard in Clark Pilcher's former office seemed to mourn the passing of a decent man. Just before we reached the next intersection, I thought I heard a hideous scream. It was long and drawn out and seemed to span several ascending levels of pain before it reached its peak. Then it was drowned out by the clack of keyboards and business-as-usual at Vivi-Centerre.

Mother stopped momentarily. Her back was turned to me, and I could see by the movement of her shoulders that she was having trouble breathing normally. "Good-bye, Clark," she said haltingly.

"Excuse me," I called.

Mother turned around.

"I'm sure you couldn't help noticing Dr. DeJong's obvious suggestion that we know each other," I stated.

"Silly, wasn't it?" said Mother.

"Well, we don't, do we?" I asked.

"I've never seen you before in my life, until this morning," said Mother, her green eyes staring at me unblinkingly. They were the kind of green that reminds you of a lonely mountain tarn, the depth of which is unknown, the color suggesting both verdancy and stagnancy as equal possibilities.

"Of course not," I agreed. "Have a good day."

I hurried from Mother's presence, certain of two things in this world, one of them good and one of them immeasurably bad. To her, I was nothing more than a simple tag man, known perhaps for my marksmanship, but definitely not for my relationship to her or Justice August Nash. That was fine with me, for it would allow me to work my plan in secrecy. On the other hand, to Captain Levi Coffin, I was known for only one thing at the moment. I was late for moving target Monday.

And I was about to be fried.

"The point of a gun was the only law that Liberty understood. . . ."

—From "Music as History,"
Premillennial Archives, vol 1.

THE BASEMENT RANGE WAS QUIET, WHICH could mean only one thing. Roll call had begun, and Captain Levi was probably standing in front of some poor, quaking tag man, cutting him to pieces with those arrogant eyes of his.

"So, you think you're really something?" I heard him shout as I poked my head around the corner of the range's main entrance and peered into the low-ceilinged room. To my surprise, I saw the tag man he was addressing was Tiller, and Tiller was at a loss for words.

"What's the matter?" continued Captain Levi. "You had plenty to say a minute ago. Well, let me tell you something, Tolles. I don't give a rat's backside what you shot against McSwain. I could beat you with a slingshot if you had the guts to challenge me."

"I've got the guts, sir," Tiller said quietly.

"What's that?" asked Levi. He had moved on to some other victim down the line and had not expected a rebuttal from my partner.

"I said, I've got the guts, sir," repeated Tiller, this time with more confidence.

"Oh, do you now? Well, we'll just see about that," replied Levi, smiling cruelly. He looked down the line. "Fowler!" he shouted.

"Yes, sir," answered a wiry novice, snapping a little straighter to attention.

"Reset the barricades for thirty feet," ordered Levi. "We'll shoot from twenty-five yards."

"But, sir—" said Fowler, aware that thirty feet in the moving target event would only allow each shooter three seconds to perform.

"Don't 'but, sir' me, grunt," shouted Levi. "If a professional like Tolles can't bring down a Long Shadow at twenty-five in less than three seconds, then he's got no business being paid for what he does. Now either you do as you are told, Fowler, or you can start looking for another job, too. I can guarantee the benefits won't be as good as this one."

Fowler ran to his task, and I moved farther inside the door behind a row of bleachers, where I could watch the spectacle.

Captain Levi's back was to me. I could see the hard pack of muscle between his shoulders shifting as he loaded his infamous Smith & Wesson. It was a heavy stunner, the first off the line from a company that refused to allow itself to go under just because the government banned the sale of bullets to citizens around the year 2000. Their creation of a weapon that could be sold to the public as a crime deterrent, but which also had a selector switch model for sale to law enforcement agencies, had won S&W a huge contract with VC—one that had catapulted them back into the front of the pack. Levi's gun was a throwback from the days when the barricade was less of a precision event and marksmen had not yet felt obliged to go auto. But the gun was his baby and he was good with it, so he never made the switch. He had won back-to-back Bianchi Cups with "Old Stopper," as he liked to call it, setting a world record for optical sights both times—facts that silenced most critics who considered questioning him about his choice of arms. Those few who blundered ahead with their inquiries sometimes found that Levi Coffin's body, as well as his gun, was capable of enormous leverage.

He had a neatly cropped salt-and-pepper beard, the kind that you could shave the cheek hairs from and still leave a flawless black goatee. He never wore it like that, however, because he believed in staying warm whenever he had winter tracking to do.

"Narrow the firing area by half a foot," said Levi to no one in particular. "I want Tolles to feel the heat." He glared at Tiller.

Several other novices hurried to obey, and I turned my eyes toward my partner, who was tending to his Colt semiauto. His short blond hair bristled beneath the hot lights of the range, and he seemed just about ready to step into the firing area when Levi barked again.

"I wish that cocky partner of yours was here to see me humiliate you, Tolles. I'd school him, too, if he was. You're both cut from the same loser fabric, aren't you?"

To this day I have no idea what came over me, but suddenly I found myself standing and walking out from behind the bleachers.

"Were you looking for me, sir?" I said. When I spoke, my voice sounded like it was coming from the bottom of a distant well.

Captain Levi whirled around, and his lips curled back to expose a row of perfect teeth.

"Well, if it isn't the latecomer," he said. "Do you have a legitimate excuse, or did you just decide to drop by because you had some spare time on your hands?"

"I had business to take care of, sir," I replied.

"Your business is to be here at 9 o'clock sharp," shot Levi.

"I do my best, sir."

"Your best is pitiful," said Levi with disgust. "Line up with the rest of the tags, Nash. Tolles and I are about to give a little demonstration. I think you'll find it interesting."

"Pardon me, sir. But I'd like to take you up on your offer," I said.

"What offer was that?" asked Levi.

"The offer to school me in moving targets, sir. I might benefit from the education."

"Ohh, lieutenant," breathed Captain Levi. "You do love to make it happen, don't you?" He chambered his last round, and clicked the selector switch on Old Stopper. "All right," he said. "I'd just as soon make a fool of you as your friend. But when I'm through with you, you're both out of here. You got that? You and Tolles are through with the tags. I'm sick and tired of you prima donnas being sent down here by VC just because you can plink a can off a fence rail. Well, this isn't BBs with the boys, you know. This is serious work. This is for the greatest good. For all I care, every last one of you can be out there on the streets with Nash and Tolles and the rest of those stinking Long Shadows," said Levi, looking around at the ranks. No one said a word.

"Go get your piece, Nash," said Captain Levi, noticing I had not been to my locker yet. "And make it snappy. You've got people waiting here."

"My partner's will do, sir," I replied, motioning for Tiller to loan me his Colt.

"The drama unfolds," mocked the captain. "The man's not even going to use his own gun. That shows real guts, Nash. I admire someone who takes risks. Ladies first," he said, motioning me toward the firing area.

The murmur of our peers drew down to a crackling hush, while I knelt in the firing area, donned earplugs, and checked Tiller's weapon. When I was ready, I nodded at Fowler, whom Captain Levi had ordered to keep score.

"Roll 'em," said the captain, and someone behind me pushed a button.

The *thwack* of gears squeezed whatever adrenaline was left in the troops into a pool of angst, and the hologram figure of a businessman darted from behind the left barricade.

Blam! I shot a gaping hole in the target's brow.

"Keep 'em coming," growled the captain.

Out came several figures simultaneously; a nanny, a fireman, a sharply dressed executive in her thousand-dollar pantsuit. Lightning-quick, they crisscrossed the range, each of them wearing a brightly flashing bracelet. Occasionally, a young person was interspersed to keep the shooter honest.

Blam! Blam! Blam! the Colt rang. I was shooting cleaner than I'd ever shot before. But the targets began coming at a furious pace and I could hear Captain Levi laughing above the roar of the gun.

"Now he'll miss," predicted the captain.

But there were no misses in Tiller's gun that day. Hologram after hologram flew by me on its track, each with a new, crisp hole in the appropriate spot. Even as the last two bolted from behind the barricades and I saw they were aligning in such a way that a clean shot would be possible on only one of them, I took command of my breathing, estimated the exact point where one would overtake the other, and squeezed the trigger just as the targets crossed paths.

When I removed my earplugs, I was surprised to find that an awkward hush had fallen over the room and everyone except Captain Levi was looking at Fowler.

"Perfect score," said Fowler timidly.

"Impossible," hissed the captain as he reversed the tracks to check my last two holograms. Even he was unable to hide his astonishment when he discovered I had bagged an investment banker and an attorney with one incredible shot. "Nothing but luck," he said, still staring at my handiwork. Suddenly remembering a meeting he was late for, Captain Levi flew from the room in a cloud of profanity.

"I guess that means we keep our jobs," said Tiller, which brought nervous laughter from everyone present. On the way to pick up our towels for the sauna, Tiller lavished me with praise. "Man, I knew you were good, but I've never seen anyone shoot like that before. Where'd you learn that last trick?"

"Plinking cans in my spare time," I replied. Again, we suppressed our joy, uncertain whether Captain Levi was really out of earshot. At the desk, we found that news of my X-count—as well as Captain Levi's tantrum—had already spread. The man in charge of towels went out of his way to congratulate me, pumping my arm up and down as if I were some dignitary. After I extricated myself from the man's praise and the two of us were heading for a shower, I glanced around to see if our resident member of the opposite sex was present to witness all the attention being given to me.

"Does she leave any hot water for the rest of us?" I asked.

"Who? McSwain?"

"How many other *she*s do you know in the tag corps?"

"I'd forget about her if I were you," warned Tiller.

"Well, you're not me. But while we're on it, why should I forget about her?"

We turned the corner toward the locker room and Tiller swung his towel over his shoulder. "Haven't you heard?" he asked, looking at me as if I had posed an unforgivably stupid question.

"Heard what?"

"McSwain was transferred from VC North as a last-ditch effort before dishonorable discharge."

I had to laugh. "What'd she do, use someone's razor to shave her legs in the shower?"

Tiller came to an abrupt halt in the hallway. "Sarah McSwain is pregnant," he announced.

A chill raced along my arms, and I knew that if Tiller had not been looking down the hall in the direction of our fellow tag men, he would have seen me shiver. Quickly, I regained my composure. "So?" I replied.

"You know the rules. A woman can't give birth and be in the tags, John. It's as simple as that. You get involved with her and you're on a fast train to heartache."

"That's the pot calling the kettle black," I said sourly. "You have Lacee. Who are you to talk?"

Tiller glanced around. "Yeah, and there're times I think I'm in way over my head."

"Well, why didn't North just issue McSwain a bracelet and get rid of her?" I asked.

"Because you don't just get rid of the best female marksman in the country. I guess they thought she could be rehabilitated by placing her under Coffin's care for a while."

"I see. So she's sort of a reclamation project. Has she been cured of her maternal instinct yet?"

"You tell me. Last night she brought in a Long Shadow that Roberts and Jameson had been tracking for a year. Apparently, the target was so used to watching out for male tag men that McSwain got her. The suits were very impressed."

"Speaking of suits, I just got out of a meeting with Dr. DeJong. He was his usual cheery self."

Tiller suppressed a laugh. "Right. And Captain Levi is the strong yet sensitive type. Did our dear mechanical friend have any sagely advice for us peons?"

"No, just the routine stuff. We bug 'em, you plug 'em. Say, Tiller," I said, glancing at him, "this McSwain sounds like someone I'd like to meet."

"Well, you may not get the chance if she keeps her baby. Rumor has it VC is holding her pay until she agrees to abort. So far, she's been showing up to work for free. She's a stubborn one."

I shook my head. "She's more than stubborn. I'd bet my paycheck McSwain's got a moral compass that's been telling her to head in a different direction lately."

"What makes you an expert on her character? You haven't even met her."

"Call it a hunch. Don't you ever get that feeling that something or someone is about to explode onto the stage of your life, and when it finally happens it makes perfect sense?"

"You know, John, you are really weird sometimes. Did you do drugs when you were a kid?"

"Enough antidepressants to fill a swimming pool. What did you say her first name was?"

"I told you I'd forget about her, if I were you."

"Stop saying that."

"I just think you ought to be careful."

"Oh, what do you know?" I said, waving away his advice with the sweep of a hand.

"I know a whole lot about this kind of thing," said Tiller, lowering his voice to a whisper. "You don't think Lacee and I have kept from getting caught because we're stupid, do you?"

"Is she still seeing someone?" I asked.

Tiller gave me a blank look. "What?"

"You know, the father of the child. Are she and he—"

"How should I know?" said Tiller.

"See there? You don't know as much as you think you do."

"I know I don't want my partner to have anything to do with a pregnant tag man," said Tiller.

"Ah-ah. Pregnant tag *person*," I corrected.

"Whatever," said Tiller. "I'm just doing my best to keep my own life a secret."

"Now I understand. You think I'll blab your story in a moment of passion."

We started down the hall again without saying a word to each other, all the while listening to the grumbling of our colleagues up ahead, who wished desperately for the old days when the tag corps was exclusively male and a man didn't have to wait thirty minutes to take a shower. Eventually, I broke the silence.

"Do you ever feel guilty for doing this job?" I asked, glancing at Tiller for his reaction.

This time when he stopped, Tiller grabbed me hard by the elbow.

"That's the second time today you've made me wonder about you," said Tiller. "I mean, first you're late to the most important practice of the week—not to mention the fact it's already the sixth time this year you've done that. Now you're talking like you and I are some sort of neo-Nazis who ought to be ashamed of our occupations. Let me remind you there are people upstairs with their eyes and ears glued to those monitors," said Tiller, pointing to one of the cameras near the ceiling. He leaned closer to me and I could have sworn his voice was trembling. "I need you, man," he whispered. "You have no idea how much you keep me sane around this place."

"All right," I said, yanking loose from his grip. "I'm just tired of all the blood. Okay?"

"S-h-u-t-u-p!" hissed Tiller, moving me farther from the camera. "Who's feeding you this stuff?" he demanded.

"Nobody."

"Then why the overactive conscience all of a sudden?"

"I've been doing some reading, that's all."

Tiller eyed me with suspicion. "What kind of reading?"

"Just reading. Is there a law against that?"

"What *kind* of reading?" Tiller persisted.

"I can read whatever I want to."

"Why do I feel like what you're keeping from me is going to change everything between us?"

"Well, if a few crumpled pages from a Bible have that much impact, then I'd say our friendship was never much to begin with," I said. It felt good to admit it. Even the crumpled paper in my pocket seemed to diminish in weight the moment I said the words. The look on Tiller's face, however, suggested a definite heaviness had settled in his soul.

"That's just great," he said. "What am I supposed to do now? Get all excited and do handsprings over this new revelation? I've got a family to feed, John. I can't afford to get caught up in your guilty conscience, even if you are my partner."

"I'm your friend, too," I reminded him.

"Okay, you're my friend. But that doesn't mean I'll take the fall with you. This is dangerous stuff, John. Too dangerous for me to be around."

"It's just a couple of pages from—" I started to remove the wad from my pocket to check the title.

"For God's sake," said Tiller, grabbing me by the wrist and glancing again at the camera, which had begun to pan toward the recession in the wall where Tiller had steered me. "Act normal," he said. He took his stun from its holster and began showing it to me as if something about it were of great interest to the two of us. The camera lagged momentarily when it got to us, then continued on its arc. "Come on," said Tiller, steering me with force toward the showers. "At least there'll be some privacy in the sauna. Unless they've started putting surveillance in there, too."

Under the cloak of steam, I tried to explain to Tiller that I wasn't going religious on him. "I'm just trying to bring some order to my life," was the best I could manage. The more I tried, the more he seemed intent not on dissuading me, but on discerning whether what I was saying was really heartfelt.

"Do you know what happens to a person when VC catches them with stuff like that?" he asked, pointing toward my damp tangle of jeans in the corner of the sauna.

"Remind me," I replied sarcastically.

"Immediate termination. Whether you're a Long Shadow or not."

"I'm a big boy. I can take care of myself."

"Then you've considered what would happen to you if you got caught with that kind of . . . of *propaganda* in your billfold?"

"I'm getting tired of this interrogation."

"Answer my question."

"All right, I've considered it. I've also considered the part that says *Thou shalt not kill.* And while we're on the topic, I've considered looking after my father, too. Is that good enough for you? Is that what you're probing for?"

Tiller didn't react at first. For a moment I thought he was going to let my announcement lose itself like a drop of moisture in the sauna's atmosphere. After a further silence, he bored into me with those eyes of his, blue as ice.

"I didn't know he was yours to look after," said Tiller, lowering his voice to an unusually intimate volume, as if he were afraid someone had snuck into our midst unnoticed and was recording our every word. "The last I checked, the new assignments hadn't come out yet."

"They haven't. I'm assigning him to myself."

"You're going to kill your own father?"

"I'm going to set him free in Canada," I replied, looking away from Tiller.

"You're insane," Tiller whispered. "How long have you been planning this?"

"About an hour," I said. Then I checked my answer. "Do you really want to know?"

"We're partners, aren't we?"

"I've had the plan since I was nine."

"You know you can't just wing this job," said Tiller forcefully. "Things like this aren't done nowadays."

"Look at the things that *are* done nowadays," I replied.

"Shhh," he said, with a look of unforgettable reproach. Apparently he thought my voice could travel through a half foot of cedarwood and stone. "You're acting awfully strange, John."

"*I'm* acting strange? What about this job? We hunt people for a living. Have we done it so many times that we've lost sight of how strange that is?"

"VC's not going to put up with your nonsense."

"That's something we'll have to deal with."

"Is that a you-we or a me-we?"

"It's an us, Tiller. We're partners. Remember?"

"Yeah, yeah, so I said. We're friends, too," said Tiller. "And if it were *my* pedotrainer, I wouldn't be asking my best friend to look the other way while I disregarded company rules."

"If it were your pedotrainer, you'd have him stuffed and mounted before he could say Jack Robinson."

"That's not fair," objected Tiller. "I'm just concerned about you, that's all. You're not going to get all male-bonded with your old man, then decide to quit the tags, are you? I mean, you're only talking about helping one Long Shadow run, not changing an entire career, right? John?"

Suddenly it had become unbearably hot in the sauna.

"John?" repeated Tiller.

"What?" I replied.

"I said—"

"I heard what you said."

"So talk to me."

"What do you want me to say?"

"You *will* keep your job as a tag man, won't you?"

"I don't know."

"What do you mean, you don't know?" said Tiller.

"Like I told you, I'm tired of all the blood."

Tiller's eye twitched, and the twitch spoke volumes about some enormous cause within him that he had kept hidden from me and everyone. Many times since that day I've thought of that twitch, and I've wished I had hastened to read what it was trying to say about him. But no sooner had it come, than the twitch was gone and Tiller's face returned to normal. He drew his voice down to almost inaudible decibels.

"Do you swear not to tell anyone what I'm about to say to you?" he asked.

"It depends on—"

"You've got to swear!" said Tiller.

For a moment or two I stared at him in silence. "All right, I swear," I said at last.

"Would it surprise you to know I'm tired of the blood, too?" he said suddenly.

I stifled a laugh. "You? Tired of the blood? That'll be the day."

"For your information, you're not the only one in VC with a sense of morality."

"Yeah, right. I suppose next you're going to tell me you're the mysterious Shadow Train, and all those citations for completed bounty contracts hanging in your locker are just figments of my imagination."

Tiller neither confirmed nor denied my words. He just sat there, cross-legged on the bench, staring at me. Presently it came to me that he wanted my last statement to be trimmed of sarcasm and reweighed for its true measure.

"You can't be serious."

Once again, he said nothing.

"Tiller, the Shadow Train is just a legend. Besides, the Shadow Train doesn't kill its clients, it helps them. I've seen you bring Long Shadows down at two hundred yards with a single shot."

"But did I kill them?" asked Tiller.

"Of course you k—"

"Name one," demanded Tiller.

"I can't recall them without looking at the records."

"Why not, John? You don't seem to need the records to accuse me of murder. Name one incident."

"Well, there was the Harjo gentleman down in Roman Nose. He was that accountant who kept a dozen of us employed last January." I was grasping.

"And?" said Tiller.

"What do you mean *and?*" I replied. "You shot him in the second lumbar."

"With my stun switch on and he fell off a cliff," said Tiller. "When we got back to VC, did you ever bother to check the medical report for cause of death?"

"No."

"No. That's right. You didn't. You never do. I'm always the one who's left with the paperwork. If you had bothered to look, you would have seen it was the fall that killed him, not a bullet wound."

I was just preparing to defend myself when someone stuck his head inside the sauna, and it sounded like he was feeling around for something on the bench. When I thought he was gone, I continued my defense just barely above a whisper.

"I shirk my share of the paperwork because I'm starting to wonder if I'm right for the job," I said.

"That's all well and good, but you still think I'm a murderer," said Tiller indignantly.

"What am I supposed to think? That you're some kind of traffic cop or something? For crying out loud, Tiller, you're one of the top commission earners every year!"

"I won't be after the baby arrives," lamented Tiller. "I'll be so tired from changing diapers all night, I won't be able to shoot straight."

"Forget firearms, Tiller," I said, shifting the subject. "I've seen what you can do with a team of dogs, too. I've been there when the fur flies and the screams begin."

"If you're thinking of that time in Leavenworth, it was purely circumstantial," said Tiller. "It wasn't my fault the collar broke. If you stopped to think before shooting your mouth off, you'd see that I'm not as evil as you imagine I am. Check my records, John. Check all of them."

"What will I find there?"

"You'll find that 90 percent of the people we brought in last year were still alive when we got to VC. They were alive because I went for a leg or an arm, rather than a kill shot. Truth is, if you hadn't come bungling up on many of those scenes, I'd have—"

"You'd have what?" I asked.

"Never mind," said Tiller, gathering his towel around him.

Suddenly, we heard the door to the sauna pull softly closed, and I realized somebody had been listening to us the whole time. I started to stand, but Tiller grabbed my wrist.

"Let him go," he said.

"Okay. But I'm not letting go of what it was you were going to say a second ago. Something about me bungling up on you."

"You wouldn't believe me if I told you, anyway," said Tiller.

"Try me," I insisted.

"Come on," said Tiller, ignoring my question. He pushed open the sauna door and walked briskly toward the locker area. "Let's talk while we shave. I could use your help on some research."

"Research? For what?"

"An old assignment of mine—something DeJong handed down to me a while back."

"DeJong?" I said with surprise. "Well, it must be something pretty important if he cared enough to get involved."

We shaved next to each other at adjacent sinks, while all around us our colleagues splashed cologne on their young faces, combed their hair, brushed their teeth, and, in general, gussied up to go out into the world and terminate their fellow man. Tiller finished before I did and went quickly to his locker to dress himself. He was sitting there, tying his shoes, when I found him.

"I'd like to hear about that old assignment of yours," I said.

From the showers, a block of pale light fell across Tiller and the wooden bench on which he sat. He stared at me for a moment while a word formed on his lips, struggled to assume sound, then passed with a sigh as quickly as it had come. When he finally spoke, both of us knew that what he had intended to say had vanished forever.

"There's another reason I think you ought to stay as far away as possible from McSwain."

"Is there now?" I replied with skepticism.

Tiller paid unusual attention to his shoes as he tied them. "They're going to make a cyborg out of her," he said quickly.

I burst out in laughter. "Oh, that's funny—that's very funny. Of all the crazy reasons a person could come up with to keep me from—"

Tiller stood up. "I'm not kidding," he snapped. He walked around to the other side of the lockers to see if anyone was dressing there. When he came back he had the look of a man who, having made up his mind to say something, was now going to say it quickly before he had a chance to change his mind again.

"There's something going on up in SimTech," he breathed.

"There's *always* something going on up in SimTech."

"Not like this," said Tiller. "They're talking about taking all the really good tag men and doing something to them to make them more, more . . . I don't know, more efficient or something."

"It's called cybermorphosis, Tiller. They've been considering it for the last ten years."

Tiller poked his head around the lockers again to check for eavesdroppers. "Well, this time they're through considering. Rumor is, they've already got a bunch of prototypes in the field and they think McSwain is perfect for the experiment, seeing how she's been stirring up morale with her attitude, anyway."

"It's not like I'm going to ask her to produce a matri-sak with me," I assured him. "I just want to get to know her, that's all."

"You don't understand," said Tiller, his words suddenly leaning down over me. "They're like wild animals, perfect killing machines, with brains that can think as well as you and I. You want to be involved with an animal?"

"Sounds like you're afraid of being made into one, too."

"Wouldn't you be, if you had a family to think about?" asked Tiller, clearly terrified at the thought.

"Could we just forget the whole topic?" I asked. "From now on if I want to get to know McSwain, I'll leave you out of it. Okay?"

"Get your shoes on," said Tiller suddenly. I started to object, but he opened my locker and threw a pair of boots in my direction. "Hurry up. There's free lunch in the club for the guys who brought in twenty Long Shadows last month."

Before I could tell him lunch with fellow killers did not appeal to me, Tiller had taken me by the arm again—he was always doing that—and led me out the steaming glass doors.

"On second thought, lunch can wait," he said as we set off into the vast, arterial hallways of Vivi-Centerre. "There's someone I want you to meet."

4

SO, WHO'S THIS SPECIAL SOMEONE?" I ASKED Tiller as we rounded the corner of the hall. I noticed that he continued past the door marked Research.

"Be patient and you'll find out soon enough," said Tiller, pausing in front of the third door which was slightly ajar. He pushed against the solid oak and it made a whispering sound against the carpet.

"Captain Levi!" I exclaimed when I saw my superior standing at the illuminated end of a dark room. I tacked a hasty 'sir' on to avoid the usual reprimand, then filed in after Tiller, who took an abrupt right face, leaving me to stand at attention by myself. The room was completely dark, save the bluish glow of a wall-size monitor that served as backlighting to the captain and made it impossible to see any of his features except the distinct vertical bulge on the side of his neck. His carotids always betrayed his anger.

"You seem to have a rather familiar attitude with your superiors, Nash," said Captain Levi, rising from his desk.

"Yes, sir. I—"

"That's an attitude that can get you in a lot of trouble."

As my eyes grew accustomed to the dark, it became evident to me that the room was semi-filled with tag men. Some

I recognized immediately, even saw them flash dim signs in my direction to show they knew exactly how I felt at the moment. But others, particularly those nearer the front of the room, were strangers to me. I had only enough time to guess that they were visitors from neighboring VC regions before Captain Levi was yelling at me again.

"I bet you think you proved something out there today, don't you, Nash?" he said, stepping toward me in the dark.

I opened my mouth to speak, but Captain Levi cut me off.

"You proved nothing," he said. "Unless you think movers at twenty-five is a definitive display of prowess."

"I thought your invitation was genuine, sir."

"It was, but I never forget a subordinate who shows me up in front of grunts," growled Levi. For an instant, I thought I saw a flicker of a smile come to his lips. Before I could confirm it, he ordered me to take a seat. Finding one in the back of the room, I leaned against the cool wall, content to lose myself in the shadows.

I felt a pat on my knee and smelled the familiar odor of peppermint and cigarettes. "Way to go," whispered Tiller.

"What's this about?" I demanded.

"Give it a second. It'll all make sense to you," said Tiller. He seemed to be on the edge of his chair, ready to ask a question, but not quite sure when to interrupt Captain Levi, who had returned to whatever it was he was talking about before we blundered in. Behind him on the monitor, images of a military tank snapped into motion again, and I quickly deduced that this was some type of training presentation—one to which I had not been invited. At least there had been no notice of it from Maggie.

"Were you informed of this?" I whispered to Tiller, who told me to shut up again. He was beginning to irritate me.

"In the early fourteenth century, Europeans used guns in battle for the first time," boomed Captain Levi, awash in blue at the front of the room. He held up a thin glass vial filled with an undisclosed substance. It was not unusual for Captain Levi to lapse into long, historical goose chases whenever he taught. Actually, he saw no reason to limit himself to history when there was so much of every topic that he was armed with, and so little classtime in which to deploy it. We were often bombarded with short-range pontifications and intercontinental soliloquies that rendered divots in even the stoniest of minds. Nevertheless, someone told me once that history was his favorite and that he had studied it in college, back before the Academy revisionists made the past more "suitable" for the masses.

"The Europeans' secret was gunpowder," continued Captain Levi, holding out the vial so that everyone could see it. "Everyone but their enemies extolled the virtues of this volatile mixture of chemicals that exploded when lit. Over the years, all wars have sung its praises. But gunpowder has its limitations. Can any of you tell me one of them?"

"It's slower than a grunt," came an officer's voice from several rows ahead of me. A volley of laughter rose to the ceiling.

"Correct," replied Captain Levi. "It is indeed a dreadfully slow propellant. Slower than some veterans I know on Monday mornings, too." He fixed his eyes toward me in the back of the room and waited for the remark to take root in my heart before continuing. "As you well know, around the turn of the Millennium a team of Army-sponsored researchers at—" he paused to query the class—"what university?"

"Texas in Austin, sir," came the answer.

"Precisely," said Captain Levi. "A team of researchers at Texas in Austin demonstrated a revolutionary new technology that changed the way we looked at warfare. Overnight, we had the power to kill each other with far more efficiency than gunpowder could ever provide. And what, pray tell, is that revolutionary technology to which I am referring?" A buzz went around in the dark. "Speak up," ordered Captain Levi. "This is not a game show."

"Electromagnetic rail guns, sir?" someone responded.

"Is that a question or a statement?" replied the captain.

"Electromagnetic rail guns, sir," declared the same respondent, this time more confidently.

"My, we are lucid today," said Captain Levi. "I noticed on the board this morning that some of you are up for evaluation in the near future. I suggest you bone up on your history of armaments."

Captain Levi went on to remind us of the law of physics behind EM technology.

"It is an awesome law when you stop to think about it," he said, referring to the fact that an electric current can intersect with a magnetic field and generate force which accelerates projectiles to more than ten kilometers per second. "Thank God, government banned bullets from the public. Weaponry like this would cause havoc for us if it ever fell into the hands of disgruntled Long Shadows," Captain Levi continued. "But it's bulky and expensive still. Actually, it's never been installed in anything smaller than a tank. That is . . . until now."

The room erupted in curious murmurs, and I felt Tiller edge farther ahead on his chair.

"Captain, sir," he said, with his hand extended high so that Captain Levi could see him in the dark.

"Not now, Tolles," snapped the captain. "I've arrived at the most astounding part of the story. After all, it's not every day that something comes along that makes our jobs easier. It's always the other guys finding new ways to bump us off when we least expect it."

"How heartless of them," said someone sardonically.

Captain Levi did not appreciate the laughter that followed. Angrily, he clicked several images forward until he found what he was looking for. It was a picture of a demolished border blockade, complete with tag men strewn across the asphalt like rag dolls. In the background was a road sign that read, "Welcome to scenic Alberta."

"You'll think *heartless* next time you're sent to do time on the Canadian border," shouted Captain Levi, and the room fell as quiet as a morgue. "Our friend, Benny Newsome, had that same attitude, too, until last weekend." There was a collective shaking of heads. "That's right," said the captain. "Good old Benny from VC North. Some of you remember trying to tackle him in the interregional football championship last fall. He was a stout individual with a perilously soft heart, and not an enemy in the world. He thought all folks were just born naturally good, and couldn't care a whit about having their lives cut short at fifty. You can imagine his surprise the morning two Long Shadows drove a semi through his barricade and laid him out like a skin to dry."

"Captain," tried Tiller again.

Levi brushed him off again.

"Things would have been different for Benny if his number for border duty had come up a week later. Here's the reason why," said Captain Levi, reaching in the drawer of his desk and producing a strange-looking weapon. It had the basic shape of a pistol, but with all sorts of unusual gadgetry attached. "Raise your hand if you've ever seen one of these." he said. Not a single hand went up. "Of course you haven't. Because until this morning the only size it was available in was this." Captain Levi reversed the remote until the image of the tank appeared on the screen again. "All ten tons of her," he concluded.

"I'm not following, sir," said someone.

Recognizing the voice as belonging to a reckless tag man by the name of Stanton, Captain Levi wasted no time in drawing attention to his carelessness.

"You're not following, Stanton, because you neither care nor have ever shown the inclination to do so. In short, you are exactly the type of tag man who will probably be smoking a cigarette or reading a letter from your pedotrainer when some Long Shadow puts a bullet through your brain. But for those of you who care enough to follow, let me explain." Another click of the remote and we were looking at a cross section of the tank's insides.

"The reasons why the weapon I'm holding has been a fantasy until this morning are fairly obvious," said Captain Levi. He took a long wooden pointer and stepped toward the screen. "The challenge for those original researchers at Texas in Austin was to find a way to store the monstrous amount of electricity needed to operate an EM gun. That challenge has remained the same for forty years, with minor breakthroughs along the way but never anything to brag about. But last year an engineer by the name of Gullickson found a way to shrink the size of the flywheel and cylinder used in the Texas project, and . . . voilá." Captain Levi held up the gun. "Rather than an eight-foot-long cylinder, we have an eight-inch one capable of hoarding vast energy by spinning seventeen thousand rotations per minute."

"That's impossible, sir," I said, risking wrath again. "It would take an aircraft turbine to convert the rotational energy to electric current."

"Indeed it would, Nash—yesterday," said Captain Levi. "But today I stand before you with a gun powerful enough to stop a whole battalion of tanks, yet small enough to be concealed inside my jacket. I could go to dinner with it and no one would ever suspect I was carrying."

"Isn't that slight overkill? It's not as if we need a cannon to bring a Long Shadow down."

Captain Levi's eyes grew wild and I could see his carotids clearly again. He started down the aisle, pointing the gun straight at me, and suddenly I was not much concerned with the possibility of overkill. I only hoped the effects of the EM were swift and painless.

"Wait a minute, Captain," said Tiller, trying to position his body between us. Captain Levi shoved him aside.

"You're a burr in my saddle, Nash," shouted the captain, leveling the gun at my chest.

I ducked as he triggered the power. There was an enormous blast, and the smell of the flywheel winding down. Then everyone was looking up at the five-foot hole in the ceiling.

"You could have killed him, sir," choked Tiller, who was hanging onto the captain's arm with the assistance of several others. Apparently, Tiller had acted just before Captain Levi fired. Otherwise, I would have made an interesting wall decoration.

"I suppose it's not my lucky day for movers," Captain Levi said, eyeing me. "Now, what was it you've been trying to tell me, Tolles?"

The next words from Tiller's lips were enough to make me wish the captain had been lucky enough to finish me off.

"He's going to help his father run, sir," answered Tiller.

I was up in a flash, backing toward the door, denying anything and everything. "What are you saying?" I croaked, as I stumbled over a chair. "He's crazy, sir. He doesn't know what he's talking about."

"Is it true, Nash?" roared Captain Levi, breaking loose from the men who held him.

"Of course not, sir," I insisted, scrambling to regain my feet. "Tell him, Tiller. Tell him you were just kidding."

"What's to kid about?" said Tiller.

"Tiller, please," I begged.

Captain Levi leveled the gun at my face this time, and I felt all the fluid in my body shove its way to the bottom of my abdomen. Suddenly he began to laugh, and the more he laughed, the more I felt the need to be far from his presence. I noticed that Tiller was laughing, too. The whole room was laughing, as if they had anticipated the punch line to some joke for a long time, and were thankful now for release in their bellies.

"John," said Tiller, extending his upturned palms toward the roomful of men, as if he were introducing me to dignitaries, "Meet the Shadow Train."

I stood like a fish with my mouth wide open and gaping.

"He doesn't believe you, Tolles," bellowed Captain Levi, scarcely able to contain himself.

"There's a hole in the ceiling," I said in a daze.

"Yes, there is," said the captain. "And I'm getting tired of fixing it. Private Cox?"

"Yes, sir?" replied a tag man in the chair next to the one I had fallen over.

"Get up to maintenance. Tell them we let another grunt handle the EM rail."

There was another explosion of laughter.

"Right away, sir," said Cox, heading for the door.

When Cox had gone, I felt the weight of eyes upon me and I slumped against the wall where I was standing.

"What's the matter, Nash?" said Captain Levi. "Too much to digest in one sitting?"

"I . . . I guess I just didn't—"

"Didn't expect the good guys to be so close at hand, did you?" said the captain.

"You might say that."

"Well, don't worry about it, Nash. Everyone thinks like that at first. You should have seen your partner when he made the great discovery."

I turned to Tiller.

"He's right," said Tiller. "I couldn't believe my ears when I found out someone else in VC felt like I did."

The initials of our employer caused me to instinctively lower my voice in order to avoid surveillance.

"Shouldn't we be more . . ."

"Discreet?" said Captain Levi. "Not really. We sweep the place for bugs every morning. I also requested that the office above us be left vacant. To my knowledge it hasn't been occupied in years."

"Which is a good thing for someone, sir," laughed Tiller. "He'd have had his legs shot off by now, the way you've been getting into it lately."

"Getting into it?" I repeated.

"You know," said Tiller. "The bit about Captain Levi acting like he was going to shoot you."

"So, this is all an act?" I asked incredulously.

"That depends on what you mean by 'all,'" said Captain Levi.

"Well, this meeting . . . this, this pretense of whatever it is you call this little assembly."

"My good friend, John," said the captain, becoming suddenly more familiar with me than I'd ever imagined him capable. "There is nothing pretentious about Vivi-Centerre. It is still every bit the coldhearted killing machine it has always been. I take that quite seriously, so much so, in fact, that I am extremely unwilling to receive into my confidences every Tom, Dick, or Harry who wants to spare his favorite aunt Matilda from termination. Their kind are usually fair-weather saviors, and I have no use for them. Benevolence is a trait I've learned to trust sparingly."

Captain Levi glanced at Tiller as if to question my own trustworthiness one last time.

"He's solid, sir," assured Tiller. "How many others have you known who'd admit they read the Bible in the hallway of VC, without a second thought about the cameras?"

"He may be solid, but he's going to have to show a lot more restraint than that," muttered Captain Levi, turning back toward his desk.

We found our chairs again and leaned back against the wall.

"You're in," whispered Tiller, as the picture of the tank disappeared from the screen and was replaced by a map of the United States.

"In what?" I asked.

"In the Shadow Train," he replied as nonchalantly as he had said it the first time. He must have seen the same codfish look on my face, because I felt him pat my knee again and, in his own way, heard him reassuring me in the dark.

"What did you think this was?" he asked. "Some sort of discussion group?"

"Do you mean to tell me everyone has been in on this but *me*?"

"Not by a long shot. You heard the captain. VC's as committed as ever to 'the greatest good.' There're just a few of us who buck the system."

"It's too good to be true," I said, shaking my head.

"Yeah. Isn't it great?"

"Why didn't you ever tell me?"

"It's not the kind of thing you talk about around here. Captain Levi gives us strict orders not to tell anyone, unless we're absolutely sure they think like us. I can't tell you how many times I hoped you would come around."

"But . . . but the way you acted in the hall—"

"Oh yeah, sorry about that. Anyway, you'll learn real quick that you can't be part of the Shadow Train and go around flashing pages from the Bible."

"Okay, I'm new at this. But tell me something," I said, leaning closer to Tiller. "Where in the world does Captain Levi fit into this? In my wildest dreams, I couldn't imagine him going against VC."

"Didn't you ever pay attention in history class?" asked Tiller.

"What's that got to do with anything?" I replied.

"Levi Coffin, man," said Tiller. "He was the captain's distant grandpa. That's where he gets his name."

A sudden chill raced down my arms. "Are you talking about *the* Levi Coffin, president of *the* Atlantic Underground Railroad?"

"Was there more than one?"

"Tiller, slavery ended almost two hundred years ago."

"Tell that to a Long Shadow."

"But—"

"Shhh," said Tiller. "Now we get down to business."

On the map, a pinpoint of laser light darted from town to town, and all eyes were riveted to its movement.

"All right," said Captain Levi. "Last month we had a half dozen Shadows use the Nishnabotna route, so I think we'll back off of that one for a while. Sioux City might be open again, if the heat's off, that is. Does anybody have the stats on Sioux?"

"Nine tag poles are out of commission, sir," said Cox, who had returned from maintenance with materials for patching the ceiling.

"Did anyone in maintenance seem suspicious about your questions?" asked Captain Levi.

"Not really, sir," answered Cox. "The poles were right there being worked on. Anyone could have asked."

"The entire poles were there?" asked Levi.

"Yes, sir. As far as I could tell, sir."

Captain Levi chuckled. "Okay, who's been having fun in Sioux City?"

A hand went up near the front of the room.

"What were you using, Martinelli, a rocket launcher?" asked the captain.

A good-natured Italian colleague stood to attention. "No, sir. Night scope on a shoulder-held stunner. I guess I got carried away."

"I guess so," said Captain Levi. "Remind me never to issue you an EM rail. You'd be a menace to society."

The room began to tease the overzealous tag man. I, on the other hand, was caught between the desire to cheer and the incredible fear that I was being swept into something that could swallow us all if VC ever caught wind of what was going on here. Ever since I was a child in the Academy, I had had it drummed into me that you never touched a tag pole—units placed by the thousands throughout the country for the purpose of sounding their alarm whenever a Long Shadow whose T-date has expired passes by. Now, here were these colleagues of mine blasting the very pillars of VC's vast tracking network and laughing about their exploits. It was indeed too much for me to digest at one sitting.

"So Martinelli's done his share in Sioux City," said Captain Levi. "How about the rest of you guys? Anybody bother to check with dispatch to see how many tag men are still being sent to this area?" With his laser light, Captain Levi marked a narrow corridor alongside the Floyd River, between Sioux City, Iowa, and its neighbor to the north, Orange City. He waited for a response. When no one made a sound, he slammed his desk with his hand and glared at the screen.

"I will not let that route be jeopardized on account of irresponsibility. It has been in existence since before the Civil War, and if you think I'm going to stand by and—"

"I'll check with dispatch," interrupted Tiller.

"See that you do," shot Captain Levi. "I aim to use the Floyd River route this month, maybe even with our new friend, Nash. What do you think, Nash?" he asked, looking straight at me. "Is there someone on your assignment list you'd like us to set free?"

Now, if there is a time in every man's career where he reaches a point of no return, and upon his arrival must make the decision to either press farther up the ladder or take the plunge into occupational suicide, then this was that point for me, and I was terrified.

"Yes there is, sir," I answered. "He's not actually my assignment."

"And who would that be?" asked Captain Levi.

"My father," I said, swallowing dryly.

The room fell silent.

"Ahh, yes. Supreme Court Justice August Nash," amplified Captain Levi, as if he wanted to formalize the matter. "He's due for termination in a week, is he not?"

"Yes, sir," I replied.

"Well, then . . . that does change things considerably," said the captain, as the room came alive with the excited whisperings and half-concealed gestures of men trained to be wary of their closest friends.

I turned to Tiller. "*What* changes things considerably?"

"He means that since your father is such a high-profile Long Shadow, maybe the highest ever, he'll be watched like a hawk by every tag man looking to make a dollar. It won't be easy getting him to Canada."

"Class dismissed," said Captain Levi suddenly, and someone in the back of the room turned the lights on.

"Looks like that's it for today," said Tiller, standing to leave.

I started to protest, but the others were filing past us now, assuming once again the loud, bravado voices of men who kill for hire and have long since ceased to feel guilty about it.

"That's it?" I said, standing on tiptoe to see over the heads of those who had come between Tiller and me. "We just got here. We haven't done anything yet."

"That's because we got here late," said Tiller. "The excitement of your little tiff with Captain Levi disrupted the normal flow of things."

"So what is the normal flow of things? What do they, I mean, *we* do at these meetings?" I asked.

"Study maps, schedules, timetables, that sort of thing. It's a huge task moving large quantities of human beings across hostile territory without being detected. Last year alone, we liberated over three thousand Long Shadows."

"This has been going on for years? Right here in VC?"

"Yep. Right under your nose."

All the while we were talking, Captain Levi was shutting down the screen and stuffing his lecture notes into his briefcase and dimming the lights. Finally, he called for Tolles.

"Coming, sir," said Tiller. He turned to me and whispered, "Look sharp, now. The captain takes best to those who take him seriously."

"Hurry up," commanded Captain Levi. "And bring that friend of yours up here. I can use a good shot like him in the Shadow Train."

We navigated between rows of chairs to the front of the room and stood stiffly beside the captain's desk. Several uncomfortable moments passed wherein Levi silently scrutinized me from head to toe. The only sound in the room was that of his heavy breathing.

"I'm sorry I was late this morning, sir," I offered.

Captain Levi paused to recall my tardiness. "I was rather hard on you, wasn't I?"

"You were doing your job," I replied.

"Job or not, I'd like to put it behind us," said Captain Levi, offering to shake on the matter. When I took his hand, he jerked me forward until we were nearly chest to chest. "You have no idea how hard it is for a man to maintain an evil facade, when deep down he's really a lamb. Can we forgive and forget?" he asked.

"Consider it done," I replied.

"Good," said the captain, releasing my hand. "Now that that's taken care of, tell me what I can do for your father."

"Maybe you can help me find him, sir," I said.

Levi cleared his throat and Tiller looked away, as if he had already heard what was about to be said and felt embarrassed for keeping it to himself.

"Unfortunately," said the captain, "the finding of your father will not be that difficult."

"That's good, isn't it?"

"Not exactly. You see, Nash, upon your father's departure from Rivendale—"

"How did you know about that?" I interrupted.

Tiller cleared his throat. "We have our ways," he said quickly.

"What ways?" I demanded, backing away from the two men.

"Easy, Nash," said Captain Levi. "What your partner is saying is that we keep a constant watch on all high-risk Long Shadows. When we think they're about to run, we tighten our surveillance even further. In the case of your father, he ran straight to his house before we could intercept him. By the way," said the captain, breaking into a relaxed smile. "Our sniper reports that you looked pretty silly trampling those petunias."

Tiller laughed.

"Anyway," said Captain Levi, "a Long Shadow's house is the first place VC looks upon notification of an escape. Ten minutes after August's psychiatrist called, there were two dozen tag men waiting on his doorstep. When they accosted him, he hardly struggled. He seems to have lost his will to fight."

"That's not fair," I protested. "He had six full days until his T-date."

"It's not going to help things by talking about what he had," said Tiller. "The immediate problem is how to get him to Canada. He's under house arrest, so our job is to smuggle him out while distracting his jailers."

"Or perhaps by having them removed from the scene altogether," suggested Captain Levi. "Sooner or later, there's always a changing of the guard. A team of us could slip in quite easily."

"It was a stupid thing for him to have gone home," I said, sulking.

"Look, Nash," said Captain Levi. "There are a thousand reasons why a Long Shadow gives up prematurely. I suspect your father has been burdened with the weight of considerable guilt ever since his writing of the majority opinion. You can't blame him for wanting to put an end to things ahead of time. You and I would do the same if we were in his position."

"He's all right, isn't he?" I asked anxiously.

"Most assuredly," said Captain Levi. "But heavily guarded, nevertheless. They take little enough chance with average Long Shadows. You can imagine the lengths VC is willing to go to in securing Justice Nash's death."

"Yeah," said Tiller. "I could just see the headlines if they were to blow it. 'Author of *Long Shadow* Vacations in Quebec.' The people would go crazy."

Captain Levi nodded. "And the greatest good would be seen as a farce. VC would have a war on their hands, which is fine for us, but bad news for them. After all, the fitting collapse of Southern economy followed not long after its slaves were gone. Do you suppose VC wants history to repeat itself?"

"No way, man," said Tiller. "We have six days to get him out of that house. If we put our heads together, we can free him before his time is up."

"How?" I demanded.

Captain Levi glanced at Tiller and a thousand nuances seemed to pass between them.

"It will have to be an inside job. Way inside," said Tiller, looking up through the hole in the ceiling as if he could see into the various little mole holes of VC secretaries and counselors and technicians and then into the larger ones of its attorneys and executives.

"We'll have to ingratiate ourselves to someone of importance," said Captain Levi. "Any suggestions for who to begin with, Tolles?"

"Yes," he said immediately, as if he had been considering this plan for a very long time. "I think I know the woman for our purposes."

Unexplainable panic washed over me. "Who is it?" I asked.

"Your mother," said Captain Levi. "Is that going to be a problem for you?"

"In what way, sir?" I asked nervously.

"Would it be a problem for you if we were to ask your mother's assistance in getting your father out of the country?"

Tiller looked at me expectantly.

"Yes," I said at last. "I would have a very big problem with that."

5

SHE'S A BEAUTIFUL WOMAN," REMARKED Captain Levi. "I've always thought it odd that the two of you don't speak to one another. Especially since she does her filming here full-time now."

"She'd have contact with me every day if she knew who I was," I replied.

"Why don't you tell her?" probed Tiller.

"Because I don't trust her."

"That's strange," said Captain Levi.

"What is?"

"That you would save the life of the man who created this mess, but have contempt for the woman he cheated on."

"How do you know about that?" I asked, suddenly defensive. I had never discussed my parents' divorce with anyone.

"Partly because we have enough mistrust for Roberta Nash ourselves that we did a background check on her a long time ago," said Captain Levi. "Your father fooled around on her when you were nine, didn't he?"

"What's the other part?" I demanded.

"The other part is . . . we knew you would come around someday."

"Come around?"

"Yes. We figured when you finally began to see things from our perspective, it would behoove us to understand the nature of your relationship with Roberta Nash in case the opportunity for you to influence her ever arose."

"And with all your snooping, what did you discover?"

"That you have never quite accepted the fact that she left you at the Academy. Your marks there indicate you were always rather melancholy."

"She didn't have to leave me," I said angrily. "It wasn't mandatory then."

"Yes, but it was profitable," said the captain.

"Excuse me," I said irritably, "but what does all this talk about my mother have to do with getting my father to Canada?"

"Everything," said Tiller. "Have you happened to notice who's in charge these days of the VOX executions?"

Of course I knew who was in charge of the executions. Mother had become director of VOX not long after the dissolution of her marriage. I was in the Academy when she took the job, so what little I saw of her on weekends and holidays abruptly vanished as VC required more of her time.

"Who says we need the director of VOX to get the job done?" I said.

"We don't," agreed Captain Levi. "That is, if you can think of some other way to get past the guards at your father's house and out of the country without getting shot by crack marksmen, who, by the way, I happen to have trained myself."

"What he means is, we're sunk without an insider," said Tiller.

"But he's a harmless old man," I said. "For once in my life, I just want to go far, far away with him and do whatever normal fathers and sons do, like . . . fish, or play catch, or something."

"When you're in Canada, you can fish until you're sick of it," said Captain Levi. "But first we have to get you there. And to do that, we're going to have to contact your mother. There's no other way. I'm sorry."

In my gut, I felt pressure of a nature I had never felt before, at least not since childhood. Had I the courage to define it at the moment, I would have recognized it as the pure, undiluted pain of a nine-year-old boy, standing on the curb, watching his nanny, his nurse, his love, his life roll slowly away on taxi wheels. It was the pain of rejection and I could not bear it again.

"I'll get my father out by myself," I said through clenched teeth.

"You'll get yourself killed, and your father, as well," said Tiller.

"I'll take my chances."

"Look here, Nash," said Captain Levi. "We've been suspicious for a long time that your mother is playing both sides of the fence to line her own pocket."

"I could have told you that, sir. She puts the 'e' in expedient. That's why I want nothing to do with her."

"That's also why we must find out once and for all if she's safe to do business with," said Tiller. "What better time than when her ex-husband's life is at stake?"

"Wise up, Tiller," I said. "He's not her 'ex' for nothing. She can't stand the man. She'd just as soon watch him die as anything."

"Maybe. Maybe not," replied Tiller.

"Don't tell me your background check discovered she's been sending him care packages at Rivendale because she's secretly in love with him."

"No," said Captain Levi, "but the reality is your father wasn't always in favor of Long Shadow. He spent the winter of '12 in the congressional library with clerks' memos up to his ears, picking through every case on mercy killing, on health care costs, on patients' rights. He ate *amici curiae* for breakfast, lunch, and dinner."

"I know all that," I said automatically, though what I really meant was that I didn't want to discuss it.

"Yes, but did you know that somewhere in the middle of spring, someone got to him? Or maybe a lot of someones got to him, with a lot of money, or sex, or power, or something. I'm not trying to say he was innocent. Heaven knows, August Nash had his problems. I just know that by the time your father finished writing in late July of 2013, the majority opinion that eventually became the backbone of Long Shadow legislation looked nothing like the majority opinion he set out to write. Roberta knows that more than anyone, John. I think you ought to know that, too."

I rolled the revelation over in my mind, sitting silently.

"This could be a breakthrough for the Shadow Train, John," coaxed Tiller. "Your mother's likely to still feel sympathy for your father. Maybe even love. Just think what it would be like to have someone in VC as powerful as her on our side."

"I am not going to talk to her!" I shouted.

"Fine!" shouted Captain Levi in return. "Go on back to your precious little tag man job. I'll never tell a soul you didn't have the guts to help a Long Shadow. Go on back to 'the greatest good.' With every T-date that comes and goes, you can join the long, pathetic queue of people who turn away from the horror and, in doing so, embody the reason why our country is such a stinking cesspool of hatred and murder! But so help me, Nash—" Captain Levi put his face in mine, so that I could smell the rich tonic in his hair, and nearly estimate the gold in his teeth every time he opened his mouth for an angry gasp of air. "If you ever say a word about what you saw in this room today, I swear I'll come to you on tiptoe some night when you're sleeping like a baby, and I'll carve you a smile from ear to ear."

"All right," I said at last. "I'll meet with her."

"Excellent," said Captain Levi. "We knew you'd see it our way, once you had some time to think about all the lives at stake."

"As far as I'm concerned, sir, there's only one life at stake, and that's the life of my father. After he's safe, you can do what you want, and I'll keep my mouth shut. But I have no desire to make a career out of the Shadow Train."

"Fair enough," said Captain Levi. "Then we have an agreement?"

"Yes, sir," I replied. "You help me get my father to Canada and I'll never tell a soul about your Shadow Train."

After a moment or two, Captain Levi got up from his chair and strolled back to his desk, where he took a pouch of tobacco and a pipe from his top left drawer. It was an expensive blend, the kind only government employees are privileged to have. He took his time in tamping and lighting the pipe, presumably to measure his next piece of indoctrination for a Shadow Train novice, and when he came back to where Tiller and I were sitting, he was wearing his game face.

"You'll have to meet with her as soon as possible," he said, blowing a ring of smoke toward the ceiling. "Now that your father's T-date is just around the corner, he could go on VOX as soon as his speech is scripted."

"Who does the scripting?" I asked.

"High-ranking policy wonks who have nothing better to do with their time," said Tiller. "They take the task pretty seriously when it comes to someone like August Nash."

"Let me put it this way," said the captain. "When Joe Blow Long Shadow goes on VOX to give his two cents' worth of credence to the greatest good, it usually nets at least a week or two of decreased T-dodging in the populace at large. A well-known celebrity can bring as much as a month of compliance, depending on the script, of course, and how well it was delivered. Now imagine what the public's response will be when they see and hear the founder of Long Shadow praising the virtues of

Vivi-Centerre. They'll fairly storm the place to have themselves terminated! It's called the power of repetition and suggestion, Johnny-boy. Why else do you think the Academy gave out candy to the best memorizers?"

"But sir, do they really think they'll get him to read it word for word?"

Captain Levi looked at Tiller as if to say, "We've got a green one here." But when he addressed my question, there was an absence of condescension.

"Are you that estranged from your mother, that you've never asked how she does an interview?"

"I've never gotten around to it."

"Well, it's rather elementary. Do you remember the old blue screens they used to use in filmmaking?"

"I remember."

"Okay. Well then, you see, VOX knows better than anybody that death—no matter how you dress it up—is still death. Knowing that, however, they continue selling people on the notion that T-dates are noble, even desirable undertakings."

I thought of all the billboards around town. *The highest sacrifice for the greatest good.* "All right," I said, "so where do the blue screens fit in?"

"You have watched a complete interview before, haven't you?" asked Tiller.

"Of course."

"Then do you believe there are really waterfalls, and tropical birds, and sandy beaches present when a Long Shadow breathes his last?"

"I assumed VC kept its promise about making termination as pleasant as possible."

"Have you ever known VC to make things pleasant for people?" asked Captain Levi.

"I guess not, sir."

"You guess right. They are in the business of making a profit, pure and simple."

"From whom?" I asked. "Long Shadows are terminated free of charge. It's a publicly funded service."

"Nothing's free," said Tiller, absorbed in some concern of his that was not quite on the fringe of our conversation, but near enough that the allusion to money brought him back to us.

"Think, Nash," chided Captain Levi. "You work hard. You get paid. You put a little in the bank, a little in your wallet. Then where does the rest go?"

"To Washington," I replied.

"To Washington," said the captain. "And what does Washington do with your money?"

"Well, I suppose they spend it, sir."

"That's right, Nash. They are very good at spending it. They spend it on highways and waterways and just about any other way they want. But most of all, they spend it on votes. They send it all over the country wherever the largest block of potential constituents resides. Believe me, John, there are an awful lot of votes involved in the VC network. We're not just talking about the insurance companies and the doctors and the grunts like you and me. We're talking about all the little people out there who never want to go back to having their futures mortgaged by the elderly. So in a roundabout way, VC makes a profit off the same poor citizens it terminates. Sure, they call it nonprofit. But who are they fooling? We all know one or two fat cats who are doing just fine on their six figures' worth of government payroll and still finding ways to make a profit."

"No tropical waterfalls?" I asked.

Tiller shook his head.

"No sandy beaches?"

"Blue screens," said Captain Levi. "Smoke and mirrors for the sake of the greatest good."

"In fact," said Tiller, "as we speak, there are people being given their shots of sodium pentothal in rooms less attractive than the one we're sitting in now."

I thought about meeting with my mother. "So, what do I say when I see her?"

"The truth," said Captain Levi. "If she's really one of us, she'll be glad to do everything within her power to help us. And believe me, Nash, we're going to need a lot of help to get your father free."

"And if she's not one of us?"

Captain Levi's eyebrows fused themselves into a single black line across his forehead. "We'll be a whole lot wiser," he said.

"Which do you think she is?" I asked.

Captain Levi and Tiller looked at one another again. "It's hard to tell," said the captain.

My heart sank, not because I wanted to preserve some childhood hope about a mother-and-child reunion, but because what I had always suspected of Roberta Nash was likely true; that her bitterness over my father's affairs had grown so disproportionate to all her other feelings, she could kill him without blinking an eye.

"But you can expect her to say things that will make you think you're talking to the queen conductor of the entire Shadow Train," said Tiller.

"Such as?"

"Such as 'The Floyd River route is open clear to Ely, Minnesota.' That's her signature line. She's got some connection with a place called Tonsus Abbey."

"A monastery?"

"We'll explain it to you at length when we have more time," said Captain Levi. "Right now, time is of the essence. VC wants Augustine Nash on VOX so bad they can taste it."

"Can I find her in her office?" I asked.

"She's off today," said Tiller. "I heard she's the one VC chose to be in charge of the script. She's probably somewhere planning Nash's farewell speech."

"You know," I said, shaking my head at the sudden craziness of it all. "With all due respect, the two of you may be as evil as they come and I may be the biggest dupe of all time. But for some reason, I feel better right now than I've ever felt before."

"It's called belonging, John," said Captain Levi. "You're in. You're one of us. You are finally about to do something worthwhile for a change."

"So, if she's not in her office, where do I start?" I asked.

"Our records show VC has moved Roberta again to a new location over in Mission Hills. Here's an address," said Captain Levi, handing me a slip of paper.

Tiller gave a low whistle and rubbed his thumb and middle finger together. "Mission Hills! She must have taken your father's shirt in the settlement."

"I don't think he minded much," I replied as I walked over to the door and opened it. "Apparently he didn't have any use for it at Rivendale. Oh, yeah. One more thing. Will she try to play me for a fool?"

"She'll play you like she's been playing others for the last few years," said Captain Levi. "Sweet, innocent—"

"Benevolent?" I asked.

"Very," said the captain. "That's why I think you should fit her with this," he added, handing me something that looked like a miniature thumbtack.

I studied the device curiously.

"It's a surveillance probe," said Captain Levi. "We would like to know just how benevolent your mother really is."

He looked at me with his own probing eyes.

"I'll trust her sparingly," I said, pocketing the device. And I closed the door softly behind me.

6

"China, Vietnam, North Korea, and Indonesia have all implemented population-control programs. The successful ones shared a dirty little secret: extreme coercion."
—From a source at VC National

THE RIDE UP IN THE PARTICLE TRANSPORT gave me a few seconds to pinch myself and see if I was dreaming. Then I was out into the fresh afternoon and halfway down the stairs of VC before I noticed Mother's address was missing from my pocket. Remembering what Captain Levi said about time being of the essence, I bolted back to the transporter and searched its confines without success. A thorough check in the hallway outside the room where we had met also proved unfruitful. When I passed the conference room, Captain Levi and Tiller were nowhere in sight, and the EM rail was still on the desk where the captain had left it. A minute later, the gun was in my shoulder holster and I was heading back up the transporter, resolved to go on what I could remember from the slip of paper, when I heard someone behind me.

"You're very clever," came a woman's voice.

I turned around to see a stunning brunette leaning against the wall, her shoulders thrown back like a young cadet.

"Pardon me?" I replied.

"Don't act naive. I watched the whole thing."

Instinctually, I looked at the ceiling camera. "You must have the wrong person."

"Oh, you're the right person, all right. I'm a good judge of character. You're an accomplished thief. By the way, I disconnected the camera, in case you're wondering."

"Have a nice day," I replied, turning back toward the transport.

The woman persisted. "It will be a shame if that gun in your shoulder holster has a grip that's only activated by the fingerprints of the man you stole it from."

When I wheeled back toward her, my eyes must have registered some concern at the prophecy, for a look of satisfaction settled over the woman's face and she pressed ahead with confidence.

"Tell me about Mr. Harjo in Roman Nose last January. That sounds like an interesting case."

"So, you're the eavesdropper," I said, remembering the visitor in the sauna.

"The name's McSwain," said the woman.

My jaw dropped ever so slightly. "Sarah McSwain?" I asked. "*The* Sarah McSwain?"

"Well, I had a great aunt with the same name once, but her T-date occurred when I was in the Academy. So I guess I'm the only one left. You needn't worry about me being in the sauna. I didn't see a thing. There was too much steam. But I heard enough to make me dangerous, if you know what I mean."

"You make an interesting first impression."

"Some people call it irresistible."

"Some call it extortion," I said, though I agreed with her self-assessment. I glanced at Sarah's stomach. She showed no signs of the pregnancy, yet. "What did you mean by dangerous?" I asked.

"That I could be a problem for you if you don't tell me everything I want to know."

Sarah put her hands on her hips and stared at me with strangely familiar eyes. In an instant, I knew where I had seen those two sensuous gray spots of pigment. Their pleasant yet cynical expression had looked out at me on more than one occasion from the covers of *Rifleperson* magazine, and it seemed there was a rumor or two that went along with the pictures. Being with her in the flesh, however, made me forget whatever they were.

"First, there's a couple of things I'd like to know," I said.

"Fire away," replied Sarah.

"All right, for starters you can tell me why someone as attractive as you works in a place like this."

"The pay is good," she said flatly.

"Good enough to support the two of you?" I asked, nodding toward her stomach.

"That's none of your business."

"It was none of your business to listen in on my conversation in the sauna, either. You're not even supposed to be in that bathroom when the men are occupying it."

"Are you trying to hide something?" she asked.

"If I were, I could have found a better place to hide it than the sauna."

"You're hiding things right now," insisted Sarah. "Remember, I heard every word you said in that room this morning. Bottom line is, you've got something I want, and I'll do whatever is necessary to get it."

My pulse quickened. "I won't be blackmailed."

"Did I say blackmail? I've never liked the word *blackmail.*"

From the depths of my brain, Tiller's advice for me to forget about this woman came floating to the surface of my consciousness and I wished that I had never acknowledged her voice in the first place. Still, her beauty was irresistible.

"What do you want?" I asked. "Is it money?"

"Heavens, no."

"What then? A share of my assignments? I can arrange to have a portion of my territory parceled to you."

"I don't want your belongings."

"Look, I'm tired of playing this game," I said, turning toward the transport.

"I want to know how soon you'll be leaving for Canada," said Sarah suddenly, as if it were the only thing in all the world she was curious about. For a moment, I thought I saw a glimmer of vulnerability in the way she leaned toward me to extract an answer.

"And if I choose not to tell you?"

"Then I'll choose not to keep your little secret from Captain Levi."

"You don't give a guy much of a choice, do you?" I said.

"What's it going to be?" asked Sarah. "Do I tell the captain who it was that pocketed his new toy? Or do you and I have a long talk about the Shadow Train?"

At the mention of those last two words, I crossed the ten feet of crimson carpet that separated us and clamped my hand over Sarah's mouth before she could make another sound. She was as strong as many men I had wrestled, and twice as vicious with her kicks, but I held her back against my chest, until her arms went limp and she stopped trying to gouge my shins with her heels.

"You are not going to jeopardize my plans," I breathed into Sarah's ear.

She let loose with another flurry of kicks and muffled threats.

"Are you going to be quiet? Or do I have to keep your mouth covered?" I asked, glancing around the hallway. "Look, everyone has a different reason for wanting to get to Canada. If it will help to cut through the game-playing, I'll tell you right now that I already know about the cyborg experiment."

Suddenly, I felt the shock of incisors breaking through the skin of my forefinger.

"Oww!" I yelled, letting go of Sarah.

She sprang into the transport and the door *whooshed* shut. There was a stairwell to my left, so I took it, racing upwards.

When I burst onto the cool, marble floor of the main level, Sarah was nowhere in sight. Frantically, I checked the counseling rooms and the Post-Conceptive Services rooms and even the transport again to see if she was hiding there, but she had vanished.

An icy tremor registered in my spine.

She's going to report me, I thought, as I hurried to the big front doors. I flashed a smile at the cameras (undoubtedly these had not been disconnected) and shoved out into the sunlight. *How could I have been so stupid as to take the rail? She's bound to do something with this new information.* Professionals like her never missed an opportunity to better themselves, even if they did claim they didn't want your money. But there was no time to worry about my predicament. I broke into a run for the People Mover at 75th and Ward, unable to forget the way I felt when I first saw Sarah McSwain in the hallway. *That's great, Nash, just great,* I chastised myself. *You're infatuated with the person who's going to turn you in. That's a real winning combination.*

"Mission Hills," I said to the late-model cyborg, as I boarded the People Mover. He made a harsh sound in his metal gullet and took my ticket. I took a seat as far away from people as possible. Soon, I was speeding south to find my mother.

Her face was everywhere, it seemed; on billboards, boxcars, the sides of tall skyscrapers. Of course, every night there she was again, a hundred stories of Roberta Nash beaming out to the city, spinning happy bedtime tales about the greatest good. I tried closing my eyes and replacing her image with the newly minted one of Sarah McSwain I had acquired, but to no avail.

"Know which terminal you want off at, mister?" droned the cyborg. "We can stop at Ward or Prairie Village. That way you won't have to walk from Nall."

"Prairie Village, if it's no trouble," I replied.

There was a click in the cyborg's throat and he continued with his answer, obviously preprogrammed for the occasion.

"No trouble at all. We don't have much volume this time of day. There's talk of shutting us down for good. Something about intensive labor costs between peak hours. I just do my job, keep my mouth shut."

"You wouldn't happen to know a Roberta Nash, would you?"

The cyborg paused. "Are you kidding?" he said, lowering his voice to a tinny murmur. "Everybody knows that woman. She's on VOX at ten, five, and nine. Best thing VC ever did was couple a fresh face like hers with the greatest good. VOX ratings shot up so fast, you'd have thought it was a soap opera. She's . . . ," the cyborg scrolled for an appropriate response "She's like a mother to us all."

"Do you know where she lives?" I asked, hurriedly.

"I don't know everything," said the cyborg. "But I know someone who does."

Ten minutes later, I stepped off the Mover at Prairie Village and ran across the empty four-lane into a tobacco shop owned by an immigrant, named Rossi, from Samsun. After a brief interrogation, I realized he would answer no questions until I had spent a substantial amount of currency on his wares. So for the better part of an hour I forced myself to sample various blends, while feigning interest in Rossi's monologue on the Turks' unsurpassed romance with Lady Nicotine. All the while, the afternoon was fast receding.

"You got to cut dee plant before it gets too old," said Rossi, as if he thought I was interested in going into business with him. "Dot way dee nourishment goes to dee few leaves and not dee many."

"Cut before they're old," I repeated, nodding.

"Dot for sure. May or June," said Rossi. He had a fake diamond in his left front tooth, and the fact that his identification bracelet was blinking fast signified he was probably in the final days of his forty-ninth year. "You like a pack?" he asked, pointing to a shelf full of merchandise.

"No, thanks," I replied.

"Can't get enough of a good ding," he insisted.

"No. Really. Thank you."

"Okay by me. But you remember what old Rossi tells you." He leaned as close to me as the counter would allow for his belly, and I detected the sugared heaviness of Turkish blend on his clothes. "Cut dee plant before it gets too old," he repeated. "You see?"

I said that, yes, I saw, but by that time the store had filled with such a haze that Rossi himself was nothing more than an apparition, and his wisdom a coagulation of hot air and socialism. All the while I was figuring madly how I was going to find Mother's house. If only I hadn't lost that slip of paper.

"Say, Rossi," I said, "you wouldn't happen to know where I can find a woman by the name of Roberta Nash?"

Rossi went rigid like a stick. "You with dee tag men, aren't you?" he said suspiciously.

"She's my mother," I replied.

"Dot makes no difference," said Rossi, stepping from behind the counter and hurrying me toward the door with polite gestures. "My neighbor in dee house behind me had a son in dee tags too. He tracked her all dee way to Montana and brought her back in a long, black bag. Come again sometime."

"I'm not going to terminate my own mother," I said with as much ire in my voice as I could muster. It must have been enough, because Rossi stopped coaxing me along with his enormous girth and seemed to be considering whether he should offend a customer or take the chance of betraying a kindred soul.

"Besides," I added quickly, "she's not a Long Shadow. She's with VC. Remember?"

"I know dat. Everybody know dat Roberta Nash is dee head of VOX. Such a sweet, pretty lady. How'd she have a son who looks like you?" said Rossi. Luckily, his greed had overruled his scruples and he seemed pleased once more to curry my business.

However, he still demanded to see a photograph of Mother, insisting that, "All good boys carry pictures of dee pedotrainer."

"Here," I said, producing the only photo of Mother I had in my wallet—a ten-year-old one, which would have to do. I was beginning to wonder what would happen if the country ever lost faith in that attractive face that addressed them daily on VOX. Rossi examined the photo and immediately warmed to Mother's countenance.

"Ahhh," he exclaimed. "She is like dee Euphrates at dawn. If Rossi had dee time and dee wherewidall, he would go and find her himself. Dot for sure. She's like a mother to us all."

"So I've heard. Do you know where she lives?" I asked impatiently.

"Where all beautiful women live," said Rossi.

"And where is that?"

Rossi smiled and there was that silly diamond again, winking at me through the smoke. "In my dreams," he replied.

I cast a silent curse on every tooth in his mouth, and crammed the photo back into my wallet. "I'm sure she'd appreciate the compliment," I said, turning to leave.

"More smokes for dee road?" asked Rossi again, snatching a pack of hand-rolled perique from the shelf. "See here," he added. "Dey are dee oldest cigarette from my country, and very, very good. Dey say dee members of dee Shadow Train smoke dees very brand."

I froze at the mention of the Shadow Train.

"Is something dee matter?" asked Rossi.

"No. I was just wondering what they're called, that's all."

"Zolphyrs," said Rossi.

"Zolphyrs," I repeated. "No, thanks. I'm trying to quit."

Outside in the street, I blinked my eyes to rid them of tobacco sting. I could feel the rumble of the People Mover moving southward beneath my feet and I almost wished for the days of traffic and pollution. Mass transit is a wonderful thing, but it makes life unbearably quiet above ground. As far as the eye could see in either direction, there was not a privately owned vehicle on the road, unless you wanted to count the Personal Rapid Transits, but PRT's weren't really owned by individuals and they definitely weren't *on* the road.

If you have never been on the Personal Rapid Transit, rest assured it's everything it's cracked up to be. It's nice to lean back and leave the work to a computer, sort of like those old monorails, except PRTs have wheels that can swivel and negotiate ninety-degree turns. And the best thing about the PRT is you avoid the crowds of the People Movers. Still, I prefer untethered driving whenever the option is available, and I miss the surge of adrenaline I used to feel whenever Uncle Ames narrowly missed running us into some unsympathetic object. (He never could talk and drive at the same time.) However, if I must get around by rail or track, there is nothing better than the PRT. Whoever originated its concept were prophets of enormous stature. To think they envisioned it without scrapping the existing networks of mass transit and aboveground highways makes it all the more an impressive genesis.

As I walked, a memory from my childhood haunted me.

It was not my guiding principle that got me sent away on my ninth birthday, but the fact that I carved it into Mother's kitchen table with a butter knife. Over and over I traced the words until a deep, abiding wound appeared in the Formica, and the laminate was laid bare in much the same way my parents' divorce had exposed me to pain.

Do unto others as they have done unto you: That was my gilded rule.

I remember looking up from my work and seeing the crooked shape of Mother's mouth as she backed toward the telescreen. Two hours later I stood with my suitcase on the curb outside Northeastern Academy. The year was 2022. I was crying when she left me.

At Mission and Tomahawk, good fortune smiled upon me, and I found I had no need of Captain Levi's slip of paper. When

I look back upon it now, I realize that in varying degrees Mother had been avoiding me in much the same way I had avoided her for years. But like the two sides of an angle, we were bound to converge on a common reference point eventually. Father was our reference point. His pending death was the thing that drew us together.

On the corner acreage sat an abandoned strip mall and behind it the usual things one finds behind forgotten establishments; rusted skeletons of Acuras and Lexuses predating the PRT and the People Mover era, gutless washing machines, old shopping carts with missing wheels. It was there I came across Mother. She was on her hands and knees at the base of an industrial waste ionizer, wearing an expensive pantsuit, calling ever so softly into the half-foot of darkness beneath the enormous contraption.

"Here, Comfort. Come home to Mama," she whispered. When she heard my boots scuff against the sidewalk, she gave a start and, looking up, crossed her wrists in front of her face, as if she expected a blow. It was obvious she had strayed from her circle of movement, which at the time were heavily monitored restrictions on one's geographical range. As technology brought about more effective ways for the government to keep tabs on its citizens, these circles were gradually done away with, and once again people were free to go anywhere they wished. Of course, they were never free of being monitored.

"You're a long ways from home aren't you, lady?" I said.

"I was looking for my cocker spaniel," came the reply. She studied me more closely. "Wait a minute. I recognize you. You're the one from the meeting this morning."

"Let me help," I offered, stooping down into the evening shadows. "It's refreshing to see a human being care so much for an animal. Most people wouldn't risk it." I would have known that perfume anywhere. Wrapped in its scent was a memory— a wisp of hair against my face, a lullaby, something about a cradle falling. Mother caught me looking at her left hand.

"I know what you're thinking," she said.

"Pardon me?"

"You're thinking if this woman would just settle down and find a man with whom she could produce a matri-sak, she wouldn't have to be crawling around beneath a dumpster at midnight."

"I wasn't thinking that."

"Well, most people do."

"So have you?" I asked, staring at her face. She had exceptional skin for her age, or maybe she, too, knew a good plastic surgeon.

"Have I what?"

"Have you found a man?"

"I don't have to answer that," she interrupted.

"Of course not. I was just making conversation. But if you don't mind me saying so, you ought to stick more closely to your circle."

"Thanks for the advice," said Mother. She stood to brush the knees of her suit, looking one last time behind the ionizer before turning to leave. There was no sign of the mongrel. She turned to go.

"I know more about you than you think I do," I said hurriedly. The words seemed only to slow her pace. I tried again. "Head of VOX at Vivi-Centerre. Must be quite an honor. I could still report you for this transgression."

She kept on walking, the click of her heels against the sidewalk collaborating with my heart's maniacal pace.

Say something, you fool. "Mother!" I shouted.

A four-legged shadow bolted from a nearby stairwell and we both watched it disappear around the corner of the mall.

She quickened her pace, "Ignorant animal! He acts more like a cat every day," said Mother, adding, "I'm quite certain I don't know you."

"I'm quite certain you do," I insisted, working enough moisture into my mouth to say the words that had filled my fevered dreams for years. "And you know a certain birthday, the way a certain head of hair gets curly when it's left to air dry, the certain sound of a nine-year-old crying at a curbside. You know these facts so well they haunt you."

Mother stopped.

"That's right," I whispered. "We might still be a family if it wasn't for that stupid majority opinion."

A little, gasping sound eminated from her lips.

"It's probably hard for you to imagine that your son actually made something of himself, isn't it?"

Mother whirled to face me, the expression in her eyes suggesting she would have liked to say my name but could not bring herself to do so. She looked like a convict waiting for the worst of sentences.

"I take it you weren't counting on this reunion the day you dropped me off," I continued, trying to make things easier for her.

"John?" cried Mother. "My John? Is it really you?"

In the distance, VOX bullied the skyline with scenes from an ancient western. The quiet whir of a spy glider became a momentary buzz as it dipped into the neighborhood south of us, looking for circle violators.

"Yes, it's really me," I answered. "Do you mind if I call you Roberta?"

"But you sound so . . . old, like your voice has gotten hard, or something."

"It's called puberty. You weren't around for it."

"You were too much for me," Mother countered quickly.

"I was too much for anyone," I said. "Still am, if you want to know the truth. Are we just going to stand here, or do you know of a safer place to talk?"

"I can't take a stranger home with me."

"I never said anything about home. But, anyway, I'm not a stranger. I'm family."

"Prove it," said Mother.

"Does this ring a bell?" I undid my watch and handed it to her. Its rich, gold case heralded the fact that I could well afford life's frills. Mother drew the watch close to her hazel eyes and squinted.

"*Do unto others as they have done unto you,*" she read on the back of the case. Her hands began to shake again. "What *have* you made of yourself, son?" she asked.

My heart tripped over the word *son*, but I quickly dashed whatever emotion I was feeling. "Don't act so surprised," I said. "We've both made monsters of ourselves. You just happen to get paid more for your monstrosities than I do." With a sweep of my finger toward VOX, I changed the subject. "There's nothing worse than reruns," I said, eyeing the hundred-story testimony to motion capture technology, where an Indian braced his foot on the chest of a blue-clad soldier and retrieved his arrow with a yank.

"If you'll let me explain, John, I can tell you why I had to join VC," said Mother, defensively. Already I could sense her shifting into the exact script that Captain Levi had predicted.

"Can we go?" I interrupted. "Those gliders are getting awfully close. I'd prefer not to be caught with a circle violater."

"I'd like to find Comfort first," said Mother.

"Wouldn't we all."

"You don't understand. This is the fourth time he's run away from me. You've never had a dog do this to you."

"I've never had a dog," I corrected her. "Come on, Roberta. I promise I won't touch your furniture this time."

We ducked into a tangled copse just as two bright globes spilled over the trees onto the ionizer. The glider came in low, tracing a wide arc around the perimeter of the parking lot. I heard the communication system squawking coordinates and the sharp curse of a man insisting he'd seen something.

"Do you do this often?" I asked when the glider had gone and Mother's breathing had returned to normal.

"No. Never. I'm not sure what would happen to me if they knew."

"That seems like a detail you ought to be sure about," I said. "You *are* involved in policy making, aren't you?"

"Yes, but there are a lot of upper level secrets in VC."

"I thought you guys at the top stood for utopia, choice, things like that. What's our slogan? I can never remember it."

"'The highest sacrifice for the greatest good,'" said Mother by rote.

I found I was enjoying playing this game with her. "That's it," I said. "It sounds so benevolent."

"It is a benevolent idea. Really. It's just that one's choices are somewhat limited . . . sometimes."

"Your dogma has its tail between its legs," I replied.

After a mile of branches barring our way, we emerged torn and scratched from the copse to find ourselves standing in one of Kansas City's few undeveloped meadows. The moon dangled like a hangnail on the edge of ominous clouds, and the air smelled like rain. Across the street that ran along the meadow's east side, I saw a string of apartment lights and I laughed inwardly.

I have always thought it absurd how people like Tiller look at such dives and gasp as if they've seen the Taj Mahal. Call me pessimistic for saying it, but I doubt Kansas City will ever regain the beauty she once was known for.

When the new millennium began, designers were challenged to be bold, different, individualistic. The public, in a stimulated state of mind, demanded architecture that was imaginative and even wild. Bubble and dome configurations ruled this period. Everywhere one looked, curvilinear construction caressed the landscape, and the sharp, square edge of the twentieth century was a rare sight. Then came the carefree age of deco-tech, with its patented panels made of wood, steel, aluminum, ferroconcrete, and high-performance plastics. Even Frank Lloyd Wright would have dropped his jaw at the way these panels were extended beyond their anchor point, resulting in "fins" and other unusual visual forms. I recall one July when there was no better place for a boy to enjoy lemonade than in the shade produced by sunlight on the fins.

About the time Long Shadow legislation was set in motion, deco-tech gave way to biomorphism, and the art of nature was upon us. Organically designed buildings in harmony with humanity were the order of the day. This architecture was inspired by the Art Nouveau style of the early twentieth century, prompting some to laud it as Nouveau Art Nouveau. I, on the other hand, always thought a house was for the purpose of keeping the rain off your head, not looking like a shell, or a tree, or a network of creeping vines. Still, biomorphism was considered beautiful and it remained that way for a good long while.

So, whatever it was that possessed men to plow biomorphism under in exchange for the ratty dwellings that Mother and I faced on the edge of that meadow is beyond me. I surmise that money and creativity were eventually funneled away from the upkeep of the aesthetic and into the practical task of promoting the greatest good. Whatever the reason, that is how the nouveau riché reside today; deceived into thinking they live like kings and queens, because VC says it's so.

"Would you think badly of me if I wanted to touch your face?" asked Mother as we stood there. "I couldn't bear to get caught and never know the way it felt." She reached with hands delicate and white like the moon.

"Don't," I said.

Mother dropped her hands to her side. She stood stone still, as disappointed as Lot's wife discovering she could not go back. After a moment or two, she pointed in the direction of her home.

"Mine's the one with the porch light off," she said. "I didn't want the tag men suspecting I was out after curfew."

"It's hard to fool us," I replied. "We're a clever bunch, you know. Now stay low. Drop if you hear something like a cat purring."

We started across the meadow. All the while I kept one eye on the purplish black vacuum above the ridge of trees behind us, for the gliders sometimes track with infrared. Like mad rats we scurried over the dewy grass, until we reached the door and Mother dug into her pocket for her access card.

"Hurry," I whispered, keeping an eye on the far end of the street. Suddenly I heard a whir and saw a glider dart around the corner. It was followed by two others. Mother found the card and jammed it into the slot, but the pasteboard broke apart in the lock.

"Not now," she groaned.

"Patience, Roberta. Panic kills," I said, stepping in front of her. The gliders were nearly to us now, slowed only by their dutiful probing into neighboring windows. A hundred feet away, I watched a man frantically trying to make it to his home before he was caught breaking curfew. I removed the card piece with a pair of tweezers kept for just such occasions, then shoved the tweezers hard into the slot. I pushed my weight against the door, heard a click, and the door sprang open. I tumbled in on the carpet, Mother on top of me—perfume, hair, half-remembered lullabies—the glider lights dancing all around her meager house.

"Shut the door!" I snapped.

Mother kicked it closed.

We sat up quickly, breaths snatched short, backs ramrod straight against the door. I remember leaning there with Mother in my arms as the gliders nudged the panes on either side of her porch. I think it must have been her first happy moment in years, which is a terribly odd possibility considering the danger she was in. For as everybody knew then, not even VC executives were supposed to stray from their designated circle of movement. Only us tag men were allowed to roam. When the glare finally faded from her living room walls, Mother made no attempt to move.

"I've missed you," she said, fishing for a warm word in return. I ignored the bait and craned my neck to see over the edge of the windowpane.

"They're gone," I replied. "Are you in one piece?"

She took inventory of her limbs. "I'm okay. Do you think they saw us?"

"No. They wouldn't have left so quickly if they had. We've dodged a bullet."

Mother grasped my left hand and veered sharply back toward sentiment. "You're alone," she said, passing judgment on my empty ring finger as I had done to hers earlier.

"You're one for talk," I replied. "Why haven't you remarried?"

"VC won't allow it," replied Mother. "Who would want to produce a matri-sak with me, anyway? Every man I meet is a man who thinks I'm going to murder him someday."

There it was again; her attempt at convincing me that underneath that executioner's hood she was really Florence Nightingale, miserably misunderstood. I helped her to her feet and we felt our way to her darkened kitchen where she hastily prepared sandwiches and peppered me with questions about my face. I stalled by pretending to be shocked at the kind of food a VC executive kept stocked. A little meat would have been nice, and I was somewhat surprised she had none.

"Did it hurt?" she repeated, staring not so much at my present features but at the invisible snapshot of me in younger years that apparently hung in the air between us.

"What's that?" I asked.

She reached for my face again and I pushed her hand away.

"The surgery. Did it—"

"Actually, it helped," I said. "A man gets through life better if no one knows him well enough to bother him."

"And your T-date?" she interjected with suppressed eagerness.

"A clean slate," I replied. "The whole wide world is my residence and no one knows I'm home."

For an instant Mother's eyes lit up like boats adrift at the foot of a lighthouse. But they quickly dulled again as if warned of a treacherous shore.

"What do you want with me?" she inquired, taking a step back toward the refrigerator.

"Relax," I told her. "*Tag man* and *bogey man* aren't synonymous. I've come to find out if there's any love left between you and Dad."

"That love is dead," said Mother, her face a composite of hurt and wariness. "I hope you're not here to tease me, John. I couldn't stand to be teased by you."

"I'm not," I said as I studied her frame. She was still full of fire and freshness after all these years. Surely someone could have found her desirable in spite of her line of work. After one or two more cautious nibbles at the grayish paste that peered from between moldy rye, I decided to say the thing I had come to say.

"I'm going to help him," I announced.

"See there? You are teasing me," said Mother.

She was more cunning than I had counted on. But to insinuate she felt teased by the possibility of her ex-husband getting free was too unbelievable. I let her continue the guise.

"I told you I wasn't teasing," I said.

"I shouldn't have brought you here," said Mother abruptly. "Why is your generation so hateful toward mine?"

"I wouldn't call it hateful. Indifferent maybe, but nowhere near hateful."

"Indifference is worse," said Mother.

"Would you like to hear my plan?" I asked. "After all, it's only six more days until T-13."

Mother's hand moved toward the kitchen knife and curled around its handle. "Get out of here," she said, raising the knife.

"I'm disappointed in you, Roberta. Is this any way to treat a prodigal son? Or maybe it's you that's the prodigal. You've wandered so very far from your original view of life's sanctity."

She flung the knife on the floor and covered her ears. "Stop it!" she cried.

Since our arrival, rain had begun its light percussion on the rooftop. I followed the sound of it, up and down the shingles in the mounting wind. Spring is such a dreadful time of year to discuss death with a loved one. In spring, life is bulging from earth's brown belly and the horizon is pungent with possibility. With a touch of my hand on her shoulders, I led Mother into the living room.

"You could still find comfort," I said, knowing she understood exactly what I meant. On the rim of her eye a single droplet conceived and grew, then burst upon her cheek, causing my suspicions to falter.

"You'd like to help him, too, wouldn't you?" I asserted.

For a minute or two, Mother looked at the floor. "He ruined me," she said at last, shaking her head softly.

"You ruined me, too, when you left me at the Academy," I reminded her. "That hasn't changed the way I think about you, has it?"

"It certainly has," objected Mother. "It has made you gruff and detached, like a . . . a . . ."

"A monster?" I inserted.

Mother nodded silently, and I let out a laugh that sounded even to me like it came from the end of a pressurized hose.

"Oh, I'm sure there's some redeeming quality inside this old monster," I said. "What do you say? Would you like to help him or not?"

"But I'd lose everything," Mother moaned.

"Starting with what?" I said, staring conspicuously at her meager surroundings.

"You just don't get it. I'll be caught. I'll get a T-date."

"Everyone does, eventually," I said.

"Not you. You're free," said Mother.

"It's hard to say. There's no guarantee I'll make my quotas."

"If you're good with a gun, you've got a chance at long life."

"Look, I'd just like to meet the man whose last name I wear. It's not often you get to rub shoulders with a justice who wrote the majority opinion that led to legislation like Long Shadow, let alone one who is your father. But if you're not interested," I turned toward the door.

"Wait," pleaded Mother.

"I haven't got all night," I replied.

"Your father was a good man," she said, searching my eyes as if she had just declared the world was flat, and my reaction to her statement would either condemn or validate it.

"What was good about him?" I asked.

"He used to laugh a lot," said Mother. "And I recall a certain birthday of yours, where he took the entire day off from the office just to be with you."

"An entire day," I said, with mock awe. "My, he *must* have been a good man to make that kind of sacrifice."

Mother hardly seemed to hear me. "He won't want my help, though," she said, returning to pessimism. "Not now."

"Oh, I don't know. Life at its burned end makes people do funny things. Besides, the two of you have a lot in common. You're both murderers in your own special ways."

At that, Mother threw herself upon me and soaked the front of my shirt with a flood of long-deferred tears; tears that again seemed disturbingly genuine.

Watch it, Nash, I reminded myself. *Trust sparingly.*

"There now," I said. "Don't be hard on yourself. You had to make a living, didn't you? Sure, you did. We all did. Now, are you going to join me or not?"

Mother's face was still against my chest. "VC will find out. They know everything about everyone. They're an awful bunch."

"Careful. You never know who's listening," I reminded her, nodding toward the windows. "Besides, that awful bunch you're referring to is you and me."

"They're nothing like me," said Mother, almost choking on her emotion.

"You're a lonely soul," I asserted.

"Painfully," Mother agreed.

Outside it thundered, and Mother's shoulders began to quake like tender leaves against the storm. Soon she had resumed sobbing, and her sobs became so pronounced that when I drew her to me again it was easy to fit the tiny probe at the nape of her neck undetected, just like Captain Levi had suggested. At most, there was a prick when I inserted it—scarcely noticeable compared with the way Mother's conscience seemed to scourge her. It was a shame to trick her like that, for I had actually begun to believe she was not as Levi suspected. I smoothed her magnificent graying hair back into place, positive the device would remain secure.

"You wear your loneliness like an anchor," I said softly.

Mother blinked her wet eyes.

"Wouldn't it be wonderful to speak openly with someone who understood your burden? To hold that person? To have him hold you back?" I asked.

"Yes," Mother wailed.

"Then come help free him."

"But he hates me."

"Come. Please."

"Tonight?"

"When else?" I said. Then I added, "You do still love him, don't you?"

The sudden horror in Mother's eyes told that whatever intentions, whatever hope she had held for finding love and happiness, were swiftly vanishing.

"I have a report due in the morning," she blurted. "VC—"

"Forget VC!" I shouted. "Do you want love or not?"

"It's not that easy," said Mother.

"Look," I said. "Meet me at the East Plaza fountain tomorrow morning before work. Tell your driver you've got to pick some things up at the drugstore on Ward Parkway, then use the back door on Main and I'll be waiting for you."

"But Ray knows I buy all my things on Agora-Net."

"Make up a story, then. Say you just feel like shopping. Say it's for feminine items, or something. You've got to help me make a plan. We both know he'll try to run."

"That doesn't mean I have to rearrange my whole life."

"All right," I snapped. "I only wanted you to help me out. But if your own sweet skin is all you're worried about—"

"I want to believe you, son," blurted Mother. "I mean, having you come back to me and all, it's just too good to be true. Look, if I don't have any early paperwork and I can get Ray to understand about dropping me off at the Plaza—"

"What about saying you'll meet me?"

"Well, the idea certainly has merit."

"I need an answer."

"I have to think about it."

"Don't bother," I said, turning again to leave. "But just remember this; when I go, the last shred of hope you have for true love will go, too. It will vanish over that field and into the trees like one of those magnificent dreams that resists being dragged into waking hours. Then every moonlit walk you experience in reverie, every phantasmic dinner for two that comes to you between nod and dawn, every dance, every song, every longing that was ever yours will fade with the click of the door behind me. And you will be alone again with your awful bunch."

"John, please," said Mother.

I reached for the door handle. "I wish you well," I replied.

Suddenly, Mother grabbed my shoulder and forced herself between me and the door, all the while looking up at me with dark, hesitant eyes.

"Can you keep a secret?" she asked.

"Can I?" I replied.

"Will you," she corrected herself.

Here come the true colors, I thought. *If only Tiller and the captain could be here now.*

"That depends on what it is," I said.

"*Everything* depends on what it is," said Mother. "I must have your word."

"All right, you have my word," I assured her.

In possession of my oath, Mother wasted no time. "Have you ever heard of the Shadow Train?" she asked, glancing at the windows to make sure no gliders had come nosing about unnoticed.

"Sure," I said. "In stories, if that's what you mean."

"That is not what I mean," said Mother. "This is not a story, and this is not a scheme for me to reinvolve you in my life."

"What is it then?" I asked.

"The slightest wisp of a hope that you are no more a murderer than I—or your father, too, for that matter."

I swallowed hard.

"I have had one great hope in life," Mother continued. "One abiding dream that fills every hour of my day, and will not give me peace at night. But before I could reveal it to you, I had to make sure you were sincere."

"I hope I haven't let you down," I replied.

"You haven't."

"Do I get to hear the dream, then?"

Mother smiled. "It is the dream that someday your father will stand on Canadian soil with a grin on his face, lightness in his heart, and his family by his side. That is my dream, John. That is my one great hope."

"So, you're the Shadow Train," I said with feigned surprise.

"I'm the Shadow Train," said Mother. "And no one knows it but you and me and a couple of men in the tag corps who suspect more than they know. Of course, there are families scattered clear to Canada who know too. They're the ones who hide a Long Shadow for me whenever I send one north."

For a moment I hesitated, then flinging all caution aside, I asked, "Does Captain Levi know?"

The weight of my question must have landed like a blow to Mother's left temple, because for a second or two she looked down and to the right, as if she was remembering someone or some past event.

"I take it you're friends with him," said Mother finally.

"That's not what I asked," I replied. "Does Captain Levi know about the Shadow Train? Have you told him you're involved with it?"

Mother nodded. "We've done some work together in the past."

"Work?"

For a fraction of an instant, Mother seemed preoccupied. "I'd rather not talk about it," she responded.

I pressed her for an answer. "Will you meet me at the Plaza fountain, Roberta?"

Suddenly Mother clapped her hands together, and looked up at me with her face set like flint toward some distant objective.

"I have a better idea," she announced. Leaning forward, she whispered, "Meet me on the nineteenth floor of VC tomorrow and we'll go from there." She kissed me on my cheek and started to close the door behind me. "Oh, and one more thing," she added. "I think I'd rather not be called Roberta."

"Fine," I replied, turning up my collar to ward off the rain. "Then how about if I just call you—"

The door closed gently.

"—Mother," I said, the sound of her dead bolt signaling the end of our reunion.

I waited on her porch until the rain cooled to a pleasant mist and under the streetlight the adjacent lawns appeared like trays of costume jewelry. For a long time I stood there, all thoughts of Captain Levi's warning temporarily deferred for the sake of a great, abiding dream of my own. The wispy outline of a family in Canada appeared in my imagination, ensconced itself, refused to leave. Even when it flies in the face of danger, a moment comes when a man abandons the things he once coveted to pursue the thing he most desires. That was my moment outside Mother's door. She had come back for me it seemed. And neither sob nor sigh could persuade me that her motives were anything but pure.

At the corner, I flashed a reflector twice into the sky and, as if on invisible silk, my ride descended, spiderlike, to the curb.

"Hey, Tiller," I said through the dark, half-opened window of our glider.

"It's about time you showed up. What took you so long?"

"Oh, you know how pedotrainers are. Always interested in the details of our lives."

"I'm glad you had a chance to reminisce. Did you get the probe in place?"

I felt a twang of guilt. "Yeah, it's in place. I tried to get her to meet me at the Plaza fountain in the morning, but she said she'd feel more comfortable on the nineteenth floor of VC. I don't know about this, Tiller. That place gives me the creeps."

"Have you ever been there?"

"No."

"Then what are you worried about? You'll do just fine. Come on, climb in. I've got better things to do than hang up there in the sky, waiting for you. I thought I saw movement by that mall in Prairie Village quadrant. I want to check it out one more time, then we'll see what the night has to offer."

"I'm not up for socializing tonight, Tiller. Why don't you just take me home."

"Fine with me. You got anything in the refrigerator?"

"Uh, yeah . . . sure. You can come in for a minute or two. But I'd rather you didn't stay long."

"Okay, I get the hint. The hermit has spoken."

I climbed into the glider, resisting the urge for a last glance at Mom's house, and slid into the warm, leather seat next to Tiller. With the press of a few buttons, we lifted into the air.

"We've got some new equipment on board," declared Tiller. "Wanna peek?"

Usually, I would have been interested in the latest techno-gadget from VC simulation lab. Tonight I was too preoccupied to show much enthusiasm. "Nah," I replied. "I think I'll just close my eyes for a while."

"If it's your mom you're thinking about, this little number will give your mind a break," said Tiller, pushing touch pads on the board in front of us. Instantly, the skin of the glider disappeared and our chairs seemed to hover in midair.

"Hey!" I said, putting a hammerlock on my armrest. "What kind of crazy—"

"Take it easy, pal," said Tiller. "SimTech wouldn't send us something unless it's been tested once or twice. Relax. Pretend you're a bird or something."

"I don't want to be a bird," I said, gripping the armrest tighter.

"But think of all the advantages—"

"Put it back to normal. Now!"

"All right," said Tiller. "You don't have to be so testy about it." He touched another pad, and this time instead of the glider's regular skin appearing, a giant color display panel sprang up around us, startling me.

"What in the name of—"

"You should get a look at yourself," roared Tiller. At the sight of me consumed with wonder, his whole being broke into an uncontrollable guffaw.

"What is this stuff?" I asked.

It took a while for Tiller to calm down enough to answer my question, but when he finally did, I saw that someone in VC simulation technology had been very busy lately.

"Welcome to the future of air-to-ground combat," said Tiller.

"I don't believe it," I replied, touching the color display gingerly.

"Do you see how it works?" asked Tiller. "When the panels are down, you get a full view of your combat theater. When they're up, onboard computers receive info from global positioning system satellite receivers that let us see what's going on in any direction."

"I don't believe it," I whispered again.

"Believe it, John. And just think, as soon as SimTech perfects that adaptive colorant stuff for camouflage, you and I will be completely invisible. It'll make getting Long Shadows to Canada as easy as . . . well, as easy as shooting them used to be. Won't that be great?"

"It's . . . a dream come true."

"Yeah," said Tiller, "VC'd have fits if it knew what all its fancy equipment was being used for."

A minute later we were in the clouds, and as Mother's neighborhood dissolved into a speck of light, I began to wonder whether or not I had been fooled by her benevolence. It had happened before, I told myself—at the curbside of the Academy. Suddenly it dawned on me that one thing she had said was trustworthy. Terrible deeds had been done in the name of indifference—monstrous, terrible deeds. In the darkness I leaned my head against the seat, trying to forget the countless ones Tiller and I had committed. But a vision kept flashing in my brain of grown men running pell-mell beside lonely tarns, across the stubbled faces of cornfields in December, through woods and bogs and barnyards, always with their eyes glancing back to see if we were following. I saw the truth about Tiller and me. We were a microcosm of society, two of the nation's best and brightest gliding silently above the earth, while under our wings the stench of slaughtered babes and Long Shadows rose to meet the heavens. It was a truth that seemed incapable of being assuaged. Not even by a thousand trips to Canada.

*"Worldwide birth rates are declining, not rising.
The world is gaining resources, not losing them.
The truth is that all this doomsdaying is fiction."*
—From, *The Chronicles of Propaganda*,
Vol. IX, p. 13

I MET MOTHER AT VC BRIGHT AND EARLY THE following morning. Like I said, I had never been on the nineteenth floor of Vivi-Centerre, though I felt as linked to it as any other human being on the face of the fruited plains. It is where household names come to die; discoverers of vaccines, best-selling authors, athletes long past their primes but still dear enough to the public that their views on the greatest good are listened to. Everyday it is where the clear, strong signal of VOX Midwest originates.

With a lightness in her step that had not been present the night before, Mother led me through the hallways, traversing cable wires, sidestepping camera personnel, and all the while delivering a cheery *Hello, Good morning, How are you?* to those who respectfully referred to her as the diva of state television. We passed the door to the executive cafeteria, out of which floated the scent of food unavailable to the commoners nineteen stories below. Aware of the gap between the garbage I had eaten for breakfast an hour earlier and the fine things just inside that door, I turned toward Mother with what must have been a famished expression.

"Smells like they reserve the good stuff for the office," I observed.

Mother glanced around to see if anyone was listening, then she leaned her head toward mine. "You wouldn't know it by the kind of things in my cupboard, would you? Tight budget these days. Everything goes to propaganda and bounty hunting."

"Still, it must feel nice to be in the inner circle," I remarked.

"Inner circle," repeated Mother disdainfully. "There's always some smaller circumference you haven't quite made it into yet. You tell yourself that if you ever did, you certainly wouldn't make it hard for others to be admitted to it. It's funny, though."

"What is?"

"After going through what I did to make it into this circle, I became ten times harder on the outsiders than anyone ever was on me. That's something I'll have to live with."

"But you've got all the perks now, don't you?"

"You've seen my house, John. What do you think?"

I shrugged and Mother began to chuckle softly, so as not to draw attention to herself. "I don't believe there is a center anymore," she said. "If it exists, it certainly isn't here."

"Maybe it's in Washington, at VC National."

"It could be in Timbuktu for all I care. I quit looking for it a long time ago."

We walked in silence for a while, our feet leaving soft indentations in the carpet.

"I don't mean to shame you," I said after a moment. "But I've heard what you went through to get where you are."

"Ahh. I wondered how long it would take for the rumors to trickle down to you."

"Are they rumors?"

"What is that to you, son?"

"Nothing, I suppose. I just wanted to know." I had heard that Mother had slept with every young, pretentious suit that waved the carrot of extended life beneath her nose in exchange for a single night with her. Ironically, it was they who were beneath her now. That fact alone lent the rumors a disturbing corporeality.

Mother stopped several doors before the end of the hallway and lowered her voice again. "John," she said. "Which people do you think are most vocal for the greatest good?"

"The ones with no T-dates," I said wryly.

Mother nodded. "You know, I used to get furious at the fact that the people who were pro-abortion were those who were already born. So, what do I end up bankrupting myself for? The same kind of evil club that makes its circle increasingly tighter by excluding others, and has the audacity to call itself humane. I'm not proud of it. I will probably go to my grave with a great degree of remorse and self-loathing because of it. But it's a circle I am determined to destroy now. Regardless of my past, I will make sure its rules of admission and expulsion are done away with."

At the end of the hall there was a picture window, on the other side of which a window washer hung tenuously from his sling, risking life and limb so that VC executives might have an unobstructed view. Over his shoulder, I saw the top half of VOX shining proudly against a background of blue sky. A close-up of Mother's face filled most of it.

Mother studied herself through the window. "I really need to get out in the sun more often. A good makeup person might help in that department."

"Don't you have one?"

"I used to. He went on vacation last week and got caught trying to make it into Juarez."

While the window washer's feet bumped lazily against the glass, we stood gazing out over the city at the previous day's taped interview with a well-known local Long Shadow.

"I'll bet you get nervous knowing the whole midwest region is watching you," I said.

"Oh yes. I'm a worthless lump of emotions on camera. I can never get my hair right, and no matter how often I tell myself I'm just being paranoid, I can't help thinking I wore the exact same thing in my last interview. Tell me the truth, John, have you seen that scarf recently?" asked Mother, tapping on the glass in the direction of VOX. Thinking she was summoning him, the window washer stopped his work and leaned down to where he could look Mother in the eye. She waved him off and repeated the question.

"That red scarf, John," said Mother, pointing again. "Have you seen it before?"

"Sure, I've seen it. You wear it all the time on VOX."

"Are you sure I wear it *all* the time?" she asked, placing great emphasis on the word *all*.

"Mother, you didn't invite me here to talk about a scarf."

"Ohh, but I did," she insisted. "More has been tied to that bit of silk than people will ever know. And I am about to let you in on it. But first I have some business to attend to."

I followed her through the thick oak door to our left, down a narrow corridor, past a row of cells—which drew my curiosity—and finally to the observation window of a stark, concrete room. Inside, under bright lights, I saw the blanketed form of a man lying on a surgical table with his face turned away from the window. Behind him was a blue screen, already activated for use. At the other end of the room were the cameras trained upon it.

"You were probably too young to remember when your father and I loved each other," said Mother, staring through the glass at the man on the table.

"That's something I would like to remember," I replied. "It's just hard for me to believe that any woman could love a man who wrote the majority opinion on Long Shadow."

"He wasn't always like that, you know," said Mother. She sighed heavily. "Well, this is it."

The man rolled toward us, and I saw that it was Rossi from the tobacco shop. Instinctively, I took a step back from the window. He was still wearing his identification bracelet, which had begun to blink so rapidly that the intermittent break in the ring of light was almost imperceptible.

"He can't see you," said Mother.

"Why did you bring me here?" I demanded.

"Because few people ever see what we really do up here."

"I know exactly what you do up here," I said, backpedaling farther from the window.

"You know smoke and mirrors," replied Mother.

"I don't want to see this."

"If you ever want to help your father, you do." Mother reached for a button on the wall and mashed it with her forefinger. With a deafening click, a door slid shut behind me. "This is what the world is coming to, son. This is what happens when we teach our children to devalue life, then confer upon them a spate of rights commensurate with an adult's capacity to handle them. They become angry, miniature gods, John, bent on avenging the abortion of half their peers. They make the laws. We just administer them."

"Let me out of here!"

"There's only one way out."

"You're a sick woman."

"True," admitted Mother. "I'm sick of what VC expects me to do."

"You can't make me watch."

"You'll watch," said Mother. She disappeared through the door that led to Rossi.

Immediately, I turned my back to the observation window. I could hear the sound of the tropical music filtering into the room.

"Good evening," came Mother's television voice. "Welcome to tonight's edition of *The Highest Sacrifice for the Greatest Good*. Our witness tonight for the greatest good is beloved

Kansas City tobacco curator, Rossi Armitraj. We purposely refer to him as curator because for years he has been elevating the pastime of smoking to an art form for many of this city's fashionable citizens. Mr. Armitraj, please say hello to our viewing audience, and share with them your thoughts on the greatest good."

Where the wall met the ceiling, a TV monitor was angled in such a way that I could see into the termination chamber without turning around. At first I fought the desire to look, denying that what I had seen a thousand times on VOX could have anything to do with the woman who reared me. But hearing Mother's soothing voice and that of the sanguine man from Turkey, I glanced upward and was pulled in.

A beaming Rossi Armitraj was there on the screen, his jeweled smile dazzling the nation on the topic of death at fifty.

"Dee greatest good is dees," he began. "Dat a man lives life to the fullest, and dies as well as he lived."

"That's a lovely motto, sir," said Mother, patting Rossi's shoulder, while she kept her eye on the teleprompter. "For the sake of those in the audience who have never had the privilege of knowing you personally, we prepared some footage of your life and work."

For the next three minutes, I saw images of Rossi around Kansas City; Rossi as a Rotarian, Rossi playing Santa Claus at Saks, Rossi in his shop, Rossi surrounded by dozens of jovial customers. All the while, a taped recording of his ramblings on sacrifice and the greatest good commingled with music from his mother country.

When I finally gave in and turned around, I expected to see Rossi alive. Instead, his fat, motionless form was already being wheeled out of the room on a separate cart by two technicians in white lab coats, while the sound of his voice still played in the background. Close on the technicians' heels, Mother jabbed at the button on the wall and shoved past them through the doorway. Her face was peaked.

"Come with me, John," she whispered so the men couldn't hear her. "We've got a world to change."

I stood there, watching Rossi roll away from me.

"What are you waiting for?" asked one of the technicians with a smirk. "Don't you prima donnas in tags ever get to see any real action?"

I glanced at the terrible plastic snakes that protruded from under Rossi's sheet and attached themselves to the bottle on an IV pole. "But on VOX it always looks like there's more," I stammered.

"What were you expecting, a finale?" asked the technician. "Man, you guys are green. Sodium pentothal doesn't take forever, you know. When it's mixed with pancuronium bromide and potassium chloride, it's guaranteed to get the job done. T-7's dead, pal. Get used to it."

Fighting the urge to look at the body, I pushed past the men in white and hurried to overtake Mother. I saw her ahead of me, walking rapidly, almost running to make it somewhere. The door to the women's room banged open, then closed softly behind her, and I was alone in the hallway for what seemed like an eternity. Eventually she emerged, composed again, and went directly to her office without even a glance to see if I was following her.

"You're a murderer," I said the moment we were alone in her office.

Mother sat quietly behind her desk.

"I came to you in confidence, poured out my heart—"

"You have a lot to learn, John," said Mother. She opened her top drawer and removed a wallet-sized information appliance. "Close the blinds," she commanded.

"Why?"

"Just do as I say."

I turned around and pulled strings on each side of the door.

"Now, John," said Mother, pointing to a chair on the other side of her desk and ordering me to sit, "I am going to explain something to you that I doubt even our friend Coffin knows much about. You seem like someone who can keep a secret—a bit overreactive maybe—but sincere at least."

"Overreactive? Do you call sympathy for an innocent tobacco salesman overreactive? You're—"

Mother put her forefinger to her lips. "Ranting and raving will get you nowhere, son. In fact, it has never helped anyone who opposed VC. While we're at it, though, I think you ought to know you're not the only one with sympathy for Long Shadows."

"I suppose you're going to tell me you're sympathetic."

"Do you think I normally take fifteen minutes in the bathroom to powder my nose?"

"I hadn't thought about it."

"Well, think about it, John. Think about me for the last five years, getting sick to my stomach every time I have to do what you saw me do back there."

"If you're really part of the Shadow Train, you could stop it."

Mother leaned forward. "Not *part* of the Shadow Train; *the* Shadow Train," she corrected me. "Just because someone says he is a part, doesn't mean it's so. It is possible for a man or woman to claim participation in acts of heroism without possessing a single drop of courage or, for that matter, sympathy for the ones they supposedly rescue. Time alone bares all things."

"Captain Levi says—"

"There will be plenty of time to discuss Captain Levi," said Mother, putting her finger to her lips again. She rotated the small computer toward me so I could read for myself the long list of names contained on each page.

"Here they are," she lamented. "Two thousand people in the last six months, all of them Rossis with different names. I can't save them all. Not with my current system."

"What system?"

"That's where the scarf comes in. I was glad you noticed it before."

Mother retrieved her purse from beneath her desk, and fished in it until she discovered what she was looking for. "Does this look familiar?" she asked, handing me the attractive, scarlet scarf that I had seen on so many occasions it had finally become invisible. "It was given to me by someone whose grandfather used to live near Auschwitz."

Sarcasm overcame me. "I see. And the remembrance of that holocaust somehow makes you feel okay about perpetrating another one."

"Wrong," said Mother. "The scarf is my signal to a secret network of people that a Long Shadow is heading their way."

I sat in disbelief.

"Go ahead," she insisted, pushing the computer a little closer to me. "Scroll through the list. You'll find the names that are italicized coincide precisely with the days I wore the scarf on VOX. Do you want to see the tapes to make sure?"

I shook my head. "No. I think I believe you."

"Thinking you believe is worse than not believing. I may do some things while we are freeing your father that could make you doubt me. I must have your total confidence or you cannot be part of the Shadow Train. Do you trust me?"

"Why can't you save all of them?" I asked, shifting the topic. "Why couldn't you save Rossi?"

"Your confidence, John," demanded Mother. "I'll not say another thing about the way I operate until I hear the words from your lips."

"All right. You have my confidence."

"Good," said Mother, rising from her chair. "I'm canceling the rest of my schedule for today. I suggest you go to wherever it is you live, gather as much clothing and ammunition as you can pack in a small satchel, and meet me at my house tonight before curfew. From there, we'll go to see your father."

"How do you know where he is?"

"Where else would a judge be in his final hours? He's at home with his books and briefs, and about a dozen tag men still guarding him."

"Should I inform Captain Levi of your plans?"

Mother squeezed the bridge of her nose, thinking. From the great labyrinth of rooms and hallways beneath, muted and asphyxiating sounds of Vivi-Centerre were buoyed up to us through the ductwork.

"That won't be necessary," she said finally. "If I know Captain Levi Coffin, he'll be waiting at August's house when we get there."

I stood and walked toward the office door.

"One more thing, John," said Mother, just as my hand settled around the cool, metal knob.

I stared straight ahead at the door.

"I would save them all if I could," she murmured.

"I would, too," I replied, without turning around. When I stepped out into the hall and closed the door behind me, I heard the unmistakable sounds of sobbing.

WITH SATCHEL IN HAND, I MET MOTHER AT her place as soon as the sun went down. I was glad when she told me Ray was unavailable to drive us tonight, gladder still when she suggested we skip the People Mover and hail a PRT.

We had only a short walk to the nearest boarding station where Mother entered her code on a keypad and we both sat down to wait. Soon we heard our little vehicle whizzing toward us on the overhead guideway, and almost before it had settled to a stop there was a crackling sound and a congenial computer spoke over the boarding station address system.

"Please enter your destination," it said.

Mother typed in a new number. "I pay for door-to-door service after 8:30. That way there are no intervening transfers and I never have to wait in one of those poorly lit stops. What's the matter, John?"

"Nothing," I said, drawing my shoe raspingly along the sidewalk.

"Come on, son, mothers never believe that answer. Tell me what's bothering you?"

"I met a girl," I answered bluntly.

"A girl! Is she pretty? Tall? Tell me everything."

I smiled at the thought of my introduction to Sarah McSwain. Indeed, she was the most beautiful woman I had ever met. "She's . . . shrewd."

"Shrewd?" remarked Mother. "What kind of thing is that to say about a girl?"

"Let's talk about something else," I suggested. "I take it there's a debarking station near Father's house."

"As far as I know," said Mother disappointedly. She pushed another button and a green light flashed on the keyboard, indicating everything was in order. "You're sure you don't have anything else you want to say?"

"Positive."

"Suit yourself," said Mother, as she stepped up onto the metal platform and into the vehicle's tiny confines. "You know, there was a time when sons talked to their mothers."

"So I've heard."

I took a seat next to her, being careful to set my satchel gently beneath it, for fear I might damage the EM rail. When we were comfortable, Mother pressed the activator button and we sped into the twilight. Quickly, she extracted her wallet PC from her purse and placed it on her lap. In a matter of seconds she had called up a map.

"Don't you think we should wait for Captain Levi's input?" I asked.

Mother ignored my suggestion and with a light stylus proceeded to circle three towns between Kansas and the northern tip of Minnesota.

"What you are about to learn should never be repeated unless you are positive you are dealing with someone opposed to the greatest good. Do you understand?"

"I think so. But how do you know *I'm* really opposed to it?"

"Because I'm your mother," she replied simply. She traced the tip of her stylus down the face of the map until she came to Kansas City. "Let's see now, Floyd . . . Floyd. Here it is. The

Floyd River route. I've recommended it countless times for Long Shadows going north, and haven't had any trouble with it so far. Dakota City is really just a fuel stop," she said, pointing to the first red circle. "It's a rough little town. Lots of kids on the street at night. Tag poles galore for some strange reason. But the owner of the fuel station is a kind man who's sympathetic to anyone trying to get to Canada. He's got a solar generator that produces 650 kilowatt-hours as long as he's got enough sunlight that day. Long Shadows fill-up for free if they know the password. We'll recharge and get out of there as fast as we can."

"So, we'll be going untethered?"

"Uh-hm, in a flatbed truck to be exact. It's one of those kinds with wooden-slatted sides and lots of room. I'll explain more in a minute," said Mother, glancing at her watch. "We'll have to be extra careful in Dakota City. I've heard of kids going ballistic there at the slightest sign of something suspicious. Your father's robe has me worried, John."

"Who told you about his robe?"

Mother hesitated. "He had it on every time I went to visit him. I've grown to see it as his penance."

The sudden revelation that Mother had been visiting my father at Rivendale was a shock to me, because I still could not believe she would have anything but contempt for him.

"What if he refuses to take it off?" I asked.

"Oh, he'll refuse. We'll just have to keep him out of sight and make sure the glow of his bracelet is sufficiently hidden. As soon as we can get out of Dakota City and to Sheldon on the river, the better." Mother paused and looked at me remotely, her eyes possessed by something far away. "You remember our farm in Sheldon, don't you?"

I shrugged.

"Your father and I honeymooned in Sheldon. I'd like to spend an afternoon there when we pass through, just the two of us."

"That will be a risk."

"One I've calculated for a long time. There's no use turning a sick man free in Canada if he's too sick to enjoy himself. The way I see it, I've got seven hundred miles between Kansas City and Ely to love him back to wholeness."

This last statement was too much to let pass.

"After all he did to you?" I interjected.

Mother stared solemnly at me.

"After fooling around on you and leaving you and sentencing every person he ever knew to an early grave, you really have no hard feelings toward the man?"

"Like I told you, he wasn't like that before the majority opinion," replied Mother. "He never wanted it to turn out the way it did. He was a people-pleaser. By the time he got through pleasing every constituency and every interest group involved, he hardly recognized his own document. But he lacked the courage to start all over. In the end, he gave it his stamp of approval."

"And went straight to the funny farm," I blurted.

"If that's how you choose to see Rivendale—yes, he went to the funny farm."

"But not before he slept with everything that wore a skirt in Washington, D.C. I don't see how you can forget all that so easily."

"Nobody said I've forgotten it. I'm not even sure I've forgiven it. But I'm willing to try, John. God knows I've done a lot worse things than August. I can't see holding the past against him."

"He cheated on you, Mother. Get that through your head."

"Do I detect bitterness?"

I felt my cheeks filling up with blood. "He took every childhood dream I ever had and . . . and crushed it with his stupid career."

"It sounds like you're more concerned with how he cheated *you* than how he cheated me."

"Maybe I am!" I said.

It was silent for a while, except for the quiet whiz of the PRT's wheels along the guideway. When I spoke again, my voice sounded wobbly.

"Sometimes I wonder why I'm risking so much to get an old man to Canada who doesn't even know me."

"That old man used to take whole days off from work just to celebrate your birthdays. He bought you a baseball bat signed by all the Yankees. You carried that thing like a treasure everywhere you went."

"What do you get out of this, anyway? Is it money? I'll bet it's money, isn't it?"

Mother looked out the window.

"I've hit upon something, haven't I?" I said. "Tiller told me he got ten thousand dollars just last month for bringing in an East Coast bigwig. Think how many mortgages you could pay with the bounty that'll be out on Father. What's to keep you from blowing the whistle once we get him to Ely?"

Mother adjusted the PC map on her knee. "I'm sorry you had an unhappy childhood, John, but we only have a few more miles to discuss your father's future. Surely if I can set aside my bitterness, you can do the same. You said I had your confidence this morning."

"I said a lot of things I shouldn't have said," I concluded, burying my face in my hands.

Mother continued her explanation of the Floyd River route, though I gleaned next to nothing from it. For a while I sat brooding, wondering if there was any way I could get out of what I had gotten myself into. When I peered through my fingers I could just make out the top six inches of Mother's map. Circled in red were the words *Tonsus Abbey,* on the northern border of Minnesota. The voice of Captain Levi rang in my head. *"She's got some connection . . . some connection . . . some connection."* A moment later it dawned on me that Mother was asking me a question.

"Excuse me?" I said.

"Do you feel that way, too?" she repeated.

"About what?"

"About the thirty million who've been terminated since August wrote that awful thing. You do feel bad about it, don't you?"

"Of course I do," I replied.

"Well then, what do you do when you lie down at night and your conscience won't let you sleep?" asked Mother.

"I don't know. Drink a glass of milk, do some push-ups. I try not to think about stuff."

"That doesn't work for me anymore," said Mother. "Peter will have the answer for me. He always does."

"Peter who?"

Mother cast an irritated glance in my direction. "Have you been listening to me?" she said.

"I heard the word, *Tonsus*."

"Prior Peter Edmunds is the . . . oh, never mind. I'll have to tell you later. Your father's house is up ahead. Can you see it? It's the one with the mob in the front yard."

My shoulders slumped at the sight ahead of us. Since the next day was trash day, those citizens who were unable to purchase the costly Homewaste Deionizers had placed their cans by the curb. Punks set these on fire, and warmed up to them on cool spring nights. As far down the street as I could see, lights from the flickering garbage cans were surrounded by street parties. The sweet smell of hash drifted up toward the guideway. Dark figures in trench coats and military boots gathered around the burning trash. Some sang. Others shouted filth at the homes on either side of the street. The majority simply stood around sharing cigarettes and joints. Like a pile of anxious ants, youth from all over the city clogged the narrow pavement in front of my father's residence, occasionally shouting at the top of their lungs: "Death to Long Shadows! Death to Long Shadows! Death to Long Shadows! Death to Long Shadows!"

They were Academy rejects—those who flunked the most rudimentary building blocks of education (particularly the total acceptance of sacrifice for the greatest good) and then feed off society as unskilled parasites. They make their living as sort of nonunion tag men, bringing in a Long Shadow now and then to put beans on the table. And it's no secret that there is great animosity between real tag men and these renegades. Nevertheless, VC allows them to operate because they don't expect as much money per tag.

Our guideway angled gently down toward the debarking station, which was just a house away from Father's place. When our vehicle came to a stop, the door opened automatically and we scurried over the sidewalk to avoid confrontation.

"I heard the old man's days are numbered," said one greasy-haired punk, as Mother fumbled in her purse for her automatic gate opener. "Heard he's going to be on VOX real soon."

"That's a show I'm not going to miss," said the punk's girl-friend. "A taste of his own medicine will do him good."

I started to turn on them.

"Ignore them," whispered Mother, flashing her blue-and-silver VC identification card. Immediately, the mob made way for her and she aimed her opener at the gate, giving it a click. I followed her through onto the ragged, blue breast of Father's lawn and we trudged up the steps to his front door, while the mob resumed its party.

It was a dark, gloomy house, a shell of the one I remembered visiting whenever the high court was on long recess. The three of us had come there only a handful of times during our years in Washington, but the visits were significant enough that I felt as if I knew every nook and cranny of every room. It had a wooden floor that creaked as Mother and I navigated across it toward a dim, golden oval at the bottom of the stairs. Somewhere above, a light was on, and we heard a voice crying the same two words, over and over.

"I'm sorry . . . I'm sorry . . . I'm sorry. . . ."

Mother and I climbed the stairs and followed the light to its source. The master bedroom was as I remembered it; long, rectangular, cluttered to the ceiling with stacks of books and briefs, with barely enough room for a bed and an armoire. The only things that were out of place were Tiller and Captain Levi, who stood rigidly when Mother and I entered the room. She looked at me as if to say, "I told you so."

"I'm sorry . . . I'm sorry," came a voice from the far side of the room.

Tiller came toward us, extending his hand to welcome Mother, while Captain Levi remained in the corner. "It's all he ever says," said Tiller. "Every now and then he starts jabbering about other stuff. But he always comes back to the apology."

The black-robed figure of my father sat hunched over at the desk with his back to us. As if on cue, he began to quote in legalese: "Memorandum on government subsidized health care for the elderly. 22 January 2013. Inasmuch as Section 1090 of title 27 of the United States Code permits the use of DOH funds to subsidize health care, due to the burgeoning stress of such care upon the nation's budget, let it be known that DOH has acted far and beyond the requirements of the statute, and shall no longer do so. I hereby direct that you withdraw all federal funds involved in such subsidies, thereby placing the burden of care for the elderly on the private sector."

At this point, the voice dissolved into the pitiable wail again and I watched my mother's countenance fall. Without a word, she went to Captain Levi and shook his hand, while I moved into a shadow to observe.

"Evening, Levi," said Mother.

"Evening, Roberta," replied the captain. "I let my other men go early."

"That was insightful. Will they be any further nuisance?"

"It's not likely. I told them you were coming. Is the film session scheduled?"

"Just as we discussed it."

An indelible smudge of animosity seemed to color their relationship. It lingered between them for a moment, then vanished just as I touched the hem of its identity.

"There's his medicine," interjected Tiller, pointing toward a pill bottle on the edge of the desk. "As you can see, it's completely full. I don't think he's following doctor's orders."

Mother walked to the desk. "Easy, Auggie," she crooned as she smoothed his hair.

"Rob?" came a tired voice from somewhere in the folds of the robe.

"Yes, it's me, Auggie," said Mother.

Immediately, the voice launched into a defense of actions long since blurred by history. "You know, Rob, what I did was perfectly justified."

"I'm sure it was," said Mother.

"We were spending one percent of the gross national product on health care for elderly persons who were in the last years of life—"

"I brought the boy with me this time," interrupted Mother.

"You won't believe how big he's gotten. He's a man, Auggie. Our boy is a man."

"A man," repeated Father flatly, without looking up at Mother. I remember thinking his voice sounded like a taped recording. "I knew a man once. Called him Skink when he wasn't around to hear me. Chief Skink we used to say."

"Justice Swann was a wonderful gentleman, Auggie. All your colleagues were wonderful."

"He read summaries of the cases rather than the briefs—always came unprepared for conference."

"I'm sure he knew what he was doing."

"He read summaries of the cases!" repeated Father, slapping the desk with the palm of his hand. At the impact, a cupful of pens jumped and toppled over.

"Here he goes again," whispered Tiller to me. "He's been doing this since noon when we got here. Man, he's schizo."

"He has schizoid tendencies," snapped Mother, her eyes riveted to Tiller.

"It's a good thing you're coming along on this one," said Captain Levi suddenly, glancing at Mother. "You are coming along, aren't you?"

Mother returned the glance, and I was sure I saw a dubious light in her eyes. "I haven't decided yet."

With a sweep of his hand, Father cleared his desk of everything not permanently fastened. "He wasn't ready for discussion!"

Another painful slap rang out. From my vantage point, I could see that Father's right hand was red and swollen.

"Does he stay like this for long?" I whispered to Tiller.

Tiller shook his head. "He'll turn the corner soon. You'll see."

"Skink's position was unclear," mumbled Father, as if he were addressing an unseen therapist. "How could it be clear? He supported states' rights on euthanasia. But he thought the Michigan law was vague too."

"It was vague, Auggie," said Mother.

"He couldn't be clear, then. I couldn't have been expected to think otherwise, could I?"

"Of course you couldn't."

"There, it's settled, once and for all. I feel worlds better. I'd like my pass now. A walk on the grounds would do me good."

"We're not at Rivendale, dear. We're at your house."

"Yes. My house . . . my study . . ."

Father buried his head in his hands, and nothing was settled. Nothing in this familiar monologue had shifted enough to make August Nash feel anything but loathing for himself. Heavy tears began to roll down his cheeks, then splash onto the desk where they formed miniature reflection pools, and with every glint, every shimmer, every human heart present was drawn into the former judge's sadness.

"I'm sorry," he sobbed. "Terribly sorry."

Mother put her arms around his neck and leaned her head against his shoulder.

"He'll go all to pieces for a while," observed Tiller.

Captain Levi shook his head. "What's Canada going to do for him? He'd probably be much happier if we just put him out of his misery."

"Don't you dare," said Mother, wheeling around.

"Easy," said Captain Levi. "It was just a thought."

Mother wasn't pacified. She lit into Captain Levi with such thrilling scorn that for a moment I wondered if I might have to physically defend her.

"You've wanted to call the shots on the Shadow Train ever since you came on board," she said, glaring at Captain Levi. "But let me remind you, I'm the head conductor here. Not you, not Tiller, me. Have I made myself clear?"

A certain smoldering look established dominance over Captain Levi's face and he leaned toward Mother. "My sainted grandpa wouldn't think so," he replied.

"Let's put an end to this 'sainted grandpa' story," Mother said, biting off her words with impatient efficiency. "Quite a few generations have passed since your sainted grandpa actually did anything saintly, so many that it would be ridiculous to try to attach all the 'greats' in front of his name. He was a powerful man, I grant you that. He freed a lot of people, did a lot of good for the black man in the South. But I'll bet my last dollar you'd be hard-pressed to get him to say anything good about you."

Captain Levi gave a disdainful snort.

"Are you going to take orders, or not?" asked Mother.

"I haven't decided yet," mocked the captain.

"We don't have to work together, you know. I can kick you off this line just as fast as I picked you up," she threatened.

"Come now, Mrs. Nash," said Captain Levi. "We both know you're going to need me on this one."

"You're more expendable than you think."

"We'll see."

"Yes, we will."

Mother and the captain were nearly toe-to-toe, and all the while Father's sobs were becoming less distinct in the background. It was one of those moments that teeter between confusion and chaos, wherein I was so determined not to be fooled by the facade—as I had been in the captain's conference room the day before—that I sank farther into my shadow and reserved all judgment.

"Excuse me," said Tiller, after a minute or two of their bickering. "I think the judge has fallen asleep."

Sure enough, Father was slumped across his desk in a mass of disheveled slumber.

"It's about time exhaustion set in," said Captain Levi, turning toward Tiller. "Bring the vehicle around, Tolles. We'll load him in before he wakes up."

"Load him in?" I objected.

Tiller froze.

"Go on, Tolles," said Captain Levi. "You've got an order to obey."

"I'm the one giving orders here," said Mother, moving quickly to bar Tiller from the doorway.

"Excuse me," said Tiller as he tried to pass.

"We'll take him in the PRT," Mother announced.

"In the truck," blurted Captain Levi. "The PRT is much too small."

This was more than I could bear. Flinging composure aside, I sprang into the center of the room and looked from face to face with such intensity that I believe they all thought I had gone mad. "Where are you taking him?" I demanded.

"To VC," said Captain Levi. "Where else?" He made a move toward Father.

"Get away!" I shouted, stepping between the two of them.

"Son, we have to take him there," said Mother. "We have to do it fast. That's why Mr. Tolles is going to go and hail two PRTs for that very purpose. Aren't you, Mr. Tolles?"

"Don't move, Tolles," said Captain Levi, his voice fumbling unsuccessfully for the commanding note. "We're taking the truck."

"The truck stays here," said Mother. She moved aside to let Tiller pass. Later when I asked her about it, she confided that she had no idea which voice Tiller would obey. As it turns out, when we emerged from the house twenty minutes later, carrying Father's limp body, a pair of PRTs were waiting on the guideway.

"Death to Long Shadows! Death to Long Shadows!" chanted the kids in the street.

"Go on home. He's dead already," shouted Captain Levi from the guideway.

"Death to Long Shadows!" the cry continued.

"Can't you see the man has had a heart attack? Cripes, what vultures," muttered the captain as he and Tiller lifted Father into the lead vehicle. Mother and I climbed in after him.

"Help me tighten those straps, please. We wouldn't want your father to fall over on the crosstown," said Mother, hurrying to obey her own command. Against my vigorous objection, Captain Levi had given Father a shot of something that made him limper than a rag doll.

"You better have an explanation for this," I said to Mother, as the door closed behind us and we sprang away with the other PRT in our wake.

"I wanted to talk alone," she replied.

"And I want to know why we're going back to VC."

We passed through the light of a boarding station, and for the slightest moment a rectangle of watery green settled on Mother's face. She looked tired, almost unequal to the task that stretched before us. But just as the green became gray on its way to black again, I saw that same resolute expression I had seen so many times on VOX.

"Trust me, John," she murmured. "No matter what happens, trust me."

9

*"Once the precedent of doctor-assisted killing has
been established, there will be no turning back."*
—From *The Los Angeles Times Syndicate,
Premillennial Archives*, vol. IV.

IT WAS A LONG, CIRCUITOUS ROUTE BACK TO
VC, uneventful enough that I should digress for a moment and
tell you about my face. With my initial surgery, I was practically
able to order à la carte all the features God omitted the first time
around. I never did like my ears, so they were the first thing to
be altered, followed by my once noncommittal chin and set of
eyebrows that had a penchant for growing together in the middle. In their place, I received anonymity and an Adonis-like
countenance that has often been the envy of fellow tag men
who had the same surgery as myself, but with lesser results.
Since VC footed the bill, it cost me nothing save the certainty
of who I really am.

There have been other surgeries since then, minor ones to
customize me for a particular job where the client was promi-
nent and, therefore, more likely to have a web of people keeping an eye out for me. I used to wonder why Long Shadows
didn't all flock to have their faces changed. After all, the technology is available. Sure, it's expensive. But what're a few extra
dollars where one's life is at stake? That was before it was
explained to me that laws existed that restricted anyone but VC
employees from cosmetic surgery.

Tiller and I used to spend a lot of time sitting around the bar together, figuring what we'd do if we were Long Shadows. Once, when we were several sheets to the wind, he told me the first thing he would do is drink a bottle of eighty proof to numb himself, then cut his hand off.

"That's a little extreme," said the waitress who was serving us. She asked him why he wouldn't just cut the bracelet off.

"Cut the bracelet off?" exclaimed Tiller. "Ma'am, if you were any more naive you'd be a hazard to yourself."

"Is that so?" said the woman peevishly.

"Yes, that's so. The things explode if you cut into them."

"I don't believe it," she said, hurrying away to another table full of tag men. Tiller proceeded to tell me a story.

"When I was a kid, we had this cleaning lady—I think her name was Nan. Anyway, when she came to interview for the job, I was hiding behind the living room couch and I heard her tell my old man how much she charged per hour. She says 'nine dollars if I totes, ten if I don't totes'—which meant she charged more if she didn't steal things, like ink pens and toilet paper. My old man gave her twelve to keep her honest. She was the nicest Long Shadow I ever knew."

"What's that got to do with exploding bracelets?"

"Well, six months before my old man's T-date, Nan got her hand caught in some machinery at her other job. When it reached her wrist—"

"Spare me the details," I interrupted him.

"Fine," said Tiller. He chugged the rest of his beer.

Over the years, I've heard of a million other ways that VC keeps a tight rein on its clients. Besides the tag poles and the bracelets, there's the fact that electric cars issued to wealthy Long Shadows all have air bags full of a binary compound—I'm not sure which one, but it's fluorine something and it's the most reactive of all elements. I'm astonished when I meet anyone over forty who still thinks this is some sort of game.

Anyway, a half mile west of VC, I caught a whiff of sulfur and recognized the tall smokestacks of the incinerators sending forth their eternal black cloud. "We're getting close," I said to Mother, who had been using the time to sleep, or perhaps to meditate about the task ahead. When she sat up, I noticed the silver cross above her neckline.

"You've found religion, haven't you?" I said.

"No," she replied. "I've found life."

"At Vivi-Centerre? You must be joking."

Mother smiled. "Let me clarify. I found Jesus at Tonsus Abbey."

We came to a juncture in the guideway, stopped, and I felt the other set of wheels engaging for perpendicular travel. The sudden redirection caused Father to shift against the harness, and I steadied him to prevent his waking.

Mother looked at me alertly. "You weren't old enough to remember all the unforeseen consequences of the first wave, were you, son?" she asked.

"Of T-dates?"

Mother nodded.

"I don't suppose I was. Why?"

"Well, there was a decline in national agricultural production—a sharp decline. You may remember eating water on your cereal for a while, instead of milk."

A pale memory of the famine came to me. "Lots of watery soup," I murmured.

Mother nodded. "Do you know what caused the famine?"

"I suppose it was the termination of too many farmers at one time."

"Partly. But on top of that, most economists assumed farmers' sons were still eager to follow in their fathers' footsteps."

"A slight miscalculation?"

"Hindsight's always twenty-twenty," said Mother. "You're right, though. Most country boys in the twenty-first century figured that if they were going to have to be sedentary in life, they'd rather do it at a computer terminal than behind the wheel of a tractor."

"For a lot more money, too," I commented.

Mother nodded again. "The Academies pumped out droves of techno-minded workers, of whom few were willing to make a living by the sweat of their brow. A thousand calls an hour started pouring into the White House switchboards, people complaining about this shortage or that shortage and asking what someone was going to do about it. I remember your father being called to the Oval Office and feeling very responsible for it all."

"What did they do?" I asked.

"The ag department started looking for ways to keep everybody fed and happy. When they noticed that most monasteries had great tracts of land surrounding them, they snatched up the land for pennies, exempted the monks from T-dates, and took the lion's share of production."

"Is this a great country, or what?"

We crossed the Missouri and Mother gazed down upon its milky expanse. "It is a great country, son," she said sorrowfully. "It's the inhabitants who are the problem. Anyway, that's how the monasteries, like Tonsus Abbey, came to be known as safe havens. Beneath the spiritual trappings, they're nothing more than government work farms where men of peace live and work together to meet the food demand created by Long Shadow laws."

"If they really have no T-dates, then why in the world doesn't everybody go to live there?"

"I'm afraid you'll have to take that up with Peter when you meet him," said Mother. "He's got some interesting theories on the subject. Besides, Tonsus Abbey isn't exactly like all the other monasteries. You'll see. You're going to love Prior Peter. He grows the most fantastic tulips."

"You make him sound like a god."

"No, he's just a man," said Mother. "But there'd be no Shadow Train without Peter Edmunds. All routes lead to Tonsus Abbey. It's the last stop on the line."

"Don't tell me," I said, holding up my hand. "He sprinkles people with holy water and blesses them one last time before they cross over into the Great White North?"

Mother laughed. "He listens to God and passes on what he hears. He might even have a word for you, if you're not too proud to receive it."

I ignored this last comment. "How does he get people across the border?"

"Didn't I tell you? He's on the edge of Moose Lake."

"So?"

"So, he outfits Long Shadows, gives them canoes, packs, food to last a day or two. Then he sends them north."

"Right to the border guards," I said pessimistically.

Mother eyed me. "You know, I think I liked you better when you were a kid. You weren't so cynical then."

"I was vulnerable, instead. Is that a trait you want me to recapture?"

"It's a trait we should all strive to cultivate."

"Not a chance. The only way to stay alive in this world is to keep a look out for your back."

"Be careful, son. Cynicism eats the cynic." Mother paused and glanced out the window again.

"Do you believe two people can fall in love again, after there has been so much betrayal?" she asked.

Mother's question brought Sarah to mind, and I wondered if I would ever see her again. "I hope so," I replied.

"Hope is nice," said Mother. "But what do you *believe* in?"

"Me . . . my gun . . . the tendency of people's affections to congeal."

"You're a regular ray of sunlight," said Mother, sighing. "Do you have this same cheery effect on everyone you meet?"

I shrugged and pretended to be occupied with the advancing lights of Vivi-Centerre. "It will be difficult getting him out of the PRT without the night guards noticing," I said, nodding at Father.

"Let them notice," said Mother.

"They're not going to just allow some truck to drive away from the auto pool," I said.

"No, they aren't," Mother agreed.

"So, how do you propose to—"

"We're not transferring directly to the truck," interrupted Mother.

"What do you mean?"

"It's not the way we do things, John."

"What is the way we do things?" I demanded, suddenly wondering if Father was about to go the way of Rossi.

Mother leaned over and grabbed my wrist. "We're going back into VC, with your father, with Tiller, with Levi, and with the same confidence that has helped me pull this thing off a thousand times. If you want to wreck it all, then go right ahead with your suspicious questions and your father will be dead in less than an hour, I can assure you of that."

Looking back on those events today, I realize that Mother had intended to bypass certain problems by telling me more about the plan. But no sooner had she opened her mouth again, than we eased to a stop and the door to our vehicle slid open.

"Hello, Evan," said Mother to the technician who had been waiting for us with a wheelchair on the intake ramp.

"Right on time, Mrs. Nash," the man replied.

The hair on the back of my neck stood straight. Standing on the ramp was one of the two technicians who had taken Rossi away just a few hours before.

"Not a bad night for an honorable man like Judge Nash to call it quits," said Evan. "I'm sure the world will be inspired."

He moved to collect Father and I lunged into his midsection, driving him out the door.

"John!" shouted Mother.

Before we even hit the metal ramp, I felt a blow at the base of my skull and I collapsed into darkness. The next thing I remember is waking up outside the interview room on floor nineteen, strapped to a cold chair and staring at my father through the window. I tried to scream, but my mouth was taped.

"Trust me," mouthed Mother, just before she pointed to the camera and began the countdown. Three. Two. One. "Good evening," she said in her television voice. "Welcome to tonight's edition of . . ."

I shook my head to clear it of the fog from the blow, and blinked at the glass. Mother was wearing the red scarf. I blinked again. It was still there, peaking over the top of her neckline, where earlier the cross had been.

"You shouldn't have attacked us," came a voice behind me.

With effort, I turned my head and looked into the eyes of the two technicians. Their faces were shiny and their coats reeked of the sweat of their jobs. The one who addressed me was standing with a black baton in his hands.

"Relax. It'll be over soon," he said, nodding toward the window. "See? She's already turning the stopcock."

I spun around and saw Mother administering the sodium pentothal. The CD of Father's voice droned in the background, touting the virtues of the greatest good. On the table, his body lay limp and white. Then, regardless of my gag, a great scream welled up from my stomach and beat against the back side of my teeth.

"He's liable to make trouble if he gets loose from those straps," said the technician with the baton. "Wait here while I take the body down to the morgue. And don't take your eyes off him until Ms. Nash gives further orders."

In a moment, Father's body was wheeled past me, down the narrow corridor and away into the bowels of Vivi-Centerre.

The tech named Evan bent close to my ear and his hot breath stirred my hair. "I wish I'd have given him the juice myself."

On the other side of the glass, Mother busied herself with straightening the room; opening a little cabinet to the left of the table, pushing buttons on a CD player, retrieving the testimony of Father which she had apparently extracted from him on one of her many visits to Rivendale.

"It's a shame his eyes weren't open for the interview," she said coldly, as she doused the lights to the room and locked the door behind her. "He always had such handsome eyes."

"He looked every bit the wonderful gentleman he always was, ma'am," lied Evan. "It was a tribute to the greatest good, a definite tribute if you ask me."

"I'm sure it was. Run along now, Evan," ordered Mother.

Evan looked at me. "Who's going to watch—"

"Don't worry about him," said Mother. "He's the judge's only son. We should expect him to show at least a little emotion, don't you think?"

Evan nodded.

"Why don't you go and see if Richard needs help filing the report," said Mother. "And remind him to put the Nash tape in my office mail drop. I'll air it at the proper time."

"But—"

"Remember who does your evaluations, Evan," said Mother.

When Evan had disappeared, Mother was a blur of activity. In an instant, she had my gag off and my hands untied.

"I'm sorry about that scene at the PRT," she said, as she began to work on one of my leg straps. "What I was trying to say was—"

"You killed him!" I shouted, seizing the back of Mother's hair. She let out a scream of pain and immediately I heard footsteps in the main hallway, growing louder as they pounded down the corridor. The night guard poked his head into the room.

"Problems, Roberta?" he asked. I could see the barrel of a Remington stun jutting around the edge of the door.

"Just a little misunderstanding, Sam" replied Mother, standing up and smoothing her hair. "Nothing communication can't resolve. Right, son?"

"This is your son?" asked the night guard, in disbelief.

"Why, yes," said Mother. "He wanted to be present at his pedotrainer's termination, but he wasn't sure if he could contain himself. You know, one of those 'tie-me-to-the-mast-so-the-sirens-don't-get-to-me' kind of things."

The confused night guard stood with his mouth open.

"I'm sure you understand," continued Mother. "Have I never introduced him to you?"

"No, ma'am," said the guard.

"Well, I should be shot," said Mother, bending to untie the final knot in my leg straps. "Sam, John. John, Sam. I think the two of you might find you have a lot in common." We shook hands. "Sam, take my son and show him the place," Mother commanded.

"Yes, ma'am," answered Sam.

"Remember, though, he's just a tag man who's used to the field. He'll look a bit wide-eyed at everything he sees. I suggest you give him the million-dollar tour. Make sure you wind up at the morgue. I'll take over from there. I've got a thing or two to show him myself."

At midnight, Sam deposited me at the entrance to the VC morgue and returned to whatever he was doing before the tour. Tiller had arrived a few moments earlier and was sitting on a wooden bench.

"I saw her kill my father," I snarled, seizing Tiller by the front of his shirt, just as soon as Sam was out of sight.

Tiller grabbed my hands. "Shhh. Do you want to be heard? Of course you saw her kill him."

I gripped him tighter.

"That's not what I meant," said Tiller, choking a little. "It's all part of the plan. She told you didn't she?"

I must have looked at Tiller with bewilderment and understanding in equal measure, for he guessed immediately that I didn't have all the facts.

"It's how it's done, man," he croaked. "Now, do you want to see your old man or not?"

"Where is he?" I demanded.

"In the morgue," said Tiller.

I tightened my grip on his shirt again.

"*Alive,*" Tiller inserted quickly. "What do you think we do? Deliver them to Canada dead?"

For a moment I glared at Tiller, then let him go. He slumped back against the bench with a look of relief.

"This place is worse than the nineteenth floor," I said, glancing around.

"I forget you haven't spent much time down here," said Tiller. He stood, rubbing his neck, and motioned for me to follow him. "Wait until you see inside. I'm always afraid somebody's going to jump out of one of the drawers."

"Is Captain Levi here?" I asked.

"He's in the back with your mom. She wants you to join them ASAP."

"Take me to her."

With Tiller in the lead, we set off down immaculate white hallways, lined on either side with stainless-steel drawers stacked ten-high to the ceiling.

"Don't open any of these," joked Tiller nervously. "You might see someone you know."

We walked briskly until we heard my mother's voice coming from the back lab.

"Richard and Evan are my only real concerns," she said quietly. She was leaning over a map of Iowa when I arrived in the doorway. Behind her Captain Levi was scribbling something in his wallet PC.

"What about Sam?" said the captain.

"Not a threat," Mother replied. "He and the other guards play poker in the control room. They hardly ever check the monitors. I've wheeled three Long Shadows past them before, and they didn't even notice."

"Is the truck ready?"

"Same as always. Waiting at the Muley," said Mother, referring to the old feed barn next to the stockyard. Seeing that Tiller and I had arrived, she wasted no time in giving orders. "Tolles, take John to the Muley. They've got a truck charged and waiting there with a hundred bags of seed and ammonium nitrate stacked to the top rails. Make sure there're no cracks between the bags. I want to give the impression this is nothing more than a routine farm truck, carrying fertilizer. Stretch a good, thick canvas across the top to keep the rain out, too."

Tiller glanced at Captain Levi and the captain nodded. "Yes, ma'am," said Tiller.

"Thank God for agricultural supplies," said Mother, returning to her map. "People trust a truck that's carrying things to government farms. Oh, and Tiller," added Mother before we'd had a chance to disappear. "Don't forget to spread a bale or two of hay in the middle of those bags, big enough for five people to lie down on comfortably."

"You got it," said Tiller. He nodded his head for me to follow and we headed back the way we had come.

Tiller jogged ahead of me at a slightly less than sprint pace.

"So, where's my father?" I asked, trying to keep up with him. "You promised we'd see him."

"Don't worry about it," replied Tiller over his shoulder. "We've done this so many times, we could do it in our sleep. But right now we're pressed for time."

"Is he in the truck already?" I persisted. "Is that where the technician took him after the interview?"

"What technician?"

"I don't know his name. He was one of the guys at Dad's interview. I think he was the one who clobbered me."

Tiller stopped suddenly. He seemed surprised. "When did someone clobber you?"

"When we pulled up to the intake ramp. Look, I'm fine now. I just want to know where my father is."

"He's in the wall," Tiller finally admitted.

I looked around frantically at the hundreds of shining drawers. "What do you mean, 'he's in the wall?'"

"This is no time to fall apart, John."

"That's easy for you to say. He's not your father."

"John, please. Normal procedure is for Evan or Richard to bring the body down after the interview, slip a tag around the wrist and deposit it in whatever drawer your mother tells them. That's the only part they play in it. They have no idea the sodium pentothal was given at a non-lethal dosage. They probably couldn't even remember what drawer they put your father in if you asked them. They're merely doing their job, while we do ours. I'm sorry you got clobbered in the process. But, unless you want to stand around here and get yourself killed, I think we better get moving right now."

"I'm not leaving until I see my father come out of one of these drawers alive."

"Do what you want. But I'm going to get the truck," said Tiller irritably.

Suddenly, there was a flash at the entrance to the morgue and the hammering impact of a bullet hurled Tiller against the wall.

Tiller clutched his shoulder. "Get inside," he screamed, drawing his gun with a grimace. He fired aimlessly in the direction of the entrance.

"Do what?" I shouted, but Tiller was already across the hallway, trailing blood as he went, and then he disappeared with a *kerchunk* inside one of the shining drawers. I heard footsteps racing toward me, so I chose a drawer several stacks away from Tiller's and scrambled in. The footsteps stopped outside our hiding place.

My chest heaved against the cold, waxlike body of the drawer's occupant and outside I heard Evan ordering Richard to stand back from the drawer that Tiller's bloody trail led to.

"God, if you're real, don't let me die like this," I prayed. It was the first prayer I had ever uttered. Looking back on it, I recognize I left Tiller out of my request. First prayers are usually selfish prayers.

There was a click as Tiller's drawer was opened. Then a flurry of gunfire ricocheted around the hallway, then silence. *They've killed Tiller*, I thought. I waited, holding my breath until my lungs began to burn and I heard someone moving down the stacks of drawers, opening them one by one.

Kerchunk.

Kerchunk.

Kerchunk.

I tried to get my right hand up to my jacket lapel, but my hand was trapped between my leg and the body next to me.

Kerchunk.

Kerchunk.

All at once, cold fingers clamped around my wrist. Instinctively, I lashed out, screaming. My drawer swung open with a bang and I was staring at the muzzle of a stun.

"Hello, John," said a familiar voice. "Funny how we keep running into each other. I see you found your father."

It was Sarah McSwain. Over her shoulder, Mother was straining to see if I was okay. Beyond her, Tiller lay groaning on the ground. I felt the cold fingers relax around my wrist.

"I'm s-s-sorry," came a thin and raspy voice. The sheet over my father's face moved when he spoke.

"Strap him on the cart," Mother ordered. "We may have company soon." She looked at Sarah and extended her hand. "I don't believe we've met."

"Sarah McSwain," said Sarah, shaking Mother's hand. She looked at the ceiling camera that was scanning slowly in our direction, raised her gun, and knocked it out with a single shot. "I hear you're going to Canada. Can I tag along?"

"Can you shoot like this every time?" asked Mother, pointing to the men whom Sarah had disposed of. Three red spots adorned Richard's and Evan's chests and their eyes and mouths were agape in surprise.

"She can shoot," assured Captain Levi, grabbing Father by his armpits, and tugging on him with all his might. "Good heavens! How much does the man weigh?"

A moment later, Father was on the cart and I was crawling out into the light of the hallway.

"Thanks," I said to Sarah as I stood up.

"My pleasure," she replied. Her smile, like a magnet, had the knack for drawing me toward it.

"Slap a pack on Tolles's shoulder and let's get a move on," said Captain Levi. "Poker or no poker, those goons will be here any minute and we'll have a battle on our hands."

"Do you know where the Muley feed barn is?" Mother asked Sarah.

"I think so," Sarah replied.

"Good. I'll take care of Tolles. You get the truck and meet us by the clearance gate on the north side. Here're the keys. Hurry up."

"Got it," said Sarah. She raced away with her orders.

"Pull that sheet all the way over Auggie's face and make sure it stretches to the floor," said Mother. She directed our attention to the bottom of the cart. "Tiller will ride on this shelf. John—you push. If anybody asks questions, just say you're taking a body back to autopsy. Levi and I will cover you guys from the front and rear."

Outside the morgue, the lights were extinguished and we could hear the guards clamoring in our direction.

"I hope McSwain knows how to drive a stick," muttered Captain Levi.

"She looked like an intelligent woman," said Mother, as we sped along the sterile linoleum. "Be quiet now. We're coming to the place where we're likely to meet them."

No sooner had Mother spoken, than a guard appeared in the stairwell. "Everything all right, Ms. Nash?" he asked, striding toward us.

Mother smiled at him. "Boring as usual, Randall. Is there a problem or something?"

"Well, we heard some commotion down here and lost power on camera 20. I thought I should come and check."

I glanced up the hallway and saw Captain Levi flatten himself against the wall, Old Stopper in ready position.

"We're kind of in a hurry to get to autopsy before they close," I said.

"Do you mind if I have a look at the body, just to say I did my job? I'm sure everything's in order like Ms. Nash says."

Randall was genuinely apologetic as he flung the sheet back. There he discovered not one but two bodies on the cart, neither of which was in need of an autopsy. He had scarcely opened his mouth in disapproval when Tiller kicked him hard in the shins and we were off.

"How many stairs to the landing?" I shouted, pushing the cart toward the stairwell as fast as I could.

"Are you crazy?" said Tiller, clutching his shoulder with his good arm.

Two more guards came around the corner of the hallway to our left, then ducked behind the wall when Levi fired.

"How many stairs?" I screamed.

"Three or four," said Mother.

"Five," said Tiller. "Are these straps tight?"

"I hope so," I said. "Hold on. We're going for it."

We were running full-tilt by then. Out of the corner of my eye I saw Captain Levi push the selector switch on his weapon all the way forward, to full automatic. He ran to the junction of the two hallways, dived on his belly, and opened fire the moment he slid around the corner. Screams and curses mingled together for a brief moment, then died in a wrenching echo. Behind it, the voices of more guards came barreling up the hallway. It was a good thing we hadn't gone that way.

"There's another one in the stairwell!" shouted the captain.

I was moving too fast to stop.

We hit the man square in the chest and continued, airborne, to the wall. Father's body lurched but remained secured. Tiller slammed hard into the stark white tiles and left a ruddy stain. Above us, Captain Levi and Mother kept the advancing guards at bay with wild bursts of gunfire.

"Climb on, Tiller. We're almost out of here."

Tiller squinted at me in anguish as he boarded the cart again. "I'll believe it when I see it."

"You're in better shape than that guy," I said, pointing to the unconscious guard with whom we had collided. "Just one more flight of stairs and we're there."

My teeth registered each stair as we rattled down them. At the bottom, I repositioned Father, who had slid sideways in the descent and I shoved the cart against a metal door. The door held firm.

I banged the metal with a fist. "It's locked!"

"Better hurry!" ordered Captain Levi, as he and Mother hit the landing and flew down the stairs. "We're out of rounds and those guys are still coming."

"It's locked," I said again.

"Well, use a key!" screamed the captain.

Mother groaned. "I gave my keys to Sarah for the truck. I didn't think to give her just one of them."

"That's beautiful, just beautiful," growled Captain Levi. "I'll bet the judge, here, wishes he was lucky enough to have died the easy way, while he had the chance."

The voices of many guards came nearer. I tried the door again. Suddenly, it tore from its hinges and landed in the moon-lit parking lot, sending a huge cloud of dust into the air. Through the haze, I saw red parking lights and Sarah scrambling to undo a heavy chain from the bumper.

"She does more than shoot," said Mother, stepping through the door.

Captain Levi disregarded the comment and bounded toward the cab. "I'll drive," he shouted.

Tiller looked weak, but he helped me load my father into the back of the truck. We scrambled in and found a place to lie at the other end of the trailer. The smell of seed and fertilizer was thick and strong.

Outside the truck, Sarah was frantically fashioning something out of a half-full bottle of an indeterminate liquid.

"Didn't I tell you to meet us at the entrance gate?" said Mother.

Sarah glanced up. "Yes, ma'am. But when I saw the keys, I knew you'd be in trouble."

"Well, that's one order I'm glad you disobeyed. Come on. I need you up front with Levi."

"Almost finished," said Sarah. She tore a piece of her shirt-tail off, jammed it in the top of the bottle, lit it with a lighter and flung it at the open doorway. An enormous blast sent chunks of steel and mortar into the air, setting up a wall of flames too intense for the guards to penetrate.

"What was that?" I shouted.

"Diesel fuel and fertilizer," said Sarah, as she ran toward the cab. "We wouldn't want them to get a good look at us."

"I thought this truck was solar-powered."

"Who said I got it from the truck?"

"Nice work," replied Mother. "Get up there with Levi. Your job is to spot the tag poles and shoot them out before they're activated. Don't you dare go to sleep, girl."

"I won't," promised Sarah.

We roared out of the parking lot to the sound of guards firing in vain through the flames. Tiller grimaced every time we hit a bump in the road. Next to him, my father slept like a newborn. Soon we were far from the compound lights and if one looked between the rails toward the northeastern sky, the top of Cassiopeia was barely distinguishable above the horizon.

"That girl *is* shrewd," said Mother.

"Not shrewd enough to keep VOX from publicizing our escape before we reach the edge of town," said Tiller.

In the dark, Mother placed three cut wires into my hand. "Somehow I think VOX will be preoccupied for the next few hours," she said. Then she whispered to me, "VOX's light source has been thoroughly incapacitated."

"And we'll be long gone by then," I chuckled. "You're pretty shrewd yourself, Mother."

"I'll take that as a compliment," she replied, as she settled next to me in the hay. She leaned her head against my shoulder, and this time I felt differently from when I held her on the floor of her living room two days before. At least the rudiments of trust were present. I found myself wishing I had never placed that probe on her neck. Checking my watch, I saw that 2:00 A.M. had come and gone.

We rode for a couple of hours, with Father sleeping peacefully and Tiller readjusting his position whenever he became uncomfortable. He was lucky—Evan's bullet had merely grazed him. Periodically, the dull popping sound of Sarah shooting tag poles was reassuring. While the others slept, I did my best to wall in the back of the truck with fertilizer bags, so as to complete our refuge.

Suddenly, Mother bolted upright. Her breaths came in short, trembling snatches.

"No! No! No!" she shouted, waking Tiller and Father from their respective slumbers. She dissolved into a torrent of tears.

"What's wrong?" I inquired, rushing to her side.

Mother began to mumble something about the "back laboratory" and Evan and Richard surprising us. With every syllable Mother formed, she moved farther away from the fog of repose into the reality of the horrible thing she had done, until . . .

"I've left the map," she cried.

No sooner had she said these words than we felt the dull tug of brakes and Captain Levi was steering the truck to the side of the road. Tiller pulled his weapon from its holster and sat up in the hay.

"Shut up!" he hissed, listening for the sounds of the thing we both feared.

"Roadblock?" I asked finally.

"Most definitely," said Tiller.

"Any ideas?"

Tiller looked at me and flipped the selector switch on his gun.

"Off stun," he said.

10

> *"The legal arguments supporting a right to an abortion suggest that there is a constitutional right to medically assisted suicide."*
> —By rule of Federal Judge Barbara J. Rothstein,
> *Legal Archives*, vol. LXI

WHEN I CLEARED A HOLE BETWEEN THE fertilizer bags, I was surprised not to see the usual flash of glider lights one expects at a roadblock. Only the lonely pool of faded gold cast by our truck lit the asphalt and a few feet of grass on either side of it. In our headlights a man stood shouting and waving his hands—his *one* hand, that is. The right one was missing.

"All aboard! All aboard! It's a great day for traveling! All aboard!" he shouted.

Without skipping a beat, he began to sing at the top of his lungs. "He leadeth me, He leadeth me, by His own hand He leadeth me . . . His faithful follower I will be. For by His hand he leadeth me."

Mother leaped from the hay. "Peter!" she cried.

"Is that you in there, Roberta? Come on out and give me a proper greeting."

"Help me move these bags," ordered Mother excitedly.

I hurried to the back of the truck to assist her. As soon as there was a large enough hole in the fertilizer, Mother squeezed through it, jumped from the truck and ran to embrace the man.

So this is him, I thought. The way his teeth and eyes sparkled in the headlights suggested that beneath the vague contour of a holy man there was a heart that loved adventure.

"Hello, sister," said Peter, welcoming her warmly. "Is brother Augustine with you?"

"Safe and sound," replied Mother.

Peter shook his head. "Safe maybe. But not sound."

Mother looked at her feet. "No. Not really," she replied.

"I didn't think so," said Peter sadly. Nevertheless, he rebounded with a smile and in the headlights I saw that his was one of the happiest faces I had ever seen.

Captain Levi opened the door and stood on the running board. I could just barely make out his silhouette against the inky, eastern sky.

"Top of the morning. You must be Peter Edmunds."

"That's what my friends call me," said Peter.

"We didn't expect to see you so soon."

"Life is full of the unexpected. You must be Levi Coffin."

"Must be."

"How's life treating you, brother Levi?"

"It's *cheating* me just fine. Is it a clear shot to the border?"

Peter shook his head. "Roadblocks along the Floyd. Something wrong this time?"

Mother glanced at Captain Levi. "We . . . er, I, I left the map in the morgue."

This was the first Captain Levi had heard of the mistake. He stared at Mother in disbelief, then slammed his hand on the top of the cab. Behind him Sarah jumped.

"First the keys! Now the map! Got any other tricks up your sleeve?"

"Easy, Captain," coaxed Peter. "It's not time to panic, yet."

I looked at him standing there in the middle of the road and I wondered if there was ever a time Peter Edmunds saw fit to panic. Everything about him was so completely serene.

"These are mere inconveniences," he continued. "Nothing too big for the Lord to handle. We'll just trust Him for another path. By the way, brother Levi, Roberta tells me you've been doing some moonlighting lately. What do you find helpful in situations like this?"

Captain Levi hesitated. "I can't say I've been so ignorant as to forget my map before."

"Ahh. Would that we all had perfect records like you. As for me, I lost a lovely gentleman last month, and the month before that, and the one before that, as well. It's not been a flawless year for the Shadow Train. Do you happen to have a spare map with you, Captain?"

Captain Levi glared at Mother, then reaching back into the shadows of the truck, produced a crudely folded rectangle.

Peter took the map, climbed onto the front bumper and spread it on the hood. "Sweet Jesus," he said, taking a penlight from his pocket. "If we ever needed your help, we need it now." He shone the light on the map. "Where are you, Garden City? Come on, come to Papa. There you are!" Peter looked at Captain Levi, who was still standing on the running board. "There are ten roadblocks between here and Dakota City," he stated.

"How could you know that?" asked the captain warily.

"Come now, Captain," said Peter. "Surely you don't believe the skies are run entirely by bad guys. I've got a few connections with wings. The minute they heard Roberta was coming north with Augustine, they gave me a play-by-play report of the untethered roadways. When it started to look like trouble, I asked one of them to fly me here to meet you."

"Then Floyd River is out," said Captain Levi.

Peter studied the map. "Not completely. We've just got to take a little detour. We can recharge in Dakota City and be on our way to Sheldon, same as always. I suggest we go west, through Elkhart and Roland, then back over to Dakota City. There shouldn't be any roadblocks after that."

"I hope you're right," said Mother.

Sarah let out a sudden gasp.

"What's the matter?" asked Captain Levi, leaning inside the cab.

Sarah peered into the darkness, her image-intensifier eye-piece automatically feeding images to the monochrome display that sat on the seat between her and the captain on the cab's seat. "Tag men, sir," she said abruptly.

"How many?" snapped Captain Levi.

"Three, maybe four. Check that. There's five, sir. Five tag men at twenty-two hundred meters, with lots of foliage be-tween us."

"Forget the foliage. If we can see them, they can see us. Are they packing much?"

"Nondefinitive," said Sarah, still squinting through the eyepiece. "Weapons inventory should be coming on the display, right about . . . wait a minute." Sarah started back from the window, and I saw that she was trembling. "Whatever's out there isn't human."

"Gimme that," said Captain Levi. He jerked the eyepiece from Sarah's head and took a look for himself. I watched the muscle in his jaw contract into a tight, round plug.

"Get in the truck," said the captain sharply.

The sound of something growling in the dark sent a collec-tive shiver through the group. Having awakened and heard our conversation, Tiller emerged from the back of the flatbed.

"What's the matter?" he asked sleepily.

"I said get in the truck!" screamed the captain, aiming his finger in my partner's face. He spun around and glowered at us all. "And that goes for the rest of you, too. No questions. No talking. Just do as I say. Now!"

We boarded quickly and headed west, wordless until we were at least a mile away and I decided it was safe to break the silence.

"Any clues as to what was going on back there?" I asked in the darkness.

There was no reply. Another mile and I felt someone's elbow nudge me.

"I tried to tell you about this in the locker room the other day, but you wouldn't listen," Tiller whispered.

I could hear his labored breathing next to me, and I knew he was afraid. "Tiller?"

"Yeah?"

"Are these the things SimTech was going to make Sarah into?"

"We're in deep trouble," he said.

The detour to Dakota City was hot and bumpy. There were fewer tag poles away from the Interstate, so Elkhart and Roland flew by uneventfully. In the dark, Peter conversed gently with Mother and inquired about Tiller's wound. He was the first man I had ever met who treated a Long Shadow without the usual cow-eyed condescension. He spoke to my father like a man, never feeding into his self-pity, never downplaying the seriousness of his awful sin, yet always aiming to heal with his words. And when he called my father, "brother," there was a special nuance to the word.

"What is the first thing you are going to do in Canada, brother Augustine?"

Father answered in his usual dissociated manner. "I was a centrist, you know," he said, defending himself.

"No one is a centrist," said Peter gently. "We are all of us just sheep. And eventually every sheep chooses which side of the fence to graze on."

"What did you say your name was?" Father inquired.

A puff of air escaped Mother's lips.

"That's the first question he's asked anyone in twenty years, except for me," she whispered.

"Surely he talks with his doctor."

"I detest my doctor," muttered Father, crawling away to a corner of the truck bed, where he sat alone with his knees to his chest.

Another gasp from Mother, and her words in the PRT came back to me. *Seven hundred miles between Kansas City and Ely to love him back to wholeness.*

"Can you make him normal again?" asked Mother quietly.

"Only God can do that," said Peter. "But He has a history of reforming murderers. Frankly, I'm not sure normal is what you want, though. Have you taken a look at the norm recently?"

Mother was silent for several minutes.

"I want him to be healed," she said at last.

"Umm," said Peter, "that's a big order this side of heaven."

"Not too big for God," said Mother.

"True, but sometimes a man's guilt is so great, he will not allow the healing, no matter how willing God is."

"Pray he'll be willing," Mother implored.

"I do that daily, dear sister. And I'll continue until I receive an answer."

In the field to the north of the road, the terrible growling sound resumed, this time accompanied by a high-pitched chorus like that of a hyena pack.

"Tiller?" I whispered. Immediately, I felt a sharp jab in my ribs.

"Are you crazy?!" rasped Tiller. "If those things hear us, they'll be on us in a second."

The growling intensified into a howl. Suddenly, I could hear one of them just off our right rear bumper. Captain Levi must have known it was there, too, because the truck gave a sudden lurch and sped ahead like a frightened animal. Sarah fired a shot from the passenger window.

"No!" shouted Tiller. He started banging on the window that separated the bed from the cab. But Sarah ignored him and fired again. Instantly, the pack was on our tail. A brilliant, white light shone through the cracks in the fertilizer bags, illuminating the entire back of the truck.

"Stay away from the sides!" Tiller shouted at us.

Mother rolled Father to the center of the hay, just as a silver claw smashed through one of the lower rails.

"Throw me one of those bags," shouted Peter.

The claw was groping madly for Peter's ankles, and I remember that the holy man actually had a smile on his face as he hopped back and forth to avoid its grasp.

I picked up one of the fifty-pound bags of fertilizer and heaved it across the width of the truck. Peter caught it with his one arm, dropped it on the claw and stood on top of it.

"Can the captain go any faster?" he yelled.

Mother scrambled to the window and began to pound. There was another surge of speed, this time attended with Levi's erratic, serpentine driving.

"Hold on, friends!" warned Peter. "I think the captain has figured out what we're trying to do back here. Keep tossing those bags."

I did as I was told, until there was five hundred pounds of fertilizer resting on the howler's arm, and the truck was leaning precariously toward the driver's side.

"A machine is the strongest thing in the world without a soul," commented Peter, as he watched the claw writhe beneath the heavy mound. Almost as an epithet, he added, "Strong, but not created for the long haul."

I peered through a crack in the back of the truck and noticed that the lights of the pack were indeed a good quarter-mile behind us and the howls had all but subsided. "At least its friends seem to have given up the chase," I said.

We felt another lurch left, as if the captain was trying to shake the thing from our side. Then the loud blare sounded from a vehicle headed straight toward us.

"Truck," was all Tiller could get out, before the impact of the crash separated the howler's arm from its socket and sent it spinning into the ditch. The silver claw twitched beneath the bags, as Captain Levi brought the truck to a slow halt.

"Give me a hand here, brother," Peter said, motioning for me to help him remove the fertilizer.

"Did anyone get a close look at one of them?" shouted the captain through the rails.

There was a noise behind me in the hay, and I realized that in the commotion my father had somehow been left unattended to gaze upon our attackers in horror.

"They . . . they had faces," he gasped, rocking back and forth.

Tiller rushed to Father's side.

"Faces? What kind of faces?"

Back and forth he rocked, without saying a word.

Tiller took him by the chin and forced his face upward, less than reverently. "Now, you listen, Judge. This is important to me!"

I took a step toward Tiller, but he released my father before I came any nearer.

"Was it a human's face, or just a machine's?" he implored.

"It was shiny," said Father. "Shiny like wax with oil on it."

The effort of speech shattered the rhythm of his rocking, and for a few moments Father knelt with his head bowed to the hay. I could just barely make out his form in the dim, half-light of dawn. Then he began again, this time rocking faster than before.

"It looked like a man . . . it looked like a man."

Tiller sat down, miserably, as if somebody had pushed him.

"Would someone mind explaining to me whose arm I just amputated?" asked Peter, tugging on the silvery claw until it came free from the bags. Strangely, the material that covered it had the appearance of metal, but was waxlike to the touch.

"All-Terrain Predators," said Tiller remotely.

"Better known as howlers," corrected Captain Levi through the rails. "SimTech's little secret. The future of the tag corps." He began to laugh insanely. "Oh, what a blessed future awaits us all."

I glanced at Tiller.

"What are we sitting around for?" he blurted, standing abruptly. "We can talk all morning about stinking robots, or we can get moving. The guys with skin on can't be too far behind."

"They did have skin," murmured Father, staring at the severed arm.

"That's enough!" cried Tiller.

The rails reverberated with a sudden pounding.

"It's going to be a hard ride from here on out," boomed Captain Levi. "Looks like VC is throwing everything they've got at us." The sound of a door opening and closing echoed out into the fields, and we were off again.

In Dakota City, we were greeted by a banner hanging across the road, underneath which a small riot was taking place.

"WHAT HAVE THEY DONE WITH THE ASHES?" read the banner. The VC riot squad sent to handle the matter obviously did not want that question to be answered.

Captain Levi stopped the truck a block away from the riot and came around to the back. "Are there any other side roads that lead into town?" he asked.

"It's this or back through Hubbard," said Peter, studying the map.

"No way," said Captain Levi. "We're low on solar charge and they've got that free place on Main that I want to take advantage of. You're probably the best one to drive this rig through town. Some of the guards back at Midwest got a look at my face. I'm sure that's public information by now."

"What about Sarah?" asked Peter.

"She'll be fine. I've instructed her to stow her stuff behind the seat. The two of you will look like a farmer and his daughter. If anybody stops us, simply lift up the canvas and show them the bags of fertilizer."

After the switch, we drove through the crowd at a snail's pace, each of us holding our breath, holding our triggers lightly with our forefingers, waiting for the first suspicious sound. But soon we were on the other side of the riot, cruising through downtown Dakota City. Exhausted from his stint of driving, Captain Levi fell immediately asleep.

The sun was high overhead when we reached the station. It was beginning to feel like an oven inside the truck. Tiller said he was burning up and that if nobody else was going to go inside to pay for the solar charge, he'd gladly do it just to cool himself. Looking back, I thought his offer was a strange one, seeing as the charge was free. I figured he may not have been aware of that luxury. But before I could say anything about it, Captain Levi spoke up.

"Cover that wound," he called, with one eye open.

Tiller removed his clotted shirt and slipped a spare one on. Then he crawled from the truck and walked quickly toward the store, while Peter connected our cell to the generator and gave us a good charge. In a moment or two, the captain was fast asleep again.

While we were sitting at the station, the riot progressed slowly up Main Street until it was happening all around us and I feared we might get swept up in it. I peeked through a crack. There seemed to be a core group of instigators, most of them forty to forty-five years old. Over and over, they demanded an answer to the question written on their proud and tattered banner.

"What have they done with the ashes?" they chanted, repeating the words as if they were some powerful mantra. Parallel to this group, the collective voice of another one, more savage and youthful, rose to the sky.

"Down with Long Shadows! Down with Long Shadows! Down with Long Shadows! Down with Long Shadows!"

In the middle of it all, the Dakota City riot squad wielded their batons and blew their whistles. Suddenly, the crack of a gun sounded and a bullet ricocheted off the side of our truck, startling Captain Levi from his sleep.

"Where's Tolles?" he demanded, frantically clearing a large enough opening in the sacks to fit his weapon through.

"Gone inside, sir," I reminded him.

Captain Levi mashed a meaty thumb in his tired eyes. He seemed embarrassed that fatigue had kept him from exercising good judgment.

"Idiot," he hissed. "If VC has a bulletin out on him already, that arm of his is going to get us all killed."

Another shot rang out, followed by a long silence.

"It came from the rooftop, sir," said Sarah. "It didn't sound like any gun a cyberslave would use."

Suddenly, we heard Tiller running toward the truck.

"Go!" he screamed. "Get this thing moving!"

I expected to hear shots following him across the pavement, but strangely there were none. Tiller's arm appeared through the hole in the fertilizer bags and I pulled until his whole body was inside. He winced at the pain in his shoulder.

"What kind of stupid move was that?" shouted Captain Levi.

"I . . . I was about to pass out from the heat. I knew it would be cool inside, so I offered to pay for the solar charge and buy some cookies for breakfast. I'll be darned if I didn't get inside and they told me the charge was free." Tiller marshaled a grin and handed the captain a bag of Fig Newtons. "Thanks for covering me, sir."

"I ought to kick you to the moon," muttered Captain Levi. He flung the cookies aside and hastened to the front of the bed, where he banged on the window for Peter to get moving. There was a whir and the electric motor jumped to life just as some rioter's brick hit the side of our truck. With a screech of rubber, we headed for Marble Rock.

But the conditions in Marble Rock were the same as Dakota City—as in Rockford, Rudd, Riceville, and Floyd. The whole of rural America was up in arms over the issue of the missing ashes and no one knew quite what to do. Onward we flew across the Minnesota border and into the simmering evening. Our bed of hay hovered on the brink of combustion. Only the whine of the truck's hot tires broke the silence of the countryside. I kept my eyes glued to my peephole, watching the wheat fields speeding past. They were burnt umber, thick and ready for the harvest.

"What do you see?" whispered Mother, so close to my ear that only I could hear her.

"Life rushing by," I replied.

"Did you happen to hear that old man's voice in Dakota City today?"

"I heard a lot of voices."

"So did I. But there was one that rose above the others for just a moment. It made me think of you."

"You hardly know me."

"I know you're tired of hunting human beings."

I leaned closer to my peephole. "What did the man in Dakota City say?"

"He didn't *say* it, John. He yowled it like a dog yowls at the moon. 'History repeats itself,' he yowled, over and over, until someone on the other side got sick of his message and chunked a rock at him. It happened while there was all that commotion over the shots from the station. I kept my eyes glued on the man. The rock busted his lip, but he went right on yammering and yowling. They finally knocked him down and beat him slick and red."

"Who did?"

"People like you and me, John; good people who've gone a little crazy with our world the way it is."

"Someone ought to do something about it. We've still got free speech, don't we?"

"Not if someone wants to speak against the greatest good. Did you ever hear what people said back in the 1970s about the abortion industry?"

"That was almost seventy years ago."

"Yes, it was. But you studied it in the Academy, son. You ought to have an opinion on it."

Gazing through the peephole made my eyes feel heavy, and I laid my head on the hot hay. "I'm too tired to think about stuff like that."

Mother ignored my drowsiness. "Back then, people wondered where the babies went too. They said someone has to be making money on all that tissue. Then the rumors started. Or maybe they weren't rumors. Your great-grandma gave up hand lotion because her next-door neighbor said it was full of human collagen. All over the country, ladies quit wearing makeup. Whole lines of suntan products disappeared from the market. It was like nobody wanted to come right out and say killing babies was a bad thing, but everybody wanted to be sure they weren't getting their hands dirty paying for it."

"Yeah, but I'll bet nobody got beat to a pulp for voicing his opinion."

"You're right. The media shut down the rumors before they led to blows."

"And grandma went back to her hand lotion. Right?"

Mother smiled. "No. She was still ranting about it in the nursing home when she died. But I believe a lot of people went to their graves never knowing how intricately woven their personal comforts were to the sin of this country. In a sense, it became everybody's sin."

"I don't believe in sin."

"Do you believe in cancer?"

"Of course."

"Same thing. It just keeps breaking out in different forms. You know," said Mother, changing topics abruptly, "they're after your father for a reason. He knows a secret, John," continued Mother. "It's something about VC that very few others have ever known."

I sat up. "What do you mean, 'a secret?' I thought VC was just concerned about getting him on VOX so he could praise the greatest good."

"If that was their only concern, then they really don't need your father at all. It's easy to fix up some average Long Shadow to look like August, then roll the tapes. I'm sure they already have plans to do just that."

I recalled Mother telling Richard to "put the Nash tape in her mail drop," and I quickly blocked the thought.

"What they're really worried about," continued Mother, "is your father telling as many people as possible about the thing that put him in Rivendale in the first place."

"I was always told depression put him there."

"Oh, he was depressed, all right. You and I would be, too, if we had just sentenced every one of our peers to death with the stroke of a pen. But that's only what VC wanted the public to *think* was the reason for his hospitalization."

I heard Mother shift in the hay and I sensed she was checking to see if everyone else was asleep. When she turned back, she was leaning closer to my ear.

"The real reason VC put your father in Rivendale, and *kept* him there, was to make sure he kept quiet. Like I said, he knows their secret, John."

The sudden—*pop!*—of Sarah shooting tag poles startled me.

"He knows about the ashes?" I guessed.

"Yes," said Mother.

"You mean, VC put my father in a mental institution to keep people from knowing what they did with all the bodies?"

Mother nodded her forehead against my shoulder. "They've had him making baskets and pot holders for two and a half decades. Medicated up to his eyeballs."

I felt the hot lash of anger as it all came into focus for me. "Those rotten—"

"Shh," said Mother. "We wouldn't want to wake anybody."

"He was their political prisoner," I said, seething.

"True. But it can't be proven, unless someone finds out what happened to the others who knew the secret. Even then, who would believe them? Who would believe you?"

"Who else knew?" I asked.

Mother searched her memory. "The other Justices, the secretary of health and human services, I'm not sure exactly. You'll have to check some files for all the names—if the files haven't been destroyed, that is." Mother paused for a moment. "With enough hard evidence this might be proven," she mused.

There was something else I needed to know before I drifted off into inevitable restlessness. "Mother?" I said, turning my face toward the peephole again.

"Yes?"

"Do *you* know what happens to the ashes?"

Mother hesitated. "Go to sleep, John. The morning will be here before you know it."

I lay back in the dusty darkness and waited until I was certain Mother and the others had returned to sleep. At last when the constellations had begun their descent down the back side of dawn, I raised up on all fours and crawled to the opposite side of the truck, where the Dakota City gunman's bullet had struck the wooden slats. Carefully, so as not to disturb a soul, I reached in my pocket and pulled out my knife. Because the wood was old and nearly rotten, the work was easy and soon I had retrieved the slug. Someone moved in the darkness and I caught my breath. Then it was quiet again.

Please, let me be wrong, I prayed.

I raised the slug in the moonlight and studied it closely. The scoring near the base of the cupronickel jacket was as I suspected—deep and black, the telltale signs of a gun owner who was too preoccupied with other things to have his weapon's barrel reworked. I noticed the jacket had been stripped back from the point to expose the soft, lead core and make it more destructive on impact. There were only two types of gunmen who used the dumdum bullet. One of them, the big game hunter, had been extinct ever since the outlawing of firearms for the general public. The other was a tag man.

It could belong to anyone, I lied to myself. *Just because the caliber's the same as his, doesn't mean anything.* But in my heart I knew differently.

11

*"When voluntary family planning doesn't reduce
the birth rate, the next logical step is government-
mandated population limitations. This point
should give us all pause.*

—Pete du Pont, former governor of Delaware

Ат 4:00 A.M., I REALIZED I WASN'T GOING TO
fall asleep, so I reached over Mother's still form and tapped the
Captain on his shoulder.

"What is it?" he said gruffly.

"I was wondering if we could stop for a minute or two, sir."

"You'd better have a good reason, Nash," said the captain.
"I was basking in the Caribbean."

"I'd love to stretch my legs, sir," I said.

Captain Levi started to object, but then, admitting that a
stop would probably do us all some good, he pounded on the
window and Peter exited onto the soft gravel.

I coaxed my body into action, climbed from the truck and
strolled across a cattle guard into a nearby field. The night had
given a reprieve to the oppressive heat and now the air possessed
a mysterious quality not unlike the two drastic changes of the
year. Those of us who were awake wandered stiffly in the purple twilight. I heard the rustle of grass behind me.

"Getting the kinks out?" asked Mother.

I turned and saw her dabbing her forehead with a hand-
kerchief.

"Heck of a way to travel," I replied, motioning toward the truck.

"If the mission is successful I have no complaints," said Mother.

There was a long pause in which I could think of nothing to say, so I decided to end the conversation. "I think I'll ride up front with Peter and Sarah, if that's all right with everybody else."

"You like that girl, don't you?" asked Mother suddenly.

The abruptness of her question caught me off guard.

"What makes you say that?"

Mother scuffed her foot along the ground. "I don't know. Maybe it's just a mother's wishful thinking. Maybe it was the way the two of you looked at each other when she yanked that door down at VC."

"You pick an interesting moment to notice romance."

"To a woman, every moment has romantic possibilities. By the way, I think she likes you too. Have you ever thought of staying in Canada?"

"Not seriously."

"They allow marriage there," said Mother.

"I'd make a terrible husband," I assured her.

I noticed Mother staring up at the stars.

"Do you believe there's a god who can forgive tag men?" she asked.

"I suppose there is. I haven't had much time to think about it."

What I really meant to say was that ever since I had received those few tattered pages of contraband from Uncle Ames, my heart had been filled with such unearthly fear that I did not like to think about it. Regardless of my intent, Mother turned on me quickly.

"You must *take* the time," she pleaded. "There is a God, and he is angry about what we've been doing to our fellow human beings."

"If he's so bad-tempered, why would I want to get close to him?"

"Because he is holy and he is always right."

"Not according to the Academy. They always told me right was relative."

"How do you propose to absolve yourself of all the blood you've spilled?" asked Mother.

I thought for a moment, then said the only thing I could think of, though I knew I no longer believed in the words.

"The way I see it, the universe is sort of like a great big cosmic scale. One side is for bad deeds. The other is for good. The trick is being sure that just before you die, you make one last deposit on the good side, so the scale tilts in your favor."

"So, getting your father to Canada is just part of a cosmic balancing act," said Mother.

I didn't answer her.

"Here comes Sarah," said Mother quietly. "I think I'll leave the two of you alone." She hurried toward the truck, nodding at Sarah as they passed each other.

Sarah gave a little laugh. "Where's the fire?" she inquired, after Mother was a good distance away from us.

"I think she's hoping to start one," I replied.

Sarah looked at me dubiously. "You mean . . . between you and me?"

I nodded. "She's convinced I've got some sort of thing for you. Is that funny, or what?"

"That's really funny."

"Everyone knows relationships are frowned upon nowadays."

"Particularly in our line of work."

"Mom's just a hopeless matchmaker."

"Exactly," said Sarah, pausing for a moment. "So, do you?"

"Do I what?"

"Do you have a thing for me?"

I chuckled unconvincingly. "How could I? The last time I got halfway near you, you bit me."

"I was only defending myself," said Sarah.

"Against what? The big, bad tag man with his hand over your mouth? Get serious, I wasn't going to hurt you."

"You haven't answered my question."

"What question?" I said nervously.

"Do you have a thing for me?"

Under the silver-dripping moon, Sarah's face, tipped sideways, looked at me with a bright, inquisitive smile.

I glanced at her stomach. "I thought there might be someone else involved," I answered impulsively.

"Oh, you mean the man who got me pregnant," she replied.

"I'm sorry, I—"

"Don't," said Sarah firmly.

"But it was none of my business. I should never have brought it up."

"Look, it makes it a hundred times worse when a person brings up the obvious, then apologizes before I get a chance to explain. My whole life has been like that. Take when I was a kid—" She bent down and proceeded to roll up her pant leg.

"Maybe I ought to get back to the truck," I said uncomfortably.

"Stay," said Sarah, with a note of fierce neediness. "There's something you ought to know about me." She propped her leg up on the rock between us and opened a six-inch door in the side of her calf, exposing an assembly of wires and circuitry.

Try as I might not to gape, I couldn't help myself.

"It's okay to look," said Sarah reassuringly. "Believe me, I'm used to it by now. Go ahead, touch it."

I stretched my hand out timidly. Except for the tiny seam that marked the hinge of the door, Sarah's leg felt soft and supple.

"The technology wasn't as advanced when I was a kid," recalled Sarah. "I got called everything from Peg to Captain Bly. I spent so much time crying, I almost didn't learn how to read."

I looked away into the field. "Yeah, but you probably had a mother to dry your tears."

"She *caused* my tears," replied Sarah simply.

I looked at her in disbelief.

"You know how the story goes," said Sarah. "I was Momma's fourth child, the long-awaited boy who was going to rule a household of girls and make his father proud. Daddy wasn't happy when he saw the ultrasound."

Silence, miserable and deep, settled over our heads like the surface of a pool.

"Abortions are funny things, though," said Sarah, as she closed the door on her calf, straightened her pants and stood up. "They don't always go as planned. In my case, the doctor had barely started snipping on me when I came out faster than he counted on. Rumor has it, I kicked him with my one remaining leg and he was so shaken that he never practiced medicine again."

"You don't hold a grudge?" I asked incredulously.

"Once upon a time," replied Sarah. "That's what made it easy for me to work for the tags. But now I don't have time for grudges. Not for my mom, not for that doctor, not even for the man who raped me."

My mouth fell open of its own volition.

"How else did you think I got pregnant?" asked Sarah.

"Well, I assumed—"

Sarah put her hands on her hips. "Two things you ought to know about me, John Nash. First, I am not promiscuous. Second, I am no longer angry over what life has dealt me."

"I'm sorry," I said, at a loss for words.

"Is that all you Nash men can say?" said Sarah, a smile returning to her face.

Suddenly, Captain Levi shouted from the truck. "Load up. We're sitting ducks."

I started to turn in that direction, but Sarah stepped in front of me.

"I intend to give my baby the things that I missed," she said determinedly. "Will you make sure we get to Canada?"

Here was my dream standing in front of me . . . the girl in the wheat . . . the incredible ache to care for her and her child.

"You have my word," I said.

Captain Levi shouted again, more colorfully the second time around.

"Sarah?" I said.

"Hmm?"

I considered for a moment. Then with hesitance: "I . . . I guess I ought to tell you that I have a thing for you."

"I know," said Sarah, smiling.

Back in the cab, she forgot about shooting tag poles and fell fast asleep. I, on the other hand, could not get our conversation out of my mind.

"Tell me, brother John, do you like gardening?" asked Peter out of the blue. He was wide awake behind the wheel and chipper, even at this hour.

"I like flowers," I replied. "But I don't have much of a green thumb. Why?"

"I've got some prize-winning tulips I want to show you when we finally get to Ely. I've been beside myself, wondering if one of the brothers is taking proper care of them in my absence."

"I'm sure they're in good hands," I offered.

As we drove, I noticed Peter's stub resting on the steering wheel. Try as I might not to think about it, I couldn't help recalling Tiller's story about his cleaning lady. Eventually, Peter caught me stealing a glance at his arm.

"Farming incident," he said offhandedly. "Severed it cleanly at the wrist, lost three pints of blood, maintained a hundred-and-four temperature for a week. Came through it with a renewed appreciation for life. What else would you like to know about me?"

I wanted to know the meaning of life and the certainty of absolutes and if there really was a god who forgives tag men, but I could not bring myself to ask those questions.

"Were you a Long Shadow?" I asked.

"What is that to you?" replied Peter, not a trace of ire in his voice.

"It might give me an idea of how sympathetic you are to my father's situation."

"I assure you I'm as sympathetic as they come. I get nothing out of this process, save the satisfaction of doing the right thing."

The right thing. There it was again; the notion, as Mother had suggested, that a man could actually be guided by a code of rightness set up by a God of rightness. I studied Peter's attire, which was styleless Franciscan.

"You must live a meager life," I said.

Peter nodded. "'Live' is the operative word there, brother. Others live coddled lives on their way toward the inevitable. I *live* mine richly. I'm the wealthiest man I know."

A soft murmur came from the passenger side of the truck and we both looked at Sarah, slumped against the door.

"Mom tells me you're some kind of a holy man."

"Does that affect the way you look at me?" asked Peter.

"No. But to tell you the truth, I'm not very religious myself."

"That's fine with me. It doesn't hurt my feelings if people don't think like me."

"So . . . how exactly do you think?" I asked.

"I thought you weren't into religious things," said Peter.

"I'm not—really. It's just that I've been reading lately."

Peter raised an eyebrow. "Reading?"

"A long time ago, I was given some pages of the Bible. They made me curious."

"The Bible has a way of doing that," said Peter. "Which pages are you talking about?"

"They say 'Deuteronomy' at the top."

"Ah, yes. The law of God has pierced another mercenary mind. You wouldn't by chance have been convicted by the command, 'Thou shalt not kill'?"

I shifted nervously on the seat. "It caught my eye."

"Not exactly ambiguous, is it?"

I leaned almost to his shoulder and lowered my voice. "Listen, Peter. Would you mind if I called you that?"

"I believe you just did."

"Well, I didn't know if you preferred something else or not."

"It's my name. People have been calling me by it for years."

"Okay. Fine. Peter it is," I said, clearing my throat. "So, Peter, do you think it's wrong to terminate Long Shadows?"

There was a slight hitch in Peter's breathing and I rushed to explain myself.

"I mean, obviously you think it is, or you wouldn't be doing the kind of work you're doing. But is it wrong in the *thou shalt not* kind of way?"

"For someone who's not interested in religious things, you sure seem to have an inquiring mind," said Peter, gazing at the road. His expression turned somber. "Yes, of course it's wrong."

The sky was blue-black now and as we dipped under a lonely bridge I lost sight of Peter's shining eyes. When we emerged again into moonlight, he was staring at me.

"Do you mind if I ask you a question or two?" he said.

"Not if you don't mind watching the road a little better."

Peter chuckled and redirected his gaze. "Do you believe in moral absolutes?"

"Not . . . absolutely."

"Then nothing I could tell you about life or death or law or order would ever mean much to you," said Peter, leaning his weight against the wheel. "In your worldview, killing Long Shadows is no different than taking out the trash. Sometimes you want to and sometimes you don't. It's a matter of preference to a man like you. I'm not sure I could ever change your thinking."

Peter looked at me and in the crisp light of the moon I hoped he could not detect my trembling.

"Are you serious about the Shadow Train?" he asked.

"I don't want to kill people anymore," I replied.

"But are you serious?" demanded Peter.

"Yes," I said weakly.

Peter looked out the window.

"Anyone can be serious as long as the train stays on schedule and runs neatly along its track. But let him see a friend or two get caught by VC and flung beneath the wheels of civil disobedience and right away he shows his true colors."

"I'm not a coward, if that's what you're insinuating."

"We'll see," said Peter. "But for the sake of argument, let's begin by agreeing there are some things that are right or wrong regardless of preference, and these things can be found in those recently criminalized but far from irrelevant writings we call the Bible. Fair enough?"

"Fair enough."

"Good. Then what part of 'Thou shalt not kill' seems vague to you?"

I felt suddenly ashamed in the presence of such a strange ascetic. Peter kept his eyes on the road and there was a long, unsettling pause.

"Tell me, John," he began again, "at what age does a person cease to be a person?"

"I've always been told it was fifty."

"But what does your *heart* tell you?" pressed Peter.

"I'm not certain."

"So then," said Peter, "as long as you remain uncertain, it's possible for a man on the eve of his fiftieth birthday to go to bed as a valuable human being and wake up in the morning with no more worth than a tree stump?"

"No one has ever put it to me like that."

Peter shook his head. "You've got a lot to learn, son. Do you believe in abortion?"

I thought of Sarah's leg. "No."

"Why not?"

"Because a person is a person long before his slide down the birth canal."

"Well spoken," said Peter with a smile. "Now, maybe you can see why I also believe one's personhood extends past the age of fifty."

We hit a bump in the road and Sarah sprouted suddenly from her nap with a series of yawns and stretches.

"Good morning," exclaimed Peter. "I was beginning to wonder if you might sleep all the way to Canada."

"Are we there yet?" asked Sarah.

Peter chuckled. "The Shadow Train is never actually anywhere," he said mysteriously. "We just keep moving and picking up people as we go."

Sarah yawned again and peered at Peter. "Captain Levi doesn't much care for you, does he?"

"Let's just say he seemed less than excited to meet me. It's probably a good thing we've always worked in separate regions."

Without breaking stride in the conversation, Peter steadied the wheel with his knees, reached across me, lifted Sarah's pistol from her shoulder holster, aimed it out the window and blew away a tag pole with a single shot.

"Who taught you to shoot like that?" asked Sarah.

"I'm a jack-of-all-trades," said Peter, returning the gun to her. "Roberta tells me VC's rather upset about your refusal to abort the baby."

"'Let's just say they seem less than excited about the decision," replied Sarah.

Peter laughed at her quick wit. "A lot of women over the years could have used your courage. I have this nagging suspicion that we've gotten rid of some incredibly talented individuals since *Roe v. Wade*, not to mention scores of teachers and scientists and historians and writers and Nobel prize winners since Long Shadow passed in 2013. Do the two of you ever wonder what might have become of AIDS had we not incinerated all the brilliant researchers in the name of population control?"

Outside the window a landscape of dim pastels rushed toward us, then dissolved into indistinguishable clumps of purple and black. Peter's questions were unnerving, yet I knew they were my last link to decency. If I severed myself from them, I would surely slip over the edge, into the abyss of subhuman existence.

"Tell me, Sarah," said Peter. "Would you do everything in your power to make sure the child inside you enjoys the bounty of planet earth?"

"Everything," said Sarah.

"Would you protect it from those who wanted to do it bodily harm, even if that required you to break laws, or lose your reputation, or give up personal comfort?"

"Of course," said Sarah boldly.

"Would you even give your life?"

Sarah paused and I felt her hand accidentally bump against mine on the seat. She nodded slowly.

"Then by the mercies of God, I beg you to do the same for Long Shadows. Stay with me when this assignment is completed. Join the Shadow Train. I could use a pair of young conductors like you and brother John."

"I'll have to think about it," said Sarah. "I was considering just getting away somewhere with the baby and . . . and living for a while. Working for the Shadow Train doesn't seem that conducive to family life."

Peter raised his hand suddenly and brought it down hard on the dashboard.

"It's the only thing that's conducive to family life! Don't either of you understand? This is not some happy field trip we're on. This is life and death for a half-billion people."

I thought of my awful, ratty apartment and the number of Long Shadows I had to bring in each month just to pay the rent. Something in me bowed low under the weight of my past deeds, and Peter recognized the change in my face.

"You see it, don't you, brother?" he declared, already knowing the answer to his question.

I let my chin drop to my chest.

"You are cursed occupationally," Peter pressed. "You, who were once a ruler of Paradise, who found your entire worth in the validation of a voice from heaven, now slink off from nine to five to buy a bag of self-esteem. And what do you find when you look in the bag, John? Do you feel pride at the end of a lucrative day? Or do you hear the haunting voices of those you've murdered?"

"Of course I hear them," I cried.

"God can lift your curse," said Peter. "He'll forgive you for every murder you've ever committed, if you tell Him you're sorry and really mean it."

"I think I'd like to stop this conversation."

Peter punched the solarfeed and sped toward the dawn. "No sense stopping now. We're almost to your farm in Sheldon."

Suddenly, Sarah gave a startled gasp and pulled the monochrome display closer to her eyes. "They're on the screen again," she said.

"Who is?"

"Those things we saw outside Dakota City."

Peter hit the brakes and turned the steering wheel. There was the crunch of gravel and the truck gradually groaned to a stop. With the click of a switch, he doused the lights. Everyone looked at the bluish screen.

Sarah hoisted herself up into the open window frame and peered into the distance. "What are their coordinates?" she asked.

I read her the numbers and heard her breathing heavily as she punched them into the Compulog.

"What side of the road is your property on?" asked Peter, eyeing the screen.

"West—as far as I can remember."

"They're coming right up your old farm road to the main blacktop," said Sarah, quivering with adrenaline. The look of a mother lioness had settled into her eyes, and I saw instantly that she was gathering herself for battle. There was no way she would let them hurt her baby, or be made into them for that matter.

"Maybe they're just combines," I said hopefully.

Suddenly, Captain Levi's hulking shadow blocked the moon over Sarah's shoulder, and she gave a little start when he spoke.

"They're howlers again," he said flatly.

"Do you think they're the same ones that chased us before?" asked Peter.

"Same model probably," said the Captain, as he lit a cigarette. "The ones that tried to catch us before Dakota City weren't fast enough to get the job done. These are probably down from VC North. They're quicker, with more firepower."

"Perhaps we should go another way," suggested Peter.

"Nonsense," asserted the captain. "We've come this far. We're not turning around now. Once the howlers hit the black-top, they'll probably investigate the next section to the east. They never recheck their work once their entire list of coordinates has been covered. The safest place on earth is down that road they just occupied." Captain Levi paused. "But we are not going to waste time romancing," he said loud enough for everyone to hear.

"Yes we are," insisted Mother's voice from the back of the truck.

Captain Levi put his hands on Sarah's shoulders and leaned to within an inch of her ear.

"Eventually, the howlers will finish their coordinates. And when they find us, it won't be a pretty sight. You of all people should think about that, McSwain, seeing as you were so close to being one of them. Perhaps you could talk Mrs. Nash out of her foolishness."

Sarah gave an inconspicuous shudder and turned her face toward the field, just as the howls began again.

Captain Levi spit into the roadside weeds. "Start her up," he commanded, slapping the hood of the truck. "They know we're in range, so we better get into their wake before they turn in our direction."

Peter turned the ignition key and tested the solarfeed. "Worry is like a rocking chair," he said cheerily. "It gives you something to do, but it doesn't get you anywhere."

"Yeah, but it keeps a man alive," said the captain, eyeing Peter sourly. "I'll take the wheel. McSwain, you and Tolles get in the back. I'll keep Nash and Peter for company. You up for shooting tag poles, Nash?"

"Aren't we a little close to the howlers for that, sir?" I asked.

Captain Levi turned on me angrily. "The screen says there's a good twenty miles between us and the farm. That's good enough for me."

"I suppose I could use a silencer, sir."

"Now we're thinking," the captain condescended. His terrible laugh split the night. "Full ahead," he choked, between great bursts of hilarity. "And don't stop until we reach the farm. If we're lucky, the howlers have made a mistake."

"Mistake, sir?" said Tiller.

"Yes, Tolles," replied Captain Levi. "Perhaps, the brutes have mistaken the sharecropper and his family for us."

12

ANOTHER TAG POLE SIZZLED AND POPPED
in our rearview mirror, while ahead of us, the asphalt stretched
like a thin, black snake through Carlow, Copper Notch, and
Sheldon.

"God has blessed you with an eye for accuracy," said Prior
Peter. He was referring to my shot, but I couldn't help feeling as
if he had intended something deeper, like the possibility that I
saw things as they really were. The sound of Tiller tapping on
the window meant it was getting stuffy again in the back of the
truck.

"Why don't we rearrange the sacks so they can have more
air, sir?" I suggested.

"A little discomfort never hurt anybody," said Captain Levi.

Except for the captain's snow white grip on the steering
wheel, everything else about the man was flushed and glistening. I shut my mouth and tried not to listen to the insane tapping. After a mile or so of traveling like that, we came alongside
a section of wheat that looked vaguely familiar.

"Is something the matter?" asked Peter, seeing my bewilderment. Already Captain Levi had begun to slow the truck,

and he was making a wide turn onto a ribbon of rich, brown earth.

"It's . . . familiar to me," I said slowly.

Peter patted my leg. "This is it, John, the farm your father owned before he went to Washington. Your parents honeymooned in the little house just around the bend."

As he said it, the road opened up into a long lane, flanked on either side by elms and chinaberries and I knew the place immediately. Fifty yards ahead of us a pair of thin hounds stood in the middle of the road. When they heard the truck approaching they bounded over a shallow ditch, crawled beneath a strand of barbed wire and were off across the field, parting the wheat with chiseled muzzles.

"I hope the sharecroppers are all right," said Peter.

"Not by the looks of those," said Captain Levi, pointing toward a sickly knot of steers on the opposite side of the road. "Poor things are nothing but hooves and bones. They ought to be sold while they're still breathing."

"There doesn't seem to be a soul on the place."

I opened the door of the truck and stood on the running board. A rabbit skittered along the ditch, then vanished in a thicket of gourds and thistle. The happy "over-here-o" of a meadowlark rose on the wind. Somewhere across the field to the south of us came the steady chug of a rig, lamenting the days when oil was king.

I ducked back into the cab. "Peter's right," I said. "No movement at all. Maybe everybody's still asleep. Who'd you say was working the place now?"

"Nobody said," snapped Captain Levi. He was anxious to get to Ely and resented our making a stop for something so silly as the reawakening of love and sanity. We pulled up to a small green house with white trim and parked the truck. Captain Levi was the first to get out. He went inside the house without knocking. Sarah wandered a little ways into the yard, and I noticed she didn't make eye contact with anyone.

"Looks like a struggle here not too long ago," said Tiller, poking his head around the end of the cargo rails and studying the tracks in the dirt driveway. "Two humans and one . . . two . . . four howlers. You can tell by the width of the footprints over there," he said, nodding toward a clearer sample in front of our vehicle. It was obvious someone had attempted an unsuccessful escape over the barbed wire fence. Several posts were uprooted and a piece of torn clothing fluttered in the morning breeze.

Captain Levi returned to us with something dangling from his hand. "Whoever lived here doesn't have to worry about paying their phone bill for a while," he announced. The thing in his hand was a cellular unit—or what was left of one. "I found this lying on the kitchen floor in there. The place is pretty torn up. Furniture knocked over. Books and magazines everywhere."

"What else?" asked Mother suspiciously.

Captain Levi paused. "The whole west wall is gone."

The news brought Sarah to a halt in the yard. She squatted down in the grass, letting her long hair fall in front of her face.

"What's wrong with her?" asked Tiller, nudging me.

"She has a right to be tired. She was up half the night shooting tag poles."

"Yeah, we could all use a nap," said Tiller.

Peter's voice rang out from the truck's cab sudden and bright.

"The Lord couldn't have made a more perfect morning," he said, swinging his legs onto the running board, climbing down, and walking to the back of the truck. He mopped his brow with the back of his thick, brown hand. "A little hot, maybe, but far be it from me to complain when the judge is baking like a blackberry pie in that robe of his. Can someone give me a hand? He's asleep again. It may take all of us to get him on his feet."

When we finally got Father out of the truck and propped against the tailgate, he was stiff and listless. But the moment he was aware of his surroundings, he began wringing his hands and apologizing to the wind. Peter took him by the shoulders and looked him in the eye.

"One 'sorry' is all you need, brother."

"Is he all right?" I asked.

"Not as long as he believes he can do penance to take away his guilt," said Peter. "He must throw himself into the merciful arms of God and trust that He will catch him."

Tiller yawned and looked at Mother.

"As long as we're just going to stand around like we're on vacation, I think I'll get some sleep. Is there a bed around here?"

Mother gave a nod in the direction of the green house.

"Keep your gun on the nightstand," she said. "And make sure it's loaded. I don't trust a howler to stick to his coordinates."

Captain Levi scowled at Mother. "Coming from someone who changed our coordinates for the sake of a second honeymoon, I'd say that's rather hypocritical. Wouldn't you?"

"Your optimism is contagious, Levi," replied Mother coolly.

"Let me recall the facts for you, woman," fired Captain Levi. He had kept his opinion to himself about as long as a man like him could be expected to. "We are at this moment participating in a felony that could get each and every one of us terminated immediately. We have in our possession the most famous spokesman for the cause of the greatest good. We have VC blood on our hands, a stolen truck, and a pack of howlers trying to flush us out like game birds. And you want to stop for a picnic?!"

"I'm taking August for a walk now, whether you approve or not," said Mother. "If we see a howler, we'll tell it where to find you."

An appreciable catch in Mother's voice suggested that her words were not altogether in jest. Captain Levi dismissed her and Father with a backhand to the air and stormed away muttering.

Mother turned around. "John? Peter? Would you like to join us?"

I looked in Sarah's direction. She had gotten up, and was walking in a daze toward the truck. "I've got to sort through some things," I replied.

"Peter?" said Mother, repeating her invitation.

"The offer is tempting," said Peter, smiling. "But someone has to keep a look out for danger. I'll just sit over there by that oak and have a chat with my Maker."

"I guess that leaves you and me, Auggie," said Mother, resting her hand in the crook of my father's elbow. Turning toward me, she added, "Come find us as soon as that girl of yours wakes up."

She had never in my short life referred to a member of her own gender as if she were property, much less property of mine. But here in four short words, she had conferred upon me the title of ownership and I did not know what to think of it. "That girl of yours" was still ringing in my ears when I wriggled through the little crawl space between the fertilizer sacks and found Sarah lying on the hay.

"Are you okay?" I whispered, jostling her lightly. Her arms were wet with perspiration and she bolted up the moment she felt my touch.

"This is not a good place to be."

"Shh," I said softly, putting a finger to her lips. "Do you remember when we were sniped at in Dakota City?"

"I still have bruises on my arms from you shoving me down like you did."

"Do you recall seeing Tiller, anywhere?"

"Sure, when he was running out of the store after paying for the fill-up."

"I was afraid you'd say that."

Sarah sat up in the dim, dusty light. Through a hole in the sacks, I could see Captain Levi striding swiftly toward the woods, opposite the direction my parents had taken.

"Tell me," I said, between hurried breaths. "Are you sure you didn't see him while he was in the store?"

"What's this all about?" asked Sarah fearfully.

"I don't have time to explain."

"You think he's with VC, don't you?"

"I think he might be. I think Captain Levi might be, too."

"You're going to need a lot more than circumstantial evidence if you're going to make those kinds of accusations outside this truck."

"Just work with me," I said, more gruffly than I'd intended.

"All right, I did not see Tiller while he was in the store. Is that what you're wanting to hear?"

"Sarah—"

"Look, this is the only chance I've got to save my baby. I'm not going to let you come along and ruin it just because you have some suspicion."

I tried to put my hand on her shoulder, but she pulled away.

"If you'll just hear me out, you'll see I'm not being paranoid," I pleaded. "When the first shots were fired, you said yourself that you thought they were coming from the roof of the store. Right?"

"Right."

"You also said they sounded like no gun a cyberslave would use."

"I could have been wrong about that."

"Well, you weren't wrong. That wasn't some howler firing from the roof yesterday morning. It was a Colt semi-automatic, the same one I've heard every Monday on the VC range for the past six years. The gun belongs to Tiller."

Sarah stared at me.

"Look here," I said, reaching into the pocket of my jeans. "I pulled this slug out of the side rail once we were on the road again. It matches Tiller's ammo. I checked when he was asleep last night."

"Lots of people use the same ammunition."

"It was his, Sarah. I'm sure of it."

"Why would Tiller fire a lethal weapon at his best friend, when he could just as easily use an acoustic beam or a handheld laser?"

"That's the point. He wanted to make it look like the person shooting wasn't my friend."

Sarah shook her head. "I don't want to get involved in this. It's nothing but a theory and it could ruin all my plans."

"They wanted to keep you and me from having this conversation, Sarah. I'm telling you, there is something going on that Tiller and Captain Levi don't want me to discover before we get to Canada. It's like a play with only two actors. Tiller takes the shots and plays the part of the unseen villain. Captain Levi comes off looking like the hero who has everyone's best interest in mind."

"He was paying for the fill-up, John."

"You still believe that?"

"What else do people do at filling stations?"

I paused for a moment. "Sunshine's free at Harold's One-Stop, Sarah. Long Shadows passing through on their way to Canada have total access to his generator. Mother told me that when she first laid out the plan."

This last revelation fell like ominous thunder. Sarah caught her breath and her chin began to quiver. "I told you I don't want to get involved in this. All I want to do is get to Canada, and nobody's personal vendetta is going to stop me."

"He's not what he appears to be," I said. "I can feel it."

"Well, you can keep your feelings to yourself."

"I think we're in big trouble, Sarah," I said, reaching for her field pack. "Do you have your PowerBook with you?"

"I think so. Why?"

"Here it is," I said, locating the small computer in the bottom of the pack. I quickly set it on the floor in front of us and opened the screen. "Show me how to link with National's database, and I'll show you some data on former justices that'll make your blood run cold."

"Can't we just take the truck and get out of here?" pleaded Sarah, stark panic welling up in her eyes.

"Are you going to help me or not?"

Sarah placed reluctant fingers on the keyboard and began to type. "How former do you want?"

"Ones that were sitting when my father was on the bench."

Sarah scrolled until she reached 2010, and a long list of judges' names appeared before our eyes. For a moment, I stared in silence at the screen.

"My God, it's true," I whispered finally.

"What's true?" asked Sarah.

"My father's partners are dead," I murmured.

"That's it, I'm going," said Sarah, jumping to her feet and heading for the tailgate. I tackled her before she was halfway there.

"Let go of me!" she cried.

I could just barely hear Sarah's voice. It was like I was trapped in a box with the loud, throbbing beat of blood in my veins and the names of my father's former associates weaving in and out of the rhythm.

Swann . . .

Collins . . .

White . . .

Brandt . . .

Bilbrie . . .

Zindejas . . .

Ostermann . . .

They had all died untimely deaths within two years of the majority opinion. The little, glowing numbers on the screen showed the dates of their decease.

"I said, let go!" repeated Sarah.

Now the blood in my head was like a jungle drum. I took Sarah's face in my hands and pulled it close to mine, so that she could hear it, too.

"They were terminated because of what they knew," I said.

"I don't care about your father's partners," replied Sarah. She tried to pull away, but I held on firmly.

"You need to care, or you and your baby may not make it to Canada alive. Maybe if you're scared enough you'll get some sense about you. Now all I'm asking is for you to find me some more information on this stuff!" I reached the PowerBook with my foot and dragged it across the floor. "Do you still have sources at National?" I asked.

Sarah gave a feeble nod.

"Contact them," I said, relaxing my grip on her face.

"What am I supposed to tell them? That I'm suddenly interested in dead justices? You don't know what you're asking me to do, John. I'm not even supposed to be in the tag program anymore."

"Tell them you're doing research on the disposal of human tissue for VC Midwest and you need everything they can dig up on the topic—especially information from the early days when disposal was a national crisis."

Sarah's face was colorless.

"We're onto something," I whispered.

"They'll kill us," said Sarah, placing her hands on her stomach. "I can't go back to VC, John. I won't go back. I've got a baby to think about."

"No one's going back. Trust me."

I took her in my arms, and her scintillant face came up to my own. For a moment I hesitated, knowing that if I kissed her, I would be forever wedded to the preservation of life, and could never bear to snuff it out again in order to make a living. Suddenly, I thought of Tiller napping, and I saw that it was all a pretense.

"Come on," I said, grabbing Sarah's wrist.

"Where are we going?"

"Hurry! I just hope it's not too late."

Inside, we found the house's only bed undisturbed and Tiller's gun missing from the nightstand. A sudden vision of Tiller and Captain Levi crouched in the weeds, flipping a coin to see who would take the shot and get the tag on my parents came to mind. I ran to the hole in the west wall, bounded through it and shouted to Peter under the oak tree.

"Which way did my parents go?"

"To the pond, wherever that is," he answered. "Your mother said they might skip rocks or sit for a spell. Is something wrong?"

Without answering, I grabbed Sarah and headed across the sprawling, unkempt backyard, hoping I still knew how to find the pond. We ran wordlessly through the wheat, across a creek, then up onto a ridge that led to the pond. Another hundred yards and we were out of breath.

"I don't want to be a howler," said Sarah, when we finally slowed down. A puff of wind combed through her hair and the sunlight accentuated the redness of her lips.

"They don't make howlers out of people," I said automatically.

"Tiller says they do. He says it's what happens to all the really good tag men after they turn fifty."

"Well, Tiller doesn't know everything. Besides, retired tag men get desk jobs at VC."

"The mediocre ones do. Tiller says the really good shots are—"

"Forget about Tiller," I said, striding off again at a fast pace along the ridge. "We have to keep moving."

Sarah followed along behind me until we came to the end of the ridge and the land sloped down to a shimmering oval pond. On the shore, beneath a stand of willows, Mother and Father sat holding hands. My heart beat faster and I glanced around the field to see if there was anyone else watching them.

Motioning Sarah to crouch down on the ridge, I crept closer until I was just thirty feet from my parents, and could hear everything they were saying.

"The breeze feels nice coming off the water," remarked Mother.

"Uh-hm. Nice."

"Auggie?"

"Hm?"

"Do you remember fishing at this pond on our honeymoon?"

Father smiled faintly. "I caught a turtle and an old tire."

"That's right. And then what did we do?" asked Mother, glancing hopefully at my father.

He stared at her until she finally accepted that the answer was not going to come to him, and then she pointed to a shady spot under a spreading oak.

"We knew each other for the first time in the grass over there," she said.

For a moment, I imagined the sounds of nervous discovery emerging from the overgrown weeds, then I looked back at the two of them.

"I was happy then," said Mother longingly.

Father nodded again.

"Were you happy too?" asked Mother.

"I was the court centrist," answered Father disjointedly.

Mother' face fell.

"Brandt and Bilbrie were the real oppositionists. White, too. They were ready to acknowledge a constitutional right to euthanasia. I . . . I merely wanted to strike a few of the states' laws here and there. Nothing wrong with that."

"That's over now," blurted Mother.

"But there's nothing wrong with being a centrist, is there?"

"You're a man, Auggie, not a centrist."

"But—"

"You're my husband."

"Right. I'm your husband," agreed Father flatly, and for a second or two it seemed he would lay his head on Mother's shoulder and put an end to his relentless examination of himself. But he started in again.

"Skink didn't have to assign the case to me. It was Ostermann's case. He was the senior justice in the majority. Skink was always asserting his right to assign minority cases. But he should have never given Long Shadow to me. I was a centrist, wasn't I?"

"Yes, you were, Auggie."

"And there's nothing wrong with that, is there?"

"Nothing wrong."

"There," said Father, as if he had just handed down a decision in court. "I feel much more like my old self now. If I can get my pass, would you like to go for a walk on the grounds?"

"We are *not* at Rivendale anymore!"

Father's perplexed eyes took inventory of his surroundings.

"Oh, Auggie," sighed Mother, pulling him to her shoulder. She was holding him there and tears were flowing down her face when I saw the first little patch of dirt jump on the shore behind them.

"Get down!" I screamed, no longer concerned with secrecy. Mother saw, heard, and obeyed me all in one motion. I ran toward the pond as a second shot thumped into the mud.

"I'm sorry. So sorry," sobbed Father, oblivious to the danger. He held his forehead and repeated those two words over and over.

"We've got to get him to cover," said Mother, when I reached her.

"Can you make him be quiet?" I asked.

Suddenly, Captain Levi's voice came from the direction of the woods on the far side of the pond.

"Did anyone get hit?"

He was running swiftly along the shore in a crouched position, glancing nervously into the field as if he expected an ambush at any moment. When he reached us, I noticed his pants were covered with ticks. "Is anyone hit?" he repeated.

In a flash, all rudiments of my training concerning subordination vanished and I was in the captain's face.

"You've got a crazy lot of nerve trying to pull this off a second time."

"I have no idea what you're talking about, Nash," said Captain Levi. "But it had better be good."

"I'm talking about you and Tiller playing your little games, making the rest of us feel indebted to you each time you save the day. You'd have had me fooled in Dakota if Tiller had remembered to use a different gun."

"Unless you want to get shot, Nash, you better shut up and take cover real fast."

Suddenly, a youthful voice sang out and we all turned to see Tiller coming over a little rise to the south of the pond. He was carrying two ducks in one hand and his gun in the other.

"Look what I got," he exclaimed, hoisting the limp, unfortunate pair and grinning. "I got to thinking as I was lying there, that since nobody was around this place to complain about a couple of birds missing, I might as well go out and shoot dinner. I didn't get my nap, but at least we'll be eating good tonight. Sorry if I scared anyone. I was getting awful tired of Fig Newtons." He lifted the birds again so we all could admire them.

"Help your father up," said Mother, quietly.

"Did I miss something?" asked Tiller.

"I was wondering the same thing myself," growled Captain Levi.

I pointed at Tiller. "How many shots did you fire?" I demanded.

"Umm, three . . . four. Wait a minute." Tiller stared at me incredulously. "You don't think—"

"Forget it," I muttered, grasping my father underneath his armpits and lifting him to his feet. I felt like walking into the pond until the water covered my head and the cool sediment bonded me to the bottom.

"I better get these birds over a flame," said Tiller, glaring at me. He stomped off in the direction of the green house.

I glanced at Captain Levi. The pack of muscle was shifting beneath his shirt and the veins in his neck were standing out again.

"We've still got maps to go over, and we're talking about eating duck after dark. Cripes! I hate wasting a whole afternoon!" He, too, started off, but when he had mounted the rise he turned and pointed at me. "So help me, Nash," he shouted. "If you ever insinuate again that I'm trying to sabotage this journey, I'll do you like Tolles did those birds. Right through the chest. You got that?"

"Yes, sir," I replied.

He turned and walked away, mumbling something about Dakota City and cursing the day he let me into his confidence.

There was a bite to the air on the way back to the house, a sort of May hangover from the cold months before. Unlike the others, I did not walk briskly back the same route we had come. Instead, I threaded my way along the old cow path, down into the lowland, past the northern end of the pond where the earth shoved up into a man-made dam and the black walnuts huddled like monks in the dusk. In the top of one were the remnants of a tree house, and it dawned on me that Father and I had built it not long before we went to Washington. Instantly, my count of unfamiliar things diminished by one, and in my heart I felt as if I had never really left the place. I was nearing the house when I noticed Mother had followed me.

"I'd like to talk," she said in a low voice.

I kept walking. "What's there to talk about? I made a fool of myself."

"You're right about the captain," she said abruptly.

I whirled around to speak.

"Hold it," she said, touching a finger to her lips. "He'd ruin me if he heard me say what I'm about to say to you."

Over my shoulder, I caught a glimpse of Tiller plucking feathers and a flicker of flame whenever the breeze blew the cedars.

"What do you have on him that would make him want to ruin you?" I asked.

"We both have things on each other. It keeps the balance of power. Do you remember asking me about those rumors?"

I felt a flush of embarrassment. "The ones about you sleeping around?"

"They're not rumors," she said abruptly.

I swallowed and kicked at a dirt clod, which gave me something to focus on besides my mother's indiscreet past.

"Go ahead and face it, son," she said. "Your mother slept with every boss she ever had on the way up the ladder. Fat, thin, rich, poor, bald, hairy . . . it didn't much matter as long as there was a position above them." She paused and her eyes narrowed. "I hated every minute of it."

Now I smelled the duck cooking. The wind shifted and through the trees I caught another glimpse of Captain Levi's thick body. Both he and Tiller wielded a knife, and they kept poking the pair of ducks, halfway bewitched to a golden brown.

"Do you think I'm awful?" asked Mother.

"No—I don't know . . ." Suddenly my words leaned down over her. "What motivated you to behave like a common whore?"

Mother winced. "Starvation . . . loneliness . . ."

"But you didn't have to get mixed up with VC," I inserted.

"I had to eat," said Mother steadily. She moved slowly up the slope toward me. "Maybe you're forgetting that at that time I was full of hatred too. I didn't care if I hurt people. In fact, I *wanted* them to hurt, just as much as your father had hurt me."

I said nothing.

"By the time I had slept my way through the tag force, which is where I met Levi Coffin, contempt was my driving force. I was vice-president of public affairs before I saw my first live termination. It shocked me to discover it was nothing like the way it looks on VOX. I remember thinking there's a real human being laid out on that table, real fear, real sorrow . . . real finality to life." Mother paused. "That's when Peter Edmunds came down from the north like a cool breeze. The difference between him and other men I had known was that he didn't want anything from me, except that I embrace the God who loved me and who wanted—no, *demanded* my all."

There was another lull in Mother's explanation, and I saw that she was putting some important piece of her past where it belonged.

"I decided right then that I would make it to the top of VOX Midwest, and when I did I would start the Shadow Train."

"But how could Levi ruin you now?" I asked.

"With one sordid disclosure of all the things I did to get to where I am."

"For crying out loud, Mother—"

"Shh!" she warned again.

I lowered my voice. "We live in a society where we euthanize our parents in the same way we do our pets. Do you really think people would care if they knew you used to spread yourself around a bit?"

"I'm going on what I know, son. The public likes having a 'girl-next-door' in charge of VOX interviews. It gives them a sense of security, sort of dresses up the whole affair, makes their futures less foreboding. People want to believe that when their own T-dates arrive, their hands will be held and their brows soothed by someone maternal and pure. Do you imagine they'll think the same of me if Levi ever revealed what he knows?"

"You could always take another job outside VC. Sure, you'd receive a T-date, but you said yourself that death is not the worst thing that can happen to a person."

"You're missing the point. You forget I'm no longer motivated by hunger, or loneliness, or contempt. I am motivated by love, John," said Mother in one of those whispers that embodies a message too powerful to speak out loud. "I'm sure you think that if I know anything of love it is minimal, even less when it comes to the love of husband and wife, and certainly nothing of that affection for my neighbor after being at the top of VC for so long. But you are wrong, son. I know plenty about love. The Shadow Train proves it."

I sat down in the grass. "But why would the captain want to ruin you? What's in it for him? If he's part of the same Shadow Train, it seems he'd be harming himself to turn on you."

Mother raised her left eyebrow, a sign which during my childhood meant that I had either done something terribly inappropriate or that I had hit upon some truth.

"Then I *did* guess right," I said, interpreting the eyebrow. "He's not part of the Shadow Train."

The wag of Mother's head affirmed my interpretation.

"What's he doing on this little adventure then?" I asked.

"He's doing what he's done for years, John. Making a living off of frightened souls."

I sat dumbly with my eyes glued to Mother.

"Follow the money trail, son," she said. "Have you seen anyone besides Captain Levi driving to work untethered in a fancy car?"

I shook my head.

"Correct. Everyone else takes the PRT or the People Mover. And do you know why?"

"Because no one else brings in enough . . . tags . . . to . . ." The truth fell with an awful thud. By now, Mother had come all the way up the path and was standing in front of me.

"He's a conartist, son, a coldhearted conartist who convinces Long Shadows he can get them to Canada, then lays them out stiff before they ever reach the border. Usually he turns them in himself and collects the bounty. Sometimes he sells them back to the tag man who had the original assignment, at an inflated price, of course, because after all, he did all the work."

"Then why have we let him in on our plans?"

"He would've figured them out easily enough, so it seemed more prudent to act naive."

"What about Tiller?" I asked anxiously. "Is he in it with the Captain?"

"I don't know," said Mother. "He doesn't seem to be the type who'd let himself be controlled by the likes of Captain Levi. He's a family man."

"You know about that?"

Mother looked at me in disbelief. "Son, there are no secrets at VC. I could give you a printout of every time you sneezed in the last six months."

"Why doesn't someone blow the whistle on the captain?"

"I believe someone's about to," said Mother, looking over my shoulder at the fire.

"Well, he won't make a dime off of my father, unless he intends to kill us all," I said defiantly.

There was Mother's eyebrow again.

"Courage," she said, as she stepped past me and up onto the pasture. We walked the rest of the way to the green house in silence.

Later that night we nibbled duck and made courteous small talk until every last sinew of meat had dropped from the spit into the embers and the stars poked through the canopy overhead. Once, Captain Levi even made a stab at trivializing the words he and I had exchanged by the pond. His attempt at reconciliation only made me mistrust him more.

At midnight, we were ordered to bed with a reprieve from the captain regarding our much needed study of the Quetico maps. For a long time I watched him standing by the coals, smoking and no doubt feeling smug about the way these poor, dumb sheep went along with his plans. Sarah and Mother were already asleep (or at least pretending to be) by the time I climbed into the truck, stripped my shirt off and crawled into my bag. The cool synthetic shell made me shiver. I was just zipping it to my chin when I caught sight of Peter, sitting underneath his oak again. The cross around his neck gave off a silvery glint, and he was singing a song I had not heard since I went to summer camp in the Ozarks as a child.

> Day is done . . .
> gone the sun . . .
> from the lakes, from the hills, from the sky.
> All is well . . .
> safely rest . . .
> God is nigh.

The moon winked again on Peter's cross, and the last thing I recall thinking was that it was a fortunate thing my gun was nigh, too.

13

"There is a philosophical, moral, political, legal, medical, and theological chasm between allowing someone to die and causing someone to die."
—Anonymous

SOMEWHERE IN THE NIGHT I AWOKE TO dance music, lifted the canvas flap, and strained my ear to listen. The blue-black of the wee hours had begun to slide from the sky, dragging purple and pink into view, and the truck was surrounded by the silence that occurs when the creatures of the night have just gone to sleep and the inhabitants of day are not yet roused. I groped my way out of the truck and practically ran over Peter, who was still awake by his oak.

"Not a bad idea, huh?" he said, nodding across the road toward two distant silhouettes in the middle of the field—one of them fluid and relaxed, the other stiff as a tree.

"I never knew they danced," I whispered.

"They danced," assured Peter thoughtfully. "We all did back then."

"Have they been out there long?"

"Ever since the captain went to bed." Peter chuckled. "Your mother's not one to give up on love easily."

"Where'd you get the speakers?" I asked.

"From the truck. It took a while to get them out of the dash, but once I did, the rest was easy. I got the idea when I found some old connector wire in the barn down the road. Watch out. You're about to trip over it."

I checked my step and sat down against the tree's cool, semi-smooth bark. Across the road, fireflies punched green pinholes in the darkness, and the sound of "Moon River" washed away into the distant republic.

Peter, surveyed the scene with satisfaction. "A little love never hurt anybody."

"What does a monk know about love?" I asked.

"I know it's better than a kick in the teeth. Imagine what this would be like if we could travel back to *Roe v. Wade* and recapture all our missed opportunities for truly loving another human being. I dare say a lot more grandparents would be playing with their grandchildren today."

I fingered the wires that ran from the truck, across the road, over the ditch, into the shadows. Peter's words were finding their way to my heart.

"My dad taught me about electricity," he continued casually. "He gave me a broken-down stereo for my twelfth birthday. Said if I could fix it, I could keep it. Did your dad teach you things?"

I gazed out into the field, where my father's frame moved stiffly to the tinny drip of banjos.

"He wasn't around much."

"Your mom tells me there was some relative—"

"My uncle," I interrupted. The thought of Uncle Ames brought a huge lump to my throat. I realized there was no other person I missed more.

"Ahh, yes. Ames Nash," said Peter.

"You act like you knew him."

"Of course I knew him. He was the first person the Shadow Train ever helped to freedom."

"What?" I blurted.

"I said he was the first—"

"I know what you said, but that's impossible. I saw my mother dump his ashes in a rose bed."

"You can never be sure about ashes," said Peter. "She could have been dumping a total stranger. VC's not known for its accuracy when it comes to releasing the right remains to family members. As far as they're concerned, ashes are ashes."

The look on my face must have told of my jubilation, for when I opened my mouth to inquire as to Uncle Ames's whereabouts, Peter had already anticipated my question.

"Hold on, now," he said. "That was a few years back. He was in pretty bad shape for a man his age. There's no guarantee a Long Shadow will live once we turn him loose in the Quetico. Weather gets some. Wolves get others. Once in a while we hear through the grapevine about someone making it up to Yellowknife or one of the larger cities. But just once in a while."

Out in the field, Mother pushed Father backward in continual graceless circles.

"Did you get to know him?" I asked, sitting up on my haunches.

Peter closed his eyes.

"He was angry as the devil back then. A certain brother was the target of his rage. For weeks, he was like a lunatic; thin as a sapling, sick from eating berries, a horror to the eyes if there ever was one. And he had the most ghastly tale of being tracked by men through the woods, which he kept jabbering about night and day. I felt sorry for the man. I had to do something. So, I called the brotherhood together—there were about ten of us at Tonsus at the time—and right there, we decided we would do something to help Long Shadows."

"But surely you have some idea whether he's alive or not," I pressed, hoping for even the slightest confirmation.

"Could be," said Peter.

"I'll bet he'd kill my father if the two of them met again," I said emphatically.

"Back then, he might have. But Ames made a change while he was with us. There's an extraordinary amount of love shown by the Tonsus brotherhood, love that is capable of transforming a man. You'll see what I mean when you meet the other monks. At any rate, I believe your uncle had some things he needed to say, things that your father needs to hear. If there's ever a reunion of those two brothers, we may all be surprised by the way it turns out. Did you know they used to ride horses together when they were kids?"

I shook my head.

"Oh, yes," said Peter. "It was practically all your uncle wanted to talk about. He told me horses were the only thing August ever loved, besides you and your mother. It must have been a very special part of their childhood."

"Uncle Ames could never forgive him," I insisted.

As if he could see the shame I bore over my own terrible sins, Peter laid a hand on my shoulder. "We all can be forgiven. Just like *that*." With a snap of his fingers, he dismissed every crime I had ever committed.

I turned my eyes down the road, so Peter wouldn't see them overflow.

"You don't know what kind of things I've done."

"That's true. But God does, and he's not squeamish. He loves murderers as much as he loves missionaries."

Through the intermittent lights of fireflies, I saw the shadows dancing. Round and round my parents went in a circle of forgiveness, undoing shame, embracing imperfection, sending with the occasional candle spark a message to the heavens that some day love would ignite a global flame. I wanted this love that Peter talked about, but I still could not fathom it being extended to people like me.

"We need to get moving tomorrow," I said abruptly. "The longer we sit in one place, the more likely we'll show up on glider radar."

"We already have," said Peter. "They're simply toying with us, John. It's the way the captain—"

To the right of us, a stick snapped, and for what seemed like a long time we both sat motionless.

"Hello, gentlemen," came a bristling voice. Captain Levi stepped out of the shadows. "I thought everyone had gone to bed but me. What's wrong? Couldn't sleep?"

When Peter spoke, his words were hard and flat. "I was telling John I thought the gliders would be upon us by morning."

"Nonsense, old friend," said Captain Levi. "The howlers were here already. Why would VC bother sending gliders?"

"Call it a hunch," said Peter.

Levi spit. "Of course I couldn't expect an outsider such as yourself to understand all the ins and outs of Vivi-Centerre. May I have a word with you, John? Privately?"

I felt an icy weight in the pit of my stomach. "Excuse me, Peter," I said, as I rose to follow the captain.

For a hundred yards down the dirt road I followed him in silence, wondering what it was he had to say. Suddenly, Captain Levi turned and with a violent thrust he had me in the ditch. The root of an elm ground into the small of my back, and something hard and cold pressed against the side of my head.

"So you think I'm out to get your father, do you?" hissed the captain. His hand was clamped so tightly around my throat that I could hardly speak.

"I can explain, sir," I said.

"Save it!"

The cold, hard thing pressed tighter against my head, and I flinched, expecting any moment to hear a roar and see the world go black.

"Would you like to hear a little recording?" asked the captain.

Before I could answer, I heard the click of a recorder and a voice spoke quietly in my ear.

"Man that is born of a woman is of few days, and full of trouble."

"Do you recognize it?" asked Captain Levi, clicking the recorder off. He had relaxed his grip on my throat, but only slightly.

"It's my mother," I managed to say.

"That's right, Nash. It's a phone conversation between your mother and that pious, hypocritical excuse for a monk. Did I ever tell you what an excellent job you did placing that probe on your Mother's neck? It was the last responsible thing you did. By the way," he said, reaching into his pocket and pulling out a glowing orange identity bracelet. "I found this in your Mother's purse yesterday. I can think of only one reason she'd have this in her possession, and that's to make it easier for VC to get a lead on us. So, first it was the map she left behind, and now this."

He dangled the bracelet in front of me.

"I'm sure there's another explanation."

"Shut up, Nash!" shouted the captain. With a hard backhand, he opened a cut on my cheek.

There was another click of the recorder.

"Come again," said a man's voice. It was obviously Prior Peter's.

"Man that is born of a woman is of few days, and full of trouble," repeated Mother. "He comes forth like a flower, and withers. He flees like a shadow, and continues not."

On the other end of the conversation, it sounded as though Peter had dropped his receptor unit. For a long time there was an uncomfortable silence.

"From the book of Second Kings," said Captain Levi. "Your mother and that fraud have been using it as a code for years whenever they had business to do."

My back began to burn at the place where the root was digging. But when I tried to squirm free of it, Captain Levi pressed down harder on my chest. Finally, Peter spoke again.

"Shall the shadow go forward ten steps, or go back ten steps?" he asked.

"It is an easy thing for the shadow to lengthen ten steps; rather let the shadow go back ten steps," Mother answered immediately.

Back and forth the conversation continued for a while without any interruptions.

"And what of his bones?"

"They burn like a furnace."

"And his heart? Tell me of that."

"Withered . . . all of it . . . withered and smitten like grass."

"His days, ma'am—what do you know of his days?"

"His days are like an evening shadow," said Mother without hesitation.

With this last answer, I could almost feel through the recorder that Peter had relaxed and was moving now into a sort of routine. I, on the other hand, was drenched in sweat and shaking like the leaves just visible over Captain Levi's shoulder.

"Hello, sister," Peter said, dropping the whisper and pressing ahead in a warm, yet businesslike tone.

"Hello, brother."

"God bless you, my friend. It's been too long since I've heard from you. To what do I owe this pleasure?"

At this point, Captain Levi put his face right down next to mine, and the saliva on his teeth glistened in the moonlight. "Here comes the interesting part," he said.

"I have reason to believe there'll be a Long Shadow coming your way soon," replied Mother. "Do you have a pencil?"

"Yes."

"Good. Take notes. No names. Just numbers. Understand?"

"I understand."

"The man I am speaking of is T-13. Do you have a current copy of the Shadow Census on hand?"

"2038?" said Peter, obviously searching for it. "Yes, here it is. Which number did you say?"

"T-13. That's barely a week from now. Do you have the page yet?"

"10, 11, okay . . . T-13. Nash . . . Nash. Good heavens! How could I have forgotten?"

"Can you see now why this call is so urgent?" asked Mother.

"Perfectly."

"I knew you would. Now, I'm sure you can imagine what VC is willing to do to contain him."

"Yes. It would be a blemish on their record if he were to get away. Not to mention the response of the public. What do I need to know?"

"He's coming from Kansas City. Have a man ready for him in six days."

Peter sighed. "This is the part I dread. Do you know how it feels to watch a man be taken away to die when he still has a lot of living left to do?"

There was another moment of silence.

"Yes, I do," came Mother's voice faintly. Captain Levi chuckled when he heard it.

"Could you send me something on him?" asked Peter hopefully.

"VC isn't releasing much. As you can imagine, with the certain prestige that surrounds him, there'd—"

"Yes, of course, there'd be a frenzy. Just remind me of the vitals.

"I didn't think you'd need reminding."

"It's been a long time, sister."

"Very well. Six-foot, two inches. A hundred and eighty-five pounds. Forty-nine years old."

"Obviously. Go on."

"He has a mole on his left instep."

"Ahh, yes. Now I remember."

"Will you be ready for him?"

"I can try."

"Please, you must do more than try. Coffin's on to us."

"All right. I'll be ready for him."

"There's just one more thing."

"What is it?"

"Does anybody outside Tonsus know about your basement?"

Before Peter could answer, Captain Levi clicked off the recorder, put it in his pocket and stood above me like an animal above his prey.

"Coffin's on to us," the captain mimicked. "They've got that right. I *am* on to them. And I'm not about to let some two-bit bounty hunter, like yourself, mess things up for the Shadow Train just because he can't decide which side he's going to put his trust in." He dropped the bracelet in the ditch and with both hands seized me by the collar. "Do you understand now, Nash, that your Mother's only interest in your father is his death? She hates his guts."

I closed my eyes, not wanting to understand.

"I could kill you in this ditch right now," said Captain Levi. He drew back his fist, and I believe he would have murdered me with his hands had we not heard the sudden, shrill cries of Peter coming from far up the road, and seen the fields flecked with light.

"They're here! They're here!" Peter was shouting in the distance.

Just before Captain Levi and I clambered out on the road and saw the luminous eyes of a hundred VC gliders, I had the presence of mind to snatch the bracelet from the ditch where he had dropped it.

"They're here, indeed," said Captain Levi. And when he said it, I thought for a fraction of a second that I saw him smile.

14

> *"Ten thousand people are euthanized in Holland each year. Some Dutch patients have taken to carrying a card that reads, 'Please do not euthanize me.'"*
>
> —Los Angeles Times, 1996,
> *Premillennial Archives*

FIFTY TO ONE SHE CONTACTED VC ALONG the interstate," wagered Captain Levi, as we raced up the road toward Peter's cries. "Maybe she did it when we stopped to recharge."

"She never got out of the truck, sir," I reminded him.

"Then she found another way. I've never met a shrewder woman."

The sun had not yet risen, nevertheless the gliders had trained their lights in the center of the field, causing a parking-lot-size patch to be as bright as day. Across the moist grass my parents fled, leaving behind the music and the dance.

"Wake Tiller and Sarah," ordered Captain Levi.

"They're up, sir. I saw them run across the road with their weapons."

I thought of the EM rail buried in my bag and darted toward the truck.

"Nash!" screamed Levi, when he saw me veering away from him. "I'd just as soon shoot you myself, as let the gliders get you."

You're going to shoot me anyway before this thing is finished, I thought. But I changed my course and followed him. A few of the gliders were nearly on the ground by the time we reached the field. Captain Levi ran ahead to cover my parents, while they scrambled for the nearest trees. I heard him firing and cursing as his rounds glanced off a glider's nearly impenetrable skin. Feeling a hand on my shoulder, I turned around and saw Sarah's face lit up with the glow of glider headlights.

"Looking for this?" she asked, holding my satchel out to me. "I saw you running that way, and I heard the threats. I thought you might be needing it."

I took the satchel from her and rummaged through fatigues and T-shirts until I felt something steely. Then our eyes met.

"I didn't think you'd believe me after that scene I made by the pond."

"Your Mother filled me in," replied Sarah, keeping her voice low. She started for the ditch on the south side of the field, but had only taken three steps when she turned around, came back and kissed the cut on my cheek. "Let's go to Canada," she said.

Suddenly, the lights from the sky went black. Sarah dove in the ditch, and I heard Tiller shouting to me from a nearby tree.

"They've got their panels up! You can't see a blessed one of them!"

"There's enough moonlight. Watch for the grass waving. That's the turbines touching down," I shouted.

The rail felt awkward in my hand as I aimed it at the first disturbance in the field and fired. The explosion told me I had guessed right.

"What are you doing?" shouted Tiller.

"Getting us to Canada," I replied.

The flywheel revved back up to full speed and I fired again, ripping a wing off one glider and sending it through the windshield of another. With each ensuing bull's-eye, the transparent panels of VC's precious technobabies became visible with flames.

I turned the gun toward the sky and began to pick off incoming craft, the usual purr of their turbines giving them away before they reached the ground. Direct hits brought a high-pitched scream, as red, glowing fragments cascaded into the field. Through the smoke, I could barely make out Captain Levi dodging debris and firing over his shoulder. I think we all expected to see lasers criss-crossing the field by then. But the gliders were strangely passive.

"Why aren't they shooting back?" said Sarah.

"Maybe someone warned them not to," I replied. I glanced at Tiller who had crawled up through the long weeds, but his eyes were fixed on a particular burning glider and he seemed oblivious to my insinuation.

"Maybe there's no one in them," Peter said quietly.

Then, almost as quickly as they had come, the remaining gliders took on altitude.

"They're leaving," shouted Sarah.

"No way," said Tiller, looking up from reloading his weapon.

Sarah turned her ear upward. "It's true. They're going away."

Sure enough, the gliders purred over our heads, retreating from their downed comrades until the sound of them was only a whisper in the heavens. Except for the burning wreckage, the field was completely black again.

"We better check for survivors," said Tiller, starting in the direction of the flickering heaps. He took two steps and ran into Captain Levi.

"Let them burn," he said.

"But, sir—"

"Need I remind you of secondary discharge, Tolles?"

"No, sir."

"Then why don't you take care of our first priority, which is to find Nash and get him to safety as soon as possible. Last I saw, he and Ms. Nash were heading for those trees." Captain

Levi pointed in the direction of the woods on the east side of the field.

"Yes, sir," said Tiller, hurrying off toward the trees.

A lengthy search for my parents uncovered a twisted steering yoke, some landing gear, two seats, and a cow with its legs in the air. But August and Roberta Nash were nowhere in sight.

"What'll we do now, sir?" asked Tiller.

"We get this dog and pony show on the road before our clients get themselves killed," said Captain Levi, trembling with rage. "If they make it to deep woods country, it'll be impossible for us to find them."

"Impossible for your cronies to find them, too," said Peter suspiciously. He stood up and faced the Captain. "Seems like those gliders would have had a lot more success if they had been occupied. I don't recall seeing a single pilot in the ones John split open."

Captain Levi moved ominously toward Peter. "The smoke was thick. They might have ejected. Did you consider that?"

"Come to think of it, I didn't see any chutes either."

"That's what you get for thinking," said the captain. His right hand twitched at his side, then curled into a fist.

"Maybe so, but I think you knew they were coming. I think you sent for those gliders and requested automatons as pilots, in case you had to shoot one or two of them down yourself."

"You've been out in the sun too long, old friend. A man your age ought to be more careful about his health."

The older man did not back down.

"You've been planning to kill Mr. Nash ever since we left VC, haven't you?"

"You're a fool."

"No, Captain, it's you who has foolishly underestimated your traveling companions. You've taken great pains in demonstrating your heroism; too great, actually. It's not hard to detect a fake ambush."

In the firelight, Captain Levi's carotids were shining snakes slithering up into his sideburns. He looked around to see if the rest of us mirrored his outrage.

"I've checked the records," continued Peter. "It seems you've become quite a rich man with your little scheme."

"That's a lie," said Captain Levi, lunging toward Peter's throat. But he never reached his target.

The blast from the EM rail split the black pine behind them, sobering both men instantly. The sky was just beginning to lighten, but already the air felt thick and stifling.

"Get in the truck," I shouted.

Tiller stared at me, and in his eyes was mirrored every memory of our friendship. "What's going on, John?"

"Don't make it harder than it has to be," I replied.

"Listen, John—"

"Do as I say!"

Captain Levi's hand moved toward his holster, and I blew a deep trench at his feet. It was the only time I ever saw him gulp, and he did not reach for his gun again. Somehow I think he knew my mistrust had metastasized and he was no longer dealing with a man of composure. I led my prisoners at gunpoint across the road and into the back of the truck, where I made Captain Levi tie Tiller's hands behind his back and fasten him to the rails. I checked the knots for thoroughness.

"Now it's your turn," I said to Captain Levi, forcing him to spread his legs and lean against the truck's wooden slats. I cuffed his left wrist and yanked it behind his back. When I pulled his right wrist down, his face smacked hard against the slats.

I leaned my full weight against Levi's back. "You wanted me to choose sides and not waver. Well, I've done that, Captain. I'm on the *right* side."

"You're making a huge mistake," said Captain Levi.

"I'll take my chances," I replied. I fetched the orange identity bracelet from my pocket and Tiller's face went pale as the dawn.

"That's crazy," he warned.

"So is patricide," I said.

"Surely we can reason, John," said Captain Levi, beginning to bargain. He had never addressed me with anything besides my last name or a curse word. Of course, he had never felt what it was like to be a Long Shadow either. When he saw that I was through with reasoning, his eyes became wide and anxious.

"You've got to listen to me," he pleaded. "If there are other tag men out there, they'll get a lock on me. Those gliders will—"

"That's right, sir," I interrupted. "Those gliders will pick you up on screen and search until they find you. If I'm not mistaken, most of them still carry the old fast-pack conformal fuel tanks. They can track a man from here to hell."

"I'll be terminated."

"Isn't that what you had in mind for my father?" I said, clamping the bracelet just above the captain's handcuffs. It began to blink . . . *orange, off, orange, off.* Captain Levi let loose a string of curse words. He tried to butt me with his head and I sent him to the floor with three sharp jabs. Tiller gazed at his fallen captain, then on past him to where Mother, Peter, and Sarah stood in the yard.

"You've got the wrong guys," he said in a concealed voice. "Give me two minutes and I'll explain everything to you. Trust me."

I paused to remove the cuffs from Levi, who was obviously groggy. "There are limits to every friendship," I said. "It just took me a while to define mine."

Tiller watched me with wild, animal eyes as I backed toward the wall of fertilizer bags. "Captain Levi is your only ticket to Canada," he cried.

"Like I said, I'll take my chances."

"Aren't you going to cut me loose?"

"No, just the captain. I couldn't let a man be tracked with his hands behind his back."

A strange, clucking noise began in Tiller's throat and rose to a maniacal cackle. "You always were a softy, Johnny-boy. It'll be the death of you."

"I'm sure it will," I replied. I stood on the end of the bed and hoisted the bags back into place. When the next to last bag was in place, I peered inside the hole and saw Tiller's glistening eyes reaching out to hold me back.

"It's hot in here," he said beseechingly.

I stared at Tiller for a moment, silently severing a friendship.

"Good luck, Tiller," I said sadly, as I put the last bag in place.

15

"When it comes to taking care of the elderly, protocol is AWOL."
——From a bathroom stall on the Mission Mass

IT WAS HOT ENOUGH THAT LITTLE DIRT devils rose beneath our feet as we ran along the road. Peter believed we were fairly far south of Tonsus, perhaps a difficult day of hiking through the woods and then a circuitous route around Ely to avoid being spotted. My hope was that it would take awhile for the captain to come around and untie Tiller, and by that time we would be long gone. Nevertheless, I found myself looking back over my shoulder every few hundred yards.

At the point where our dirt road crossed the asphalt we stopped and gazed at two pairs of dusty footprints.

"They cut across that field catercorner," guessed Sarah, pointing to the other side of the intersection.

"They could belong to anyone," I cautioned.

Sarah shook her head and pointed to the larger of the two. "Press your fingers into this print, right to the bottom."

I knelt down and felt the print.

"Press on in there real good," said Sarah. "It's deeper in the heel."

"Compared to what?"

"Compared to this," she said, pointing to the other set of tracks.

I put my fingers in those, too, and declared simply that they were different.

"Different in *depth*," corrected Sarah, stooping down to get a closer look. "A man carries his weight on his heels, but a woman keeps her weight forward, particularly when she's in a hurry." She stared into the field. "They belong to your parents, all right. I hope they're okay."

"All will be well," promised Peter, hurrying off into the wheat to follow the trail.

We pressed northward, through stifling bogs and droning copses alive with flies. Once we thought we heard the sound of gliders overhead and then a dull explosion several minutes later, but we took no time to relish the implications. Indeed, Peter quickened our pace, prohibiting any irreverence for human life—even one as undeserving as Levi Coffin. By late afternoon, we crested the ridge to the south of the abbey and feasted on the view.

"Sweet Tonsus," exclaimed Peter, wiping sweat from his brow. "You're a sapphire on the bosom of the wild."

Sarah observed the architectural slash of bird's egg blue against an otherwise earthtoned backdrop. "It matches the sky," she said.

"On a good day," agreed Peter. "In bad weather, she sticks out like a sore thumb."

"Well, it's a good day today," a voice said from the porch of a nearby chapel.

I peered between saplings and saw Mother seated on a split-log bench, sipping from a cup of something that sent a continuous veil of steam before her face. She appeared dirty and haggard, but content with her fistful of warmth.

They're alive, I rejoiced inwardly as I rushed down the slope toward Mother.

"Care for some coffee?" she asked, raising her cup to salute us. "Brother Reed just made it fresh."

A man in drab monk's garb approached us with a tray. When he was near enough for me to take notice of his features,

I saw that only one of his hands extended below his sleeve. He was an amputee like Peter.

"Thank you, Brother Reed," said Peter cheerily. He helped himself to the coffee, while Reed steadied the tray on his semi-useful appendage. Sarah declined, saying she was too tired to even hoist a cup to her lips.

"Where's my father?" I asked, after hugging Mother.

She pointed across the clearing to a plain, stone dwelling.

"Is he asleep?" I asked.

"You be the judge," said Mother.

As if on cue, my father's sad voice rose through the roof of the dwelling and reverberated over the lake. "It was the duty of the government to help people live out a natural life span!" he wailed. "Not to help medically extend their lives beyond that point!"

"He's gotten worse since we arrived," said Mother, slumping in her chair.

"I'm going to see him," I announced, taking a step across the clearing. Peter moved so quickly to cut me off that his cup flew from its saucer and splintered on the hard ground.

"Coddling's not the cure," he said with uncharacteristic fierceness. He positioned his big frame between me and the stone dwelling. "Many a sick man on the verge of being healed has had his illness prolonged by a well-intentioned physician. Let him be, John," ordered Peter. "Let him suffer a little longer before you shove your oar in and muddy the water."

"But—"

"Let him be," repeated Peter. He pushed me aside gently and strode in the direction of Father's voice.

"Is anyone else alive around here?" Peter shouted over his shoulder to Brother Reed.

"We've all been praying since laud, sir," said Reed.

"Good for you," said Peter with a wave of his arm. "Go get Brother Riley and tell him to meet us in the meadow. I want to introduce a friend of ours to Fishback. I assume he's still alive?"

"As far as I know, sir," said Reed. "Actually, Brother Riley is still in the meadow with him. He's been doing what you told him to do since compline two days ago. He refuses to let anyone spell him."

"Is the creature less bloated?" asked Peter with concern.

"No, sir. He's as big as ever."

"Then we must get Mr. Nash to the meadow quickly! We don't have a moment to lose," ordered Peter, rushing to retrieve my father. The rest of us waited for him to return, and when he emerged from the stone building with Father leaning heavily on his shoulder, we followed them across the clearing and through a stand of white pine. Being downwind from Father's robe was ghastly, since it had not been washed for days.

In a meadow filled with lady's slipper, we came across a man and a wretched excuse for a horse. The man, whom I took to be Riley, was stumbling with weariness. The horse, if it could be called that, looked more like a bloated leather bag on sticks, and not a little uncomfortable.

"Hello, Brother Riley," said Peter, greeting his colleague with an embrace. "I don't know which of you looks worse for the wear. Is Fishback any better?"

"I'm afraid not, sir," said Riley. "I've been walking him since you left and nothing's changed. I'll walk him some more if you like."

"That won't be necessary. You've done your part. Go and get some sleep, brother."

Riley turned and addressed us all. "They get this way when they eat too much," he said apologetically. He wandered up the forested incline and just before he disappeared, I noticed that the right sleeve of his robe was also swinging loosely. The breeze from the lake made my shoulders shiver.

"All right, dear Fishback," said Peter, when Riley was out of sight. "You're bound to burst if we don't keep you moving. Give me a hand here, Judge."

Peter offered the halter rope to my father and everyone looked to see if he would take it. "Go ahead," he urged, when Father took a step backward. "Fishback's gentle. He's about a hundred years old. But if someone doesn't keep walking him, he'll die before the sun goes down. It won't be a pretty sight." Peter placed the rope in Dad's hands. "I've got things to do," he said to Mother, who seemed to understand what he meant immediately.

"Do you need any help?" she asked.

"No. There are just some last minute details and calculations to take care of. Someone still needs to get word to our men on the border about the exact time of our arrival. As far as August goes, we'll make the switch tonight when the doctor gets here."

The words *switch* and *doctor* shot like arrows through my heart, and I struggled to suppress my suspicion.

"Can't he get here any sooner?" asked Mother anxiously. Mother glanced uneasily around at the woods as if she suspected something evil was watching her from the undergrowth.

"Captain Levi is probably dead," said Peter somberly, when he noticed Mother's fear. Then he turned to my father. "And if you don't start walking that horse, brother, he's going to end up just like Captain Levi."

Father gripped the halter and started off through the meadow.

"That's better," called Peter. "And don't you dare let him eat another bite of grass."

"Isn't there anything we can do to speed things up?" I asked.

Peter shook his head. "It's a matter of patience now," he said. "We're at the mercy of the doctor's schedule. He said he'd be here as soon as he could. You two are free to rest or explore if you like," he added, nodding at Sarah and me. "Don't wander too far, though. I'm not so sure we've heard the last of VC on this mission. We'll be shoving off to meet the mounties as soon as our canoes are loaded on the racks and the boats are packed."

"Uh . . . is there a place for us to wash our clothes?" I asked, remembering that all our clean things were miles south in the truck.

"We've got an ancient machine and dryer below my quarters, if you don't mind the surroundings. It's a typical basement. Nothing fancy . . . and a little damp. We keep it clean, though."

I remembered Peter's basement from the recording, and had built it in my mind to be an immense dungeon. It turned out to be as he suggested, sparse but adequate. The washing machine was more ancient than I expected; a broad metal basin with corrugated sides sat in the corner next to an open window well, which I quickly recognized to be the "dryer."

"I think he said his quarters are right above this room," I said, glancing back up the stairs. "It'll be nice to know exactly where to find him in the night—if we have any trouble, that is. By the way, do you have any idea what Peter meant by getting word to *our men* on the border?"

Sarah shrugged and filled the basin with water from a nearby pitcher. "I suppose he has operatives just about anywhere," she said, as she began to grate a pair of jeans along the sides of the basin.

I thought of my father starting over in Canada. "Over the lake, across the border and he's free," I said wistfully.

Sarah nodded. "I'd give anything if I knew that tomorrow was going to change that easily for me." She stopped grating and stared at her rippled reflection. "My tomorrows are always so dreadful."

"Tomorrow will be okay," I said, trying to sound positive. I had become vaguely aware of a light coming from underneath a doorway down a dark hall and to the left. "Did you ever receive that information from your source at National?"

"This morning, while we were still in the woods," said Sarah. "I kept it in my satchel—"

"Why didn't you show it to me then?"

"I didn't know if you trusted Peter."

"Let me see it," I said eagerly.

Sarah wiped her hands on her hips and pulled a crinkled list from her shirt pocket. "Maybe you can make something of it," she said, handing me the list.

I scanned it for the obvious and found nothing particularly alarming. But on a second pass, I caught my breath and remembered Mother's words. *With enough hard evidence this could be proved.*

"You received this over integrated services?" I asked.

"Private communiqué through the PowerBook," said Sarah. "I didn't want to risk interception."

"Do you realize what we have here?"

"It looks like a bunch of guys from the EPA and the Justice Department got too close to VC's secret."

"And now they're a bunch of dead guys," I whispered.

A door closed upstairs, causing us both to jump.

"I've never been a big fan of the EPA," I whispered. "But I don't dislike them enough to want them killed."

"Someone did," said Sarah.

We traced the path of footsteps across the ceiling, until they came to a halt at the top of the stairs.

"Anybody home?" came Peter's voice.

I took a deep breath to make sure I didn't sound nervous. "Just finishing our laundry," I answered.

"Well, that didn't take long," said Peter. "By the way, before you head back to your cell, I want you to stop by my garden on the south side of the building. You know those prizewinning tulips I told you I was concerned about?"

Without giving an answer, I glanced at Sarah.

"Hello?" said Peter.

"Yes, I remember you mentioning them," I called.

"Well, they'll look good as new once I've turned a little fertilizer into the soil."

"I guess you were concerned for nothing."

"Guess so."

The footsteps faded back across the floor and out of the cottage. Sarah and I quickly hung our clothes by the window and made our way anxiously to Peter's garden. He was ankle-deep in black dirt when we found him. All around him swayed the bulbous heads of tulips bursting with color.

"Look at the way they dance in the wind," he said, pointing to his flowers. "If I didn't know any better, I'd say they were almost human. VC'd be mad as hornets if they knew I wasted fertilizer on flowers." Peter glanced at me sideways. "They send it by the truckload for the wheat, but I've never been inclined to use it the way they want me to."

"Is the doctor here yet?" I interjected.

Peter looked up from his work. "You seem awfully impatient about that topic."

"Maybe that's because you don't seem impatient *enough*," I blurted.

Peter stood and squared his shoulders toward me. "And maybe that's because you want to know more than you should."

Sarah fidgeted. "Excuse me. I think I'll get my clothes from the window well. I don't want to forget them in the morning."

"And I'm going to bed," I said angrily. I announced my approval of Peter's garden, then headed to my cell.

Even though the water was only lukewarm at Tonsus, it felt good to finally take a shower. I watched a week's worth of grime form little chocolate-colored puddles at my feet before disappearing down the drain. On the other side of the wall, Sarah was showering too. I envisioned her standing under the nozzle on her one good leg, her prosthesis waiting for her on a nearby bench. I threw my head back in the spray and let the soap cascade from my hair. It wasn't fair. We were young and without say when the rules were made by Vivi-Natal. What if Sarah and I could never be together? What if I never saw her again after we freed my father?

Father!

I rinsed feverishly, dressed again and raced into the evening with my hair still dripping. Down amongst the pine and larkspur I crashed, through the lady's slipper, over low-lying blueberry and pin cherry and service berry and finally out upon the open meadow.

"Anybody here?" I cried in a thunderous whisper.

A moan rose from the far edge of the meadow and I stumbled in that direction across a tangle of sedge.

"Dad?"

The moans became intelligible.

"You were an old, old horse," came a voice from the tall grass.

I got on my hands and knees and followed the sound of it.

"I did what I could, didn't I?"

"Is that you, Dad?"

The voice continued, detached and monotone. "I walked you just like Peter said. Walked you fast. Walked you slow. It wasn't my fault you picked tonight to die."

I caught a sudden whiff of foul flesh and through the sedge I saw my father sitting naked from the waist up, staring at a grotesque shape in front of him.

"All you had to do was walk a little faster," Dad whimpered. "You could've made it through the night. You could've walked a little faster, that's all, not even a trot. No one asked you for a trot. You could've taken it easy if you wanted to. But no! You had to do things your own way."

Dad began to sob and under a pregnant moon I saw deep cuts on his back and shoulders. On closer look, I recognized they weren't cuts at all, but shiny, fibrous scars.

"You had to pop like a balloon!" cried Dad, falling forward onto the damp, lifeless mass. He pounded his fists against what was left of the horse and lay facedown, blubbering.

I had no luck drawing Dad back to reality. It was all I could do to collect his sweaty robe from the grass and drag him back up the hill to civilization. In the dull light of our cell, I found that his robe was lined with sharp wire and broken glass. How horrible it must have been for my father, all those years thinking he could bleed his guilt away. I found a T-shirt still moist from the laundry and sponged the filth from Dad as best I could, trying to ignore the image of Peter Edmunds that kept creeping into my brain.

Why did he make him walk that stupid horse? I thought, as I tucked Dad into his sleeping bag and lay down next to him. *It seems like a man of the cloth ought to have more sense than to torment a harmless Long Shadow.*

It was no use trying to sleep after what I'd seen. Fishback's belly, slick and grinning, tormented me almost as much as the mosquitoes, who were legion by the time the breeze died down. When they found the hole in the screen next to my cot they organized their assault and came through single file.

"Where are you going?" asked Sarah when she saw me fling back the covers and sit up on the side of my cot.

"Out," I said.

Sarah's corner of the cell became silent for a minute or two. Then I heard her stirring again and in a moment I felt her warm fingers groping for my mine.

When she found my hand, she clung to it tightly, and the harder she squeezed the more I sensed a wave of terror spreading from her brain, across a network of synapses, down her arm, through her fingertips, and straight to my heart, where her helplessness registered and I drew her to my chest. She was shaking like a frightened child.

"Check his basement again," she said.

"What's wrong? Did you see something when you went back for your things?"

Sarah nodded and I hugged her tighter. Suddenly, she reeled back from me. What little moonlight shone through the screen revealed that her eyes were wild with fright.

"Let's get out of this place right now and never look back."

"But the doctor—"

"There's a jar down there," said Sarah. Her lips parted as if some other revelation, too awful for words, was trying to escape. When nothing came out, she reached into her pocket and handed me an object that was warm and glowing. It was another termination bracelet, like the one I had clamped on Levi.

"When was your uncle's birthday?" she asked in a quavering voice.

I had to think for a moment. "December third," I said at last.

Sarah pointed to the bracelet and I held it closer for inspection. Etched on the inside circumference were three words that gouged a valley through the middle of my heart: AMES NASH, T-9/3.

'*Weather gets some. Wolves get others.*' *He knew all along my uncle had died.* "All lies," I whispered, hypnotized by the glowing bracelet.

"Let's get out of here," repeated Sarah.

Blind rage narrowed my vision until all I could see was an image of me and my father, holding the world at bay, paddling helter-skelter for the border.

"I've got a job to finish," I said, feeling beneath my cot for the satchel and the EM rail. Down through wilted belongings I plunged my fingers, until I came to the bottom and drew my breath in sharply.

"It's gone," I exclaimed, standing to retrace my steps. *But it can't be.* "I . . . I shot the ground at his feet . . . I made them get in the truck . . . the Captain tied Tiller . . . I put the handcuffs on the captain. I—"

"You set it down when you put the bracelet on Levi," said Sarah suddenly. She looked up at me and I closed my eyes, trying to block out the sickening truth about my stupidity. I felt her fingers again, intertwining with my own.

"John?" she said, nestling her head beneath my chin.

"What?"

"Promise you'll come back from that basement."

I hesitated for a moment, the fitful stirrings of a nearby sleeper causing me to feel more satisfactorily alone with the woman of my dreams.

"I'll be back," I said, kissing the top of her head ever so lightly. Then I moved out silently onto the grounds of Tonsus Abbey and lost myself in the deepening shadows.

16

"*Life is a precious commodity; so precious that it ought to be rationed.*"

—Levi Coffin

THE DISTANCE TO PETER'S COTTAGE FROM our cell was rather short if traveled by a straight line. By a serpentine one it was tedious. I hugged the shadows next to the brothers' dormitory, belly-crawling in the bushes as quiet as a cat. Then a dash to a stand of poplar got me clear of the light cast through their windows. The remaining thirty yards to his door were a cinch. When I tried the doorknob and found it unlocked, my hand was trembling with adrenaline. With a nudge of my shoulder, I entered Peter's private domain.

Across the musty study, past the kitchen and the sonorous sounds of Peter's bedroom I tiptoed. If he heard me at all he never let on, though I made a noticeable racket opening his basement door. The stairs were creakier than I had remembered them. One produced such a long, mournful complaint that I had to shift my weight and freeze for several moments to be certain no one was stirring above me. Then eight more stairs and I was at the bottom.

Ahead in the basement hallway, pale, yellow light showed from under a door. Without a sound I walked quickly to it, turned the knob and peered through a crack into a tiny room.

Formaldehyde.

The odor immediately reminded me why I have always hated laboratories with their frogs in jars, cats in closets hung up like dry-cleaning, Mr. Bones-on-a-pole dressed in lab coat and scrubs.

The room had the feel of a mausoleum. Being below ground it had an earthworm smell to go along with the stench of preservative. When I shone my light on the wall, I saw signs of prior flooding. Ruddy stains came in at the window and ran like blood down the cement walls nearly to the floor. A fire extinguisher conveniently hid one stain, while over another a poster of Albert Einstein had been plastered. Above a small desk hung a portrait of Peter that caught my eye.

Even on canvas the man is imposing, I thought.

I took the portrait down from the wall, turned it over and studied the writing on the back. It was a list of dates:

Born 11 October 1938—Died 8 December 2014.

Born 8 December 2014—Died 21 June.

Born 21 June 2014—Died 31 July 2030.

Born 3 December 2030—.

I turned the picture over again and checked to see if there had been more than one person in it. As I had thought, there was only one.

Nobody lives more than once, I thought as I placed the picture back on the wall and nervously searched the contents of the desk. I found them to be no more incriminating than my own desk back home. Finally, I turned my light on the opposite wall and felt the immediate desire to retch. From ceiling to floor were two steel shelves overflowing with bottles of sodium pentothal, to the right of which I spied a jar of formaldehyde with the hand of an adult male floating grotesquely inside. The imprint of a termination bracelet still encircled its wrist.

"Did you find what you expected?" came a sudden voice behind me.

I wheeled around to see Peter in the doorway, blocking out its space with his thick body.

"I was looking for my jeans," I said quickly. "I think I left them when I was doing laundry."

"So what are you doing in *this* room?" asked Peter. "The wash basin's still where you left it this afternoon."

I raced to invent something. "I . . . I was looking for a bathroom. I saw the light coming from under the door there."

Peter grinned and shook his head. "You think very well on your feet, brother John."

"I should be going," I said, taking a step toward the door.

Peter put his big forearm on the door frame and barred my exit.

"I can't help wondering if you looked on the back of the portrait," he said, pointing to the wall above the desk. "Your reaction to it is particularly important to me."

"I'd like to get to bed, sir," I said.

"Nonsense," said Peter, herding me toward the picture. "I'll only take a minute of your time."

Before I knew it I was holding the portrait of Peter in my trembling hands, staring again at the list of dates.

"Read them," ordered Peter.

In horror I mumbled, "October eleventh—"

"Louder," he said.

"October eleventh, December eighth, June twenty-first. This can't be."

"What's the matter, John? Don't you believe there's a time to die for everyone?"

I glanced at the sodium pentothal. "You never intended to get my father to Canada, did you?" I said, inching my foot toward the door.

"So what do you think of me now?" Peter asked. "Am I one of them? Or am I one of you? It's hard to trust people nowadays, isn't it? Did you ever think of how hard it's been for me to trust you? Anyone could say they were sympathetic to the Shadow Train. Take the captain, for instance."

Slowly, I moved away from the desk. "What about him?"

"He's never really been on board," said Peter. He glanced at the sodium pentothal then back at me. "I don't think he'd be able to stomach some of our policies and procedures."

"It must take a lot of gall to call yourself a holy man," I said. Peter shrugged and stared at me.

"Well, I know what those dates mean on the back of your picture. You don't help Long Shadows get to Canada—you kill them."

"Would you like me to explain about the hand in the jar?" asked Peter.

"You're evil," I stated.

"Think what you must," replied Peter. As he moved to hang the picture back on the wall I bolted out of the room.

"You'll never get across the border without me," shouted Peter, as I careened up the dark hallway. "Do you hear me, John? There's only a small window of time when the shift is taken over by our people and—John? JOHN?!"

Our people, our people.

I had long ago lost the ability to discern the difference between "our people" and the enemy. Maybe there was no difference. I ran frantically back to the cell.

"Sarah," I whispered harshly.

There was no answer.

I tripped over bodies in sleeping bags, found my father, then recognized it was someone else, then found him again in another bag and shook him forcefully.

"Come on," I breathed into his ear. "Wake up. Pleeease, wake up."

My father gave a startled snort. "What?" he said, drawing his hands up in fright.

"You're coming with me," I asserted. "Grab a warm coat and as little of your things as possible. I'll explain everything when we're on the water."

"On the water?"

"Don't ask! Just move!"

Across the blue lawn and to the beach we ran, where a dark silhouette bumped lazily against the decomposing dock. I had hoped for something small and fast, like a waterskid, but the smell of fuel confirmed my fears that Tonsus was stocked only with fifty-horsepower relics from the past. Five minutes had passed since Peter had discovered me in his lab, and I was wondering why he had not given chase.

"Pitch your gear in the back," I commanded, noting that one of the brothers had already lashed two canoes to the boat's rack. "I'll unhook the bow rope. You get the stern. I hope the running lights are decent. Hurry up. Get in."

Father set our packs next to a mound of canvas tarp, then sat down obediently on the boat's middle bench.

"Hang on to your hat and turn your collar up too," I said. "It's going to get cold once we're up to speed."

Father did as he was told and it dawned on me how child-like he had become. I wondered for the first time about his ability to survive in Canada. It is one thing to be an adult in a strange land; it is quite another to be a little boy faced with a freedom noncommensurate to his capacity to enjoy it. In his eyes I could see that guilt and medication had completely destroyed that capacity.

"Are you feeling okay?" I asked.

"A-okay," he replied.

"You're sure you're comfortable?"

Father rearranged himself on the cold, metal bench and gave me a thumbs-up, the horror of Fishback already a distant moodswing. "Have I mentioned I was a centrist?" he said, with his feet together and his hands folded in his lap.

My heart sank as I cranked the motor and pulled away from the dock, going slow enough to avoid waking anybody.

"Are you a centrist?" asked Father in his usual obsessive manner.

"No, my occupation pretty much rules out fence-sitting," I replied.

"What do you do for a living, mister?" asked Father suddenly, when we were out past the NO WAKE buoys. The question made my stomach turn.

"I'm a tag man," I said after a moment.

Except for the low hum of the motor and the water slapping playfully against the sides of the transport, there was not another sound on Moose Lake.

"Are you going to kill me?" asked Father, in the same way a child might inquire about a spanking.

I glanced at him and saw that his brow was knotted in fear. "I'm taking you home," I said.

"To Rivendale?"

"Not exactly."

Father's face relaxed. "We're taken care of at Rivendale," he said. "There's a nice man who works at the main desk. He comes to my room every night to get me for the game shows. You remind me a lot of him."

"Thanks," I said. "But there are no games tonight."

"That's okay. A lot of times the shows get canceled. Then I usually just do calisthenics or work on crafts or—"

"How many times do you have to be told!" I shouted, hitting the kill switch and allowing the boat to drift across the smooth, dark surface of the lake. "This is *not* Rivendale and there are *no* orderlies here and I am *not* going to kill you."

"Then what are we doing?" asked Father.

"We are trying to keep you alive!"

Father winced. Off in the distance a bull moose bellowed.

"I have waited all my life to do the kinds of things fathers and sons do," I said. "Now, here we are finally in a boat on a lake, and all you can talk about is that stupid, stupid mental hospital."

"I can talk about other things," said Father quietly.

"Like what? Like being a centrist? That would be new and exciting."

"I had a birthday recently," said Father simply.

I buried my face in my hands. "That's great. Happy birthday."

As if a voice had shouted to him from across the lake, my father jerked his chin up. "I remember another birthday, too," he said, closing his eyes. He stretched out his hand to take hold of the memory. "It was a nice morning. The air was . . . the air was sweet and thick."

"*He used to take whole days off from work, just to celebrate your birthdays,*" came Mother's words in the transport. I sat up a little straighter and stared at him.

"I had been cooped up in the library for the better part of the winter," he continued. "And it had been a long time since I'd seen—" For a moment Father looked at me and I thought he was going to say my name. Instead, he closed his eyes again and returned to the beginning of the story, as if he had come to this point in the memory many times before and could not bring himself to admit that I had been part of his past.

"The air was sweet and thick," he said. "Now, where could that have been?"

"Springtime in Washington," I murmured.

Something in the phrase drew another wince from Father and he sucked in a sharp breath. "Is that a place where flowers grow in the trees?" he asked.

"Every April," I replied. "Washington's known for its cherry blossoms."

Father sighed and kept his eyes closed. "It looked like snow in the branches. I can see it as clearly as if it were yesterday. And . . . and there was a little boy standing underneath those branches . . . a little boy with a baseball bat. He couldn't have been much more than—"

"Five," I said, the automatic quality of my answer setting us both back for a moment.

Father nodded. "I believe you're right," he agreed. "It was a birthday party for the happiest little five-year-old I have ever known."

"I used to be happy," I whispered. A deep longing welled up inside of me. "Do you remember anything else about the party?"

Father cocked his head sideways. "There was a paddleboat. I think it was a yellow one."

"Yellow and blue," I corrected him.

"I remember there were two of us in the boat," said Father, smiling. "It was me and the boy with the baseball bat. We went up and down the lake all day, until the water was orange from the sun. I never laughed so hard in my life."

"You told him you loved him, too," I inserted, remembering suddenly.

"I did?"

"Yes, you did. And you hugged him, too, and told him you were proud to be his father."

"Hmm," said Father. "Maybe I did. I don't actually recall it. But if you insist."

I shifted to the edge of my seat so that he could see my face clearly.

"Dad?" I said.

He opened his eyes and looked at me.

"It's me, Dad," I said. "I'm the boy with the baseball bat."

Father squinted and in the moonlight I could tell that he was working hard to keep some foundational truth pressed down inside his soul.

"No," he said, shaking his head. "The boy in the boat had smoother skin than yours and he smiled a lot."

"Don't you understand?" I said, seizing him firmly by the upper arms and pulling his face close to mine. "I *used* to be that boy, but I grew up."

Father chuckled softly. "Mister, you've got some imagination, whoever you are."

"I'm your son!" I shouted.

Father took hold of my hands and pried them from his arms. "No son of mine would be a tag man," he said bluntly.

I slumped back against the steering wheel and made one last, forlorn attempt at winning him back to me. "I am not a tag man anymore," I said.

Suddenly, there was a rustle and a rocking of the boat and the heap of canvas tarp stood up and cast itself into the water, revealing Captain Levi and Tiller. I reached for my gun, but before I could draw it I heard the sound of a hammer cocking and I looked back at Tiller. He was pointing the EM rail straight at me.

"Come now, John," said Captain Levi. "Surely you don't want to retire just when your future at VC is looking so bright."

I spun around and cranked the ignition key. Tiller lunged forward and caught my arm before I could jam the throttle down. He pressed the rail's muzzle against my neck to let me know he was serious.

"I wouldn't do that if I were you," he said.

I glanced over my shoulder and saw Father lying facedown on the bottom of the boat. Captain Levi's foot was on his back.

"Drive as slow as this rig can go," ordered the captain. "We've got plenty of time to kill before the good guys report for duty. I can't wait to see the look on their faces when I tell those pseudo guards they're under arrest for impersonation of an officer. They have no idea how long I've been onto their little scheme."

Anger filled my gullet. "You lying—"

"Now, now," interrupted Captain Levi. "There's no need for character assassination. I never pretended to be anything I wasn't. Besides, you made a nice enough living under me. You ought to be thankful you had a job."

Captain Levi and Tiller exchanged a haughty glance.

"By the way, John," said the captain. "You were so nice to leave the keys in the truck, not to mention the EM rail. However, that really was a terrible trick you played on me. Imagine, turning your own superior officer loose to be hunted like an animal. I was lucky I had taken the time to sharpen my pocket knife last week." At that, Captain Levi raised his arm, allowing his jacket sleeve to slide down and expose a thick, red scar around his wrist. "The gliders went for the bracelet like vultures on roadkill."

I thought back to the explosion we had heard in the woods.

"Naturally, we hurried back to the truck as fast as possible and Tiller drove me to Ely, where I had this neanderthalic but adequate piece of surgery performed on me." He held up his hand and wiggled his fingers. "See. Everything still works. Anyway, thanks for leaving the keys and rail gun for us. Those were either gross oversights on your part, or you are terribly generous to your enemies."

"Why all the acting?" I asked. "Why didn't you just come out and admit both of you were still with VC?"

Captain Levi took his foot off Father, but kept Old Stopper aimed at his back. "Oh, it wasn't all acting," he replied. "I assure you some of the Shadow Train players were as real as real can be. Of course, I'll never tell which ones were and which ones weren't. But I can say that from the start our goals never wavered."

"Besides cold-blooded murder, what are your goals?" I asked.

"To find out how things are run in the underground," chimed Tiller.

"You see, John," said Captain Levi. "Tonsus is just one of twenty government farms that VC suspects of running an underground railroad for Long Shadows. We'll bring them all down, eventually. I only regret that our work requires us to destroy some magnificent examples of monasticism along the way."

I thought immediately of Sarah and Mom. "What are you going to do with Tonsus?" I asked angrily.

Captain Levi read my thoughts. "Don't worry. It's highly possible that everyone has smelled the fumes by now and gotten to safety before Tiller's little device is detonated. It certainly will be a shame if innocent lives are lost, isn't that right, Tiller?" he said, nodding at my former friend.

Tiller produced a flat, palm-sized device and without a word, pressed a button on its top. Instantly, the stars above the trees to the south of us were blotted out by a tremendous burst of light. A moment later, the blast reached our ears, accompanied by screams and indistinguishable figures running ablaze amidst the trees, and finally, the most bizarre feature of those scant seconds—Tiller Tolles aiming the rail gun at his boss, and Captain Levi unable to utter a single intelligible word. For a moment, the captain stood with his mouth wide open and his eyes thoroughly bewildered. Then Tiller triggered the power and, with a mighty crash, Captain Levi fell to the floor of the boat. The holocaust was complete.

"Do you think I enjoy this?" said Tiller, when he saw me staring at the great, sucking wound in Captain Levi's chest.

I opened my mouth to speak but he aimed the rail at me to silence my reply.

"Do you think I planned it this way?" he shouted.

"What way are you talking about?" I said, eyeing the gun.

Tiller's brow was slick with sweat. "I like you, John," he said, almost mechanically. "I've always liked you."

"I like you, too," I said.

"But you have no idea how it feels to have a baby on the way and a wife who depends on you. I told you about the diapers, didn't I?"

Father was still as stone during all this. I tried to remain calm, but I was sure Tiller sensed my fear. "Why don't we talk about it?" I said weakly.

"Then there's baby food and immunizations and clothes and—"

"Tiller," I began.

"Shut up!" Tiller's voice echoed until the bigness of the lake swallowed it up and even his hysteria seemed small and insignificant. Father coughed and shifted ever so slightly.

"He was my tag all along," said Tiller.

"Who was?"

"Your father."

Suddenly every event of the last twelve days shifted in my mind, took on different light, exhibited never before noticed facets of a newly cut diamond and I finally accepted what I had been trying to deny all along. Tiller Tolles was not just under stress. He had known what he was going to do for a long, long time. He had planned years ago to betray a friend in order to gain promotion in VC.

"He was the old assignment you were talking about that day in the locker room, wasn't he?" I said.

"That's very perceptive of you," said Tiller, waving the rail in my direction.

I glanced at the water, considering how far I would get if I suddenly rocked the boat and swam for shore, but the thought of leaving Father was repugnant. "Why don't you just shoot us now and get it over with?" I said angrily.

"Who would drive me to the border, then?" said Tiller. "Look here, John—" He fumbled with a series of beginnings, finally settling on one. "I'll split the commission with you if you'll see things my way," he said, somewhat pleading.

"No thanks," I said. "I've had a change of heart since I've been on this trip."

"It's a lot of money. I'm sure you'd be comfortable for a long, long time."

"Not interested."

"Suit yourself," said Tiller. "I hope you don't take it personally when I have to kill you. You've been the best friend a guy could ever have. Now get moving."

It was a long, slow passage to the portage. The running lights cast only enough glow on the water for me to avoid treacherous rocks and root wads. By the time we reached the portage, the sun was coming up over the trees. At the beach we unloaded our things quickly. I looked at the tragic figure of

Captain Levi, his eyes wide open like the crater in his chest, then I started up the path. Overhead, I heard the whir of a glider coming in for a landing and I wondered if, before his death, Captain Levi had notified VC Midwest to send one to retrieve my father's body. Behind me Tiller barked orders.

"Leave the cushions, old man!"

He's going to kill us as soon as we reach the other side of the portage, I thought

At a turn in the path, I quickened my pace to put some distance between Tiller and me. Ahead, I saw the beach and the U.S. ranger's cabin, just as Captain Levi had described it. Across a wide inlet, where the waterfall from Moose cascaded down into Birke Lake, was the Canadian headquarters. A mountie sat on the porch, whittling something, unaware that American blood was about to be spilled on Canadian soil.

On the beach, four border guards loitered in thick fatigues. Their faces were red with sunburn and I wondered if there ever was any truth to the story about Shadow Train conductors posing as guards. A team of dogs, mostly Dobermans, slept in the sand at their feet.

So this is how it ends. Tiller tells them Dad is a runner and I'm a traitor . . . I'm shot on sight . . . Dad is flown back to VC Midwest, where he's terminated on VOX . . . and Tiller collects the money.

Overhead a loon laughed at my deductions.

They were all in it together, I thought. *That is, until the greed set in and they began to kill each other.* Then a terrible thought came crashing down around me. *There never was a Shadow Train. Every single one of them was a phony—Mother, Peter . . . Sarah?*

With a burst of rage, I bolted into the woods. The hollow thud of fiberglass on tree roots drew Tiller in a hurry. I could hear him cursing as he crashed through the undergrowth behind me. At all costs I would make it across that inlet, past the guards, over the two hundred yards of sand that sloped up to the porch where the unsuspecting mountie enjoyed the morning. And there I would be free. If only I could get to that opening in the trees ahead. To the left of the trail I was blazing, a blast from Tiller's rail cut a jack pine clean in half and exploded in the sand beyond the opening.

"You might as well give up!" shouted Tiller. He was in excellent shape and would be upon me in a matter of seconds.

At the sound of shots, the border guards came to life. I had reached the opening in the trees and could see them far down the beach, rousing the dogs, blowing their whistles, kicking up the sand as they ran in our direction. I had no idea what had become of Father. My only hope was that in Tiller's absence he would have the presence of mind to make his own escape. When I reached the beach I cut sharply to my right and veered toward the inlet. In half a dozen steps I was up to my knees in water. Another blast from the rail sent a plume of spray into the air.

The dogs were in full stride by now. The mountie, having decided that something was about to disturb his morning whether he liked it or not, had risen from his chair and was standing on the edge of the porch. Tiller fired again. Again he missed, which confirmed what I had feared all along—that he was toying with me, and that eventually he would grow tired of the game. My only chance was to duck back into the trees and circle around behind the mountie's cabin. As I ran, I felt the warm radiation of Uncle Ames's identification bracelet in my pocket and I remembered Captain Levi's chilling description during basic training of a dog's ability to track an ID bracelet's scent.

The moment I reached the woods I saw that I had made a terrible mistake. An outcropping of stone jutted up where I had hoped for passage into camouflage, its lichen-covered surface so slick with recent rain that scaling it would have been impossible. To its right and left were brambles too thick for human navigation. At its base were several cords of wood, stacked and ready for the next winter.

"Freeze!" shouted Tiller, as I dove behind the logs. On his heels, the dogs came leaping into the little clearing. With a curt command he held them at bay so he could have the pleasure of handling me himself.

"If you had waited a few more weeks, I could have let you in on our little secret and we both could have made a fortune," he said. The rail's flywheel filled the air with stench, and with a deafening roar, Tiller blasted off a half rick of lumber.

"I don't want to kill you," Tiller continued. "In a minute, those border boys will be here. It's up to you whether they find you dead or alive."

"What does it matter, just as long as you get paid?" I shouted.

"Come on, John," laughed Tiller. "My friends are more important than my paycheck."

"Was Captain Levi your friend, too?"

"I told you the tag was mine from the beginning," said Tiller angrily. He triggered the power once more and logs went flying from the other end of the pile. There was no longer any reason to pretend that I was safe behind my flimsy barricade, so I stood up with both hands in my pockets. The dogs went crazy when they saw me.

"I can't hold them back forever," said Tiller.

"I haven't asked you to," I answered. "Turn them loose and your job will be done."

"Don't you think you've taken this Shadow Train thing a bit too seriously?"

"I believed you when you said you had a conscience."

"I'm sorry I led you to believe that," said Tiller. "The fact is, I'm fairly remorseless over taking life from people who value it so little."

"You still march lockstep with the party line, don't you?" I asked.

"Meaning?"

"Meaning you use whatever logic is available to justify the abortion-euthanasia dichotomy."

"I see," said Tiller, aware that I was stalling, but too curious to change the subject. "You think I hold that our generation, and every generation that follows us, has the right to take out our collective angst on our parents, because they practiced reproductive contraception. Is that it?"

"That's it."

"Well, you're absolutely right. Skin for skin is the way of the world. You're a fool to try to change things, John. But you're a good tag. And my friend. Come back with me to VC. We'll grow old together."

"I'd rather die young," I replied.

Tiller's eyes narrowed and I saw that same twitch I'd seen in the sauna. "So long, John," he said, releasing the dogs with another command.

As they lunged forward, I snatched the bracelet from my pocket and flung it over their heads. Instinctively, Tiller caught it just as the lead dog reversed his course. The last I saw of his face intact were two wide, staring eyes and a mouth as round as any Long Shadow's at the point of termination.

From where I stood in the clearing, I could see the border guards running toward me. A few of the dogs were no longer in a frenzy. Two of them chased their tails playfully. Around and around on the moist undergrowth they whirled, until their mouths were white and shiny, and the blood on their chests mingled with their saliva. They had lost interest in Tiller after the initial lunge, and allowed the other six to drag his form into the woods to quarrel over the leftovers. Then I picked up the EM rail where Tiller had dropped it, and turned to face my captors. No doubt, he had told them I was a traitor tag man.

The first guard to arrive at the clearing was an enormous man, purple and puffing from the run. On his heels were three others of varying stature and states of exhaustion. It was obvious their jobs were void of strenuous exercise, which did not surprise me since the average border skirmish is usually settled with a gun.

"Are you okay, pal?" the first one asked, glancing at the EM in my hand.

"Yeah . . . sure," I replied, astonished that he had not already drawn his weapon. The other men had filed past us into the woods. I could hear them gagging at the grisly sight that greeted them.

"We saw you running and figured you had your hands full. Man, he was a fast customer. I don't think I've ever seen a guy move that quickly. They must really be getting 'em in shape nowadays at Midwest."

Suddenly, it occurred to me that there was a case of mistaken identity. "Of course," I said, nodding agreeably. "You were talking about, I mean, he certainly must have been in terrific shape."

"What I can't figure out is why guys like him don't just earn their quotas and be happy about what they have. I mean, look at him. He's a mess."

I turned around and saw the other men emerging from the woods, bearing a burden that appeared only slightly human. I made the mistake of averting my eyes. Luckily the guard with whom I had been talking was too engrossed with the scene to notice my nonprofessional behavior. He gave a sharp whistle and all eight dogs came bounding to his side.

"Well, we'll just get this one bagged up, then it's back to the post," he said. "Not that I think we're going to miss anything by being gone for a few minutes. We live for excitement like this, if you know what I mean."

"Excuse me," I said. "Did you happen to notice the other gentleman that he—that I had custody of?"

"You mean the man with the cut-up back?" said the guard.

"Right."

"Yeah, we met him and your two other associates who were tracking him in the glider."

I remembered hearing one overhead when we arrived at the beach. "Associates?"

"Don't act humble, pal," said the border guard. "They're a couple of real babes. Hey, with occupational hazards like that, a guy might even start looking forward to Monday mornings. I wouldn't mind trading places with you, myself."

"Did they happen to tell you anything about our assignment?" I asked hurriedly.

"Just the usual. They said the man with the cut-up back used to be some sort of important judge. Said he decided to go against the greatest good and just took off."

I watched as Tiller was slipped into a bag. "What about the, er, the body?" I asked.

"Who? Mr. Dog-food-for-brains?" The guard scratched his sun-reddened nose. "Oh, yeah. The older broad said he was the judge's son. I think they said his name was John."

"John," I repeated.

"Uh-hm. She said something about him being a tag man who finally cracked. You know, for the life of me I can't figure out why anyone in the tags would give up such a sweetheart deal. I mean, even if it was for my own parent's sake, you wouldn't find me taking a chance on receiving a T-date. No sir-ee, I aim to stay alive as long as I can make my quotas."

My knees felt suddenly feeble and I leaned against a birch tree.

"Whoa now," said the guard. "What's wrong, buddy? You okay?"

I nodded weakly, and for the first time the guard looked at me with suspicion. "By the way, what's your name?"

I formed a reply on my lips, but the words wouldn't come.

The guard took a step back from me and drew his gun. "Get over here, Wally!" he called to one of his colleagues who was still attending to the corpse. "Seems we've got a tag man who can't remember his name."

The man named Wally let Tiller's body fall with a thud and started walking toward me. "You better regain your memory real quick, mister, or you're liable to be going home in a bag too. Now, what's your name?"

"Tiller Tolles," I said.

Wally looked at the first guard, who gave a slight nod as if my reply checked out with whatever it was my mother had told them.

"All right, Tolles," said Wally. "Tell me everything I need to know to *not* put a bullet through you."

I quickly ran through a checklist of facts about my former friend; age, birthplace, identification number, firearm of choice. When I was finished, Wally seemed appeased.

"Sorry for the trouble, Tolles," he said. "Next time don't act like an idiot. We can't be too careful up here on the border. I'm sure you understand."

I produced a faint smile. "Are my, uh, associates still on the beach?"

"Nah. The older one showed me her company card and I knew right away we were dealing with a high-profile runner. She and the other babe took the truck back into Ely. Boy, that judge looked awful worn out by the time we got him into the glider."

"You say they were headed to Ely?"

"Yeah, and then to VC North in Minneapolis."

My heart sank.

"How come?" asked Wally.

"It's a long story," I said, starting in the direction of the barricade. "Do you have a vehicle around here?"

"Sure, but—"

"I'll bring it back as soon as possible," breaking into a sprint.

"Hey! We need the jeep for transportation," shouted the first guard. But by then there was a great deal of distance between us and I could see the hood of a jeep jutting from a thick stand of tamaracks. The keys would be in it, no doubt. Nobody on the edge of the wilderness fears robbery. Greater dangers plague them.

"What do you want us to do with the body?" the first guard shouted again.

I paused momentarily. "Give him a decent burial," I replied, though I knew they'd have to take Tiller back to VC.

"Don't you want the tag?" the guard cried.

I was already in the seat, turning the key and backing away from the barricade. "Add it to your quota," I called over my shoulder as I drove away.

Out on the highway, I sped south with the wind in my face and hot tears collecting on my sideburns. It would be impossible to catch a plane in Ely, but I could overtake them in Minneapolis. Who knew what I would do with them if I succeeded? I'm not sure I knew. Nothing was sure, anymore; not the Shadow Train, not the promises of a parent, not even a kiss between a woman and a man. All of Peter's words of wisdom rushed past me with the wind and the mosquitoes, and I did not try to grasp any of it.

On the horizon, a billboard loomed ominously and seemed to peer at pedestrians like a great, wise grandfather. I tried to look away from its message, to focus my eyes on the broken white line that stretched for miles ahead. But it was no use. The message was too old, too compelling, too embedded in the hearts of humanity to be ignored. I stopped the jeep on the shoulder of the road and stared up at the sign. "THE HIGHEST SACRIFICE FOR THE GREATEST GOOD," it read.

I put the jeep in park, closed my eyes and thought of the dead judge list in my pocket. Even that seemed useless now. I could not escape those seven words on the back of my eyelids.

THE HIGHEST SACRIFICE FOR THE GREATEST
GOOD.

"They betrayed me!" I shouted to the sky and forest. I
leaned against the steering wheel and buried my face in my
arms. For a moment, I imagined I heard the sound of a legendary train whistling away into nothingness. Then my mind
locked onto a single image of deceit dressed in a monk's hood.

"If the blast didn't kill him—I will," I uttered solemnly.

17

*"Let him know that he who has turned a sinner
from his wandering way will save his brother's
soul from death and will hide a multitude of his
own sins."*

—James, the half-brother of Jesus

THOUGH NIGHT HAD BEGUN TO FALL WHEN
I arrived in Minneapolis, I still wore sunglasses to disguise my
identity. Already the city was abuzz with the very thing I feared.
I found out the news when I ordered breakfast for dinner at a
dim, sebaceous diner and listened to the waitress arguing with
the cook through a little window in the wall.

"The girls over at Nick's got the night off," she said sullenly.
"How come we ain't got the night off?"

"'Cause this ain't no national holiday, sweetheart," said the
cook, who also happened to be the owner of that dingy estab-
lishment.

The waitress threw a wet rag on the counter and wiped it
around in violent circles.

"Well, it oughta be."

"The heck it should. Far as I'm concerned, we give them
Long Shadows more publicity than they deserve. It'll be a cold
day in Cuba before I pay any of my help to watch television."

"You could lose your license for not letting your employees
go to the viewing."

"I hope that ain't a threat. 'Cause if it is, then two can play
that game, sweetheart."

WILL CUNNINGHAM

The waitress tried a new tactic. "Pleeeease," she pleaded. "It's a bigwig being terminated."

"I don't care if it's the president of the United States," said the cook.

"You wouldn't want poor old Betty, your favorite night shift girl to be the only one who missed it, would ya?"

The cook's forehead turned as red as the onion he was chopping. "I want poor old Betty to pick up order number three with the side of hash browns before she finds herself unemployed!"

"Excuse me, sir," I said, playing dumb.

The cook pivoted toward me. I could tell he was standing on tiptoe, because now I saw his eyes and a bit of his red, twitching nose above the window ledge.

"Yah? Whaddya want?"

"I couldn't help overhearing your conversation, and I was wondering who's being terminated on VOX tonight."

"Geez, mister. Where ya been the last couple of weeks?"

Betty shot her boss a punitive look for his rudeness and turned to me sweetly. "Never mind him," she whispered. "He gets a little cranky whenever there's a mandatory viewing. I mean, it's good for business and everything, but all them people from the suburbs sort of make him *closter* phobic."

"So," I said, dreading the response I was about to receive. "Do you know who the Long Shadow is?"

Betty eyed the tag man emblem on my jacket and leaned seductively on the counter. "Sure I know. He's that fellow who was supposed to be terminated a couple of days ago."

I gave her a confused look.

"You know. That guy who wrote the legal stuff on Long Shadow. I think his name's Nash, or something."

My heart was racing but I continued my charade. "Nash, Nash. It rings a bell."

"Anyway, this Nash guy has been running since the first of May, and when the tags finally catch him he says—get this—he says, 'I was just trying to buy time to work on my memoirs.'"

"Where did you hear that?" I asked.

"Good gravy, mister, you work for VC. Don't you ever pay attention to what goes on on VOX?"

"Well—"

"I heard Ms. Roberta on the afternoon report tell the whole thing," said the woman, handing me my plate of eggs.

"The afternoon report!" bellowed the cook from behind a greasy cloud of steam. "No wonder you come draggin' in here at night. You ain't sleepin' during off-hours."

"He's cranky," said Betty, repeating her diagnosis. Before I could respond, she swept through a door into the kitchen, as if a hundred other cooks awaited her commands there. I looked at my food, and it seemed suddenly unappealing to me.

"Where do I pay?" I called through the greasy window.

"On the counter," shouted the cook.

I found the digit slot by the sugar, placed my forefinger in it, waited for verification of funds, then left that place with my fried eggs still staring at the ceiling.

A block away, I found a spot on the edge of the youthful crowd. There was nothing else I could do but wait for the interview, so I sat down and soon I was swept into a river of emotions.

"What's a guy like him trying to do?" said one young man, as he angrily flung a neon sport disk off into the dark. In a moment the disk came flying back to him. This time he put more venom into his toss. "If he doesn't want to live by the law, he shouldn't have written it in the first place."

"It wasn't a law, you moron," said someone nearby. "It was a majority opinion that *led* to a law."

The young man glared at his detractor. "Whatever it was, he still has a duty to turn himself in for termination, same as everybody else. That's the way we do things in this country."

To my left I saw a knot of tag men scanning the crowd for signs of disloyalty to the greatest good. It amused me to watch them, having been trained in the same techniques that allow one to look at a person and know immediately what he is thinking.

Raised eyebrow? An obvious disapproval in the last statement spoken. Foot tapping nervously? The sure sign of a Long Shadow about to run. And so forth. It was not a science, but we sure made people think it was. I felt a twang of guilt.

"Good evening," Mother's voice boomed at exactly nine o'clock.

Ten thousand heads jerked upward at the sound of her voice. The screen was filled with Mother's face, as poised and professional as every other time I'd seen her do her job. Next to her lay my father, clothed as Rossi had been, with a thin, white sheet and a feeble smile. The blue screen placed them somewhere in the South Pacific. Soothing. Inviting.

"Welcome to tonight's edition of *The Highest Sacrifice for the Greatest Good*," said Mother. "Our witness tonight for the greatest good is a man who actually needs no introduction. He is the one responsible for single-handedly curbing the rise of health care costs, at the same time emancipating our children and our children's children from ever again having to shoulder the kind of monetary burden that existed in the last century because of the elderly. Ladies and gentlemen, please give a warm welcome to former Supreme Court Justice, August Nash."

A roar went up from the crowd. "Hail to the greatest good! Hail to the greatest good! Hail to the greatest good! Hail to the greatest good!"

To my right, I heard a woman remarking that Roberta and the judge had the same last name. And beyond her, someone else shouted, "Get on with it!" But Mother was taking her time.

"Tonight I've decided to deviate from protocol," she said softly, which caused not a few tag men to shift their attention from the crowd to the screen. "As one might suspect with an organization as vast as this one, there's a need to revisit the philosophies behind what we do here at VC."

Suddenly, I noticed the scarf and I sat up straight, craning to see over the man's head in front of me. Without taking her eyes off the camera, Mother removed the familiar red garment and laid it across my father's chest.

"At the core of VC is the constant tension between perception and reality," said Mother, leaning over to the wall and pushing a button similar to the one she had pushed that morning at Rossi's interview. In the background, I heard the *whoosh* and *click* of a door shutting tight. She pushed another button, and the crowd gasped as the South Pacific faded into dingy drywall.

"Most of you perceive that you know the man lying next to me, here," said Mother. "You've read about him in history books, taken notes in freshman social studies about his contribution to government, maybe even produced your own short biography of his life. But do you really know him?" The cameras zoomed in on Father's face and I could tell that the crowd was glued to Mother's words in a way that they had never been before. "In reality he was a good man," she continued, "faithful to his principles and to the greatest good of humanity."

"To the greatest good!" cried the people dutifully. On the fringe of the crowd, the tag men rubbernecked to better scrutinize their subjects.

Mother paused and I found that I could not take my eyes off the scarf.

"When I was a child," continued Mother, "I believed in the reality of Santa Claus, largely because my father said it was true. Since Father was a good and honest man, I clung to the belief with all of my heart. Of course, it wasn't difficult making oneself believe in such a thing. Who *wouldn't* have faith in a kindly, old gentleman delivering toys through the night air?"

Mother hesitated.

"You can imagine the blow to my little girl's psyche when I discovered that my perception of Santa was more of a hope than a reality and that Father had not been completely on the level with me. With some embarrassment and not a little anger, I severed my outward allegiance to Santa. Inwardly, however, I always kept my memory of him intact."

At that point, there began a vague and hollow knock just slightly off camera, that grew louder and more incessant as the interview progressed.

"Naturally, the childish perception of Santa diminished as the years went on," continued Mother. "But the growing sentiment of public indifference toward the elderly made me secretly afraid for my imaginary friend in his sleigh. *Certainly some people still think well of him*, I remember hoping. I dreamed of meeting someone half as good as him. Then one day that dream became a reality."

Mother looked at my father, who gave her a tired wink. She squeezed his hand and continued, seemingly oblivious to the enormous pounding in the background.

"August and I were married almost immediately," she continued.

There was a perceptible gasp from the crowd.

"At first, marriage was like a gift from the celestial sleigh-driver. We cherished it throughout our early days in Washington. However, August's appointment to the bench soon changed all that. At times, he worked such long hours that I wondered if we even knew each other anymore. Then that terrible day arrived when August was asked to write the majority opinion on Long Shadow."

The pounding suddenly gave way to the sound of a blow torch.

"I suppose the pressure of the interest groups was the worst part about it all," Mother said hurriedly. "Hardly a night went by that some representative from this caucus or that caucus didn't ring our phone, pleading to see my husband, saying the most cataclysmic things would happen if he or she was not permitted to take my husband out for a drink or to the theater. It finally got so bad that we had to have police protection around the clock. Even with those measures, the pressures eventually got to him," said Mother, fighting back tears.

By then, the entire audience was looking around at one another, and the tag men seemed thoroughly perplexed. The sound of the blow torch rang hot and continuous.

"Once we found out how serious this decision was, it wasn't easy being married to a man who had signed his name to the death warrant of every friend he ever had, including his brother and his son."

What happened next was the most triumphant moment of my short life. Though weakened from the long journey to the border of Canada and back, Father sat upright on the table and stared into the camera with a lucidity I had only seen in ancient pictures of him.

"I am truly sorry for the bad piece of officiating I gave to you twenty-five years ago," he said clearly. "My intent, I believe, was pure in the initial stages of the work. Unfortunately the end product, which has come to be known as the majority opinion on Long Shadow, reflects how utterly astray a man can go when he ceases to be true to himself and his God, and embarks upon the slippery slope of pleasing everyone. I am responsible for the pain caused by widespread, active genocide, and for that I am truly sorry. As for the greatest good," concluded Father, glancing furtively at the door just off camera, "there is nothing good about the concept."

A muffled roar exploded from the crowd and now there were shouts and curse words mingling with the audio signal. In horror, I watched as an iron rod bashed a hole through the door of the studio.

Mother kicked at the rod. "Tell them about the ashes," she urged my father.

WILL CUNNINGHAM
256

"I found out what happens to the ashes when I was presiding over a case involving the EPA and some tobacco farmers in North Carolina. A lot of people discovered the secret about the ashes during that case, a lot of people who don't work in Washington anymore. Most of them are dead now, murdered by a government bent on ruining every farmer who refused to—"

The high-pitched squeal of hinges breaking loose from the wall filled the air.

"Hurry, Auggie!" said Mother.

My father pointed into the camera. "You ought to be mad as the devil at a system that allows tag men to escape their T-dates if they bring in enough Long Shadows."

The shocking news drew glares from the crowd and I could see that the tag men were getting nervous. Suddenly, the door crashed into the room, narrowly missing Mother and sending pieces of the operating table in every direction. The screen went momentarily blank, followed by a satellite feed of Dr. Solomon DeJong trying to calm the crowd. But it was too late. All hell had broken loose.

"Down with VC!" shouted someone in the crowd, followed by "Get the tag men! Don't let them get away!"

I whipped off my jacket and threw it in the gutter. Then I was running, leaping over bushes, darting up and down side streets as I desperately tried to find my way back to the jeep. Finally, in a secluded alleyway where I had parked upon arriving in Minneapolis, I found the vehicle. But someone else had found it too.

"Hello, John." The voice from the jeep was full of pain. Its owner leaned into the circumference of the street lamp's light and I saw that it was Sarah. Her jeans were wet with blood from her thighs to her shoes.

"You're . . . bleeding," I said, staring at Sarah's legs.

Immediately, she doubled over and clutched her abdomen. "I tried not to run very fast. But I saw the hate in the crowd's eyes when your father told them the truth. All I could think of was getting my baby as far away from them as possible. I never meant to . . ."

She began to sob helplessly, just as the mob rounded the corner of the alley and recognized us.

"I seen them two at the rally!" shouted one man. "They're VC!"

"Get 'em!" screamed another.

As the mob rushed toward us, I picked up Sarah and placed her gently in the passenger's seat. The last human I ever terminated arrived at the jeep just as I cranked the key and felt the engine lurch to attention. I didn't want to kill him. I hoped he could read in my eyes some sign of reformation, but he lashed at me blindly with an iron bar. When I shot him in self-defense, his eyes snapped out like streetlights in a dismal dawn. All the way to St. Paul, I saw the red on Sarah's jeans and that man's pupils rolling back into this head. At Vivi-Natal, I trusted Sarah into the hands of orderlies and ran to admissions.

"I'm sorry, tag man Nash," came the tinny voice of the automated receptionist. "According to my records you've been deceased for 9.34 hours. Please check your entry data and try again. Thank you."

I rekeyed the data and the results came back the same. "TRY AGAIN, THANK YOU . . . TRY AGAIN, THANK YOU . . . TRY AGAIN, THANK YOU . . . TRY—"

"Admit her, you stupid machine!" I screamed at the screen.

"Are you all right?" asked a passing orderly.

"No, I'm not all right!" I said curtly. "I'm trying to admit a friend. She's bleeding to death as we speak!"

"Take it easy, buddy," said the orderly. "If it's the woman I think you're talking about, then there's nothing to worry about. We got some units into her as soon as we knew her blood type. There's a doctor looking at her right now. She's going to be just fine."

The orderly hurried away and I looked back at the screen. Strangely, the word *deceased* had a calming effect on me. It was as if a thousand new exhilarating possibilities had been opened to me suddenly. For a long time, I floated around Vivi-Natal's sterile confines, waiting for Sarah, looking out through tiny windows at an unfamiliar moon, holding up my fingers and delighting at the touch of new moonlight on newly recreated skin.

According to the computer, I was deceased—yet I had never felt so alive. At last I heard the doors to the particle transport slide open and saw Sarah in a wheelchair coming toward me, followed by a doctor with a clipboard.

"She's lost a lot of blood," said the doctor, as I rushed to embrace Sarah. She buried her face in my chest.

"Thank you," I said, holding out my hand to the doctor. "Thank you for all your help."

The doctor coughed and looked at his shoes. "I'm sorry about the baby," he said quickly. "Of course, I'll need to ask you a few questions."

"Of course."

"What is your relationship to Miss . . . er . . . Miss . . ." He checked the chart on his clipboard.

"McSwain," I replied, still holding Sarah tightly to me.

"Yes, McSwain," confirmed the doctor. "And what is your relation—"

"I'm her husband," I said suddenly.

Sarah caught her breath.

"Pardon me?" said the doctor, suspiciously.

"I'm her husband."

"Are you American citizens? I mean, there are laws against marriage and babies being made outside a matri-sak."

I paused and looked at Sarah. "We're Canadians. We came down to view the termination."

"I see," said the doctor, his eyes darting to the chart again. "Well, it's not often that we deal with this sort of thing. It would help if I could see some sort of identification. What did you say your name was?"

"McSwain . . . John and Sarah McSwain."

The doctor squinted suspiciously and was just suggesting that we step into his office to contact border authorities, when his name was called over the loudspeaker and he had to hurry off in the same direction the orderly had taken.

I took Sarah gingerly by the arm. "Can you walk?" I asked, looking around, expecting VC guards to scuttle in like rats from the woodwork at any moment.

"I'll go as fast as I can," replied Sarah.

"On second thought I'll carry you, because it won't be long before someone catches wind of this." Quickly, I lifted Sarah out of the chair and rushed toward an exit.

Outside on the sidewalk, the air was crisp and invigorating. I helped Sarah into the Jeep and glanced around one more time to see if anyone was watching.

"To Canada," I said, as we pulled away from the curb. "I just hope they won't kill us at the border."

"They won't if we're already dead," replied Sarah.

"You, too?"

Sarah smiled weakly. "I told the computer I felt too good to be dead, but she wouldn't believe me. She kept coming back with, 'Please reenter data. Please reenter data.'"

"This is bizarre," I said, as I wheeled the Jeep northward toward I-35.

"Not really," said Sarah matter-of-factly.

"What do you mean?"

"When you and August left last night, Roberta was up in a flash. She and I were out of there before the explosion. She told me the plan on the way to the border, as clearly as if she had thought it through years ago and had been rehearsing it ever since."

"She never intended to take Dad to Canada?"

"Oh, yes, she did. But she and Peter knew him so well, they predicted he wouldn't let her."

"I'll kill that liar if I ever see him again."

"There'll be no need for that, John. As far as I know, he died in the blast."

"Serves him right. He was using us the whole time," I said angrily.

"Not at all," countered Sarah. "He fought for your father with all his might, and he knew him like the back of his hand. That's why he figured Fishback would turn him around. But he never suspected it would make him want to go back to VC and blow the whistle on the whole rotten system. My hunch is that was the only way your father knew to make up for his Long Shadow ruling."

"They let him go back," I whispered incredulously.

"Yes, they did," said Sarah. She hesitated, then put her hand on my shoulder. "And Roberta went back with him, because she loved him, John. Just like I love you."

My heart skipped once. "You what?"

"I love you."

"Say it again."

"I . . . love . . . you."

The words were so intoxicating that I nearly steered into a ditch.

"Watch the road," laughed Sarah, but even her laugh was a spirited tonic that went straight to my head. I had lived with the hope for so long, dreamed of it night after night exactly the same each time, waited with breath held, and now that it had come to pass I was completely out of my element, gasping for air like a fish freshly netted from the Sea of Surreal.

"Then you didn't mind me telling that doctor I was your husband?" I asked.

"No, but a formal proposal would be nice."

"If we make it to Canada, will you marry me, Sarah?" I asked immediately.

"Only if we go by Nash instead of McSwain," she replied, leaning over and brushing her lips softly against mine.

When I finally regained control of the Jeep I broke the news. "Truth is, we'll probably go by neither," I said solemnly.

"How so?" asked Sarah.

"John Nash and Sarah McSwain are dead, remember? From now on, whether we like it or not, you and I will be known as Mr. and Mrs. Tiller Tolles."

Sarah wrinkled her nose distastefully. "Does that mean—"

"Yep, I'll have to get another face job. I know a plastic surgeon on the north end of St. Paul who won't ask a lot of questions. I think he could make me look like Tiller Tolles in no time at all."

"I suppose it could be worse," said Sarah.

I looked at Sarah and then on past her to the new world over her shoulder, the newly minted trees and parks and city halls and dwelling places, all under the light of a moon that cast scarcely a shadow. And finally I looked back at Sarah.

"Yes, it could," I said, smiling ahead at the road. "It certainly could be worse."

18

*"He paid a price He did not owe, to cancel a debt
I could not pay."*

IT TOOK A LONG TIME FOR SARAH AND ME TO
recover from all the savage things we had done. The process
might have remained incomplete, had it not been for a certain
blustery night in our seventh year at King's Point, Canada, on
Basswood Lake. I had left my wife alone in our cabin to go in
search of kindling and was in a clearing, scarcely fifty yards
from the door, when I heard a twig snap.

"Wolves," I whispered to no one at all, and I looked toward
a spot in the woods where cabin light fell between fir and birch,
then dissolved to black. Suddenly, I felt a hand on my shoulder
and whirled around to see a man who, in spite of the hood that
covered his face, seemed familiar to me.

"Can I help you with something?" I asked.

The man cocked his head sideways and listened. "They
never come this close to humans unless they're right on the tail
of something weak and tasty. Probably a deer or a moose calf."
With a sweep of his left hand, he brushed back his hood.

"Peter!" I exclaimed.

"The rumors of my death are slightly exaggerated," he said,
guessing my thoughts. He grabbed me and wrapped me in a
bear hug.

"But the blast—"

"A few cuts and burns . . . no deaths. It wasn't as bad as it looked. In fact, I'm feeling better than I've felt in a long time. By the way, I want you to know I don't hold anything against you."

"Could you ever forgive me for that night in the basement?"

"Forget the basement," said Peter. "When a man discovers a room full of sodium pentothal, he can't help but suspect a VC operation."

Peter had aged considerably since we saw each other last. As we hugged, I could feel his thin backbone through his coat. Finally, he stepped back and held me at arm's length. "What have you done to your face, John?" he asked.

I smiled and extended my hand for a formal introduction. "The name's Tolles. *Tiller* Tolles."

Peter laughed heartily, the sound of it echoing around the clearing. "You're no more Tolles than I'm a poached egg."

"You have to admit I look a lot like him."

Peter studied my face and shook his head disapprovingly. "In the face, maybe. But certainly not in the heart."

"Well, what can you expect from government work?"

"Which is exactly what brings me here on such a frozen evening. Would you mind if we talked a minute about government work?" He said these last two words with some effort.

"A minute is all I can stomach," I replied, glancing toward the woods again. "Besides, those wolves—"

"Don't worry about the wolves. They've got what they were after." Peter lowered his voice, as if even in those woods agents from Vivi-Centerre might be lurking. "VC's finally caught on to what we were doing at Tonsus. They know everything about the Shadow Train."

"Everything?"

"They've closed down monasteries all over the country and replaced the monks with their own people."

"Are any of the routes still open?"

"All blocked, I'm afraid."

"Dakota City?"

Peter nodded. "Bob Harold's One-Stop is now a bar and grill."

"What about the borders?"

"VC tightened up everything the minute your Mom and Dad—"

The two of us fell silent at the mention of my parents. After a minute or two, Peter kicked at a snow drift.

"I've been wondering if the Shadow Train might be wise to pioneer some new trails," he said. "Maybe the Pacific Coast, or some of the side roads that parallel Highway 1. Vancouver would be the jumping-off point."

"Why not just retire?" I said quickly.

"I will," said Peter. "But that doesn't mean the problem retires with me. Did you know that twelve-year-olds are being allowed into the tag corps now? And termination age has just been lowered from fifty to forty-three. There's only so much a man my age can do. I don't move as well as I used to."

I was silent, but Peter pressed ahead as if he understood my fear and disregarded it at the same time.

"I want you to come to work with me," he said resolutely.

It took a moment to find my voice. "I can't do that."

"Why not?"

"I have a wife, a . . . a future—"

Peter glared at me. "There's an entire population in the lower forty-eight who dream of having a future."

A strange sense of self-preservation rose in my chest. "Is there something so horrible about wanting to live in peace?" I asked.

"No," said Peter, shaking his head. "I just thought you might have developed a little more compassion since I saw you last. I figured if you had your face reworked—"

"I had my face reworked because my mother filed a report on *my* death instead of Tiller's. It was the perfect opportunity to melt away into nonexistence. And believe me, Sarah and I are quite happy not existing."

"Did you ever stop to wonder why your mother would file a report the way she did?" asked Peter.

"No," I admitted sullenly.

"She knew exactly what she was doing, John. She wanted you to be a conductor. She dreamed of the day you would take over the Shadow Train."

"I am *not* interested in taking over the Shadow Train!" I said loudly, no longer caring about the wolves. "I am sick and tired of killing people or seeing them get killed or bringing them in to be killed or reading about them being killed. I have had it up to *here* with death!"

"The truth is," corrected Peter, stepping forward and seizing me by the collar with one hand, "you don't even want to share your private paradise with the living." He pointed to the sky with his stump of an arm. "Look up and see the heart of God," he commanded.

I obeyed reluctantly and caught a snowflake in the eye.

"He knows the name of every pinhole up there," said Peter, his eyes blazing. "He has stock in that faint, blue one to the left of Polaris, and a very special interest in that one over there on the snout of Draco the Dragon. Sometimes on summer nights, when the bugs are all out dancing and the earth has spun around for a different view, God drops everything and thinks of nothing but Orion. But did you know, John—" And this is where Peter's grip began to feel like a vise. "If a star fell every time God thought of *you*, the heavens would be empty!"

The silence of the wilderness leaned heavily on my soul.

"What's it going to be?" asked Peter. "The security of King's Point? Or the uncertainty of the Shadow Train?"

"Can't I have a little time to think it over?" I pleaded.

Peter raised his hood against the cold and regarded me with two bright sparks that burned beneath his ample brow. "There *is* no time to think it over."

Another twig snapped, followed by the brief bellowing of something soft and defenseless. Peter eyed the woods. When he spoke again his voice was hauntingly soft.

"I had a grandfather who lived near Auschwitz in the late 1930s. His name was Jack. He went to a fine, big church in the village, and the church happened to be located right next to the railroad tracks. 'Believe me, son,' he used to say when I was young, 'it was a godawful place to worship on those Sundays when the führer was shipping Jews to be burned. You could hear them screaming for our help as they rumbled past. It was almost as if they had flung their last hopes on us, the gentiles, and if we couldn't save them, nobody could. Problem was, we knew we couldn't. It quickly became our custom to schedule our choral worship just as the trains were passing by. Sing a little louder!—the choir master used to implore us. So, we closed our eyes, lifted our hands to heaven and sang a little louder. And none of us ever heard the pathetic cries or the terrible condemnation of our own cowardice.'"

"I told you a long time ago that I'm not a coward," I said angrily.

"There's coward in us all, boy," asserted Peter. When he addressed me as *boy*, instead of *brother*, I felt for a moment that I was a boy, standing in some other bank of snow, in some other time, but with the same terrible lump in my throat. I stared at Peter as if he were a phantom.

"It's one of the sins of our fathers," he murmured. "It comes down to us in the genes—mixed up with the brown eyes and the black hair and the varying shades of skin. Grandpa Jack had a little coward in him. He passed it to his son, Edward, who passed it down to me and my brother."

Peter paused to contemplate his next words.

"Now I could never summarize my own cowardice, since I'm a man and it's the nature of men to minimize their own shortcomings. But I can tell you succinctly that my brother used his portion of that dark inheritance to write the majority opinion on Long Shadow."

I choked suddenly and backed up into the six-foot patch of light that bounced into the yard through the cabin's only window.

"You heard correctly," said the man, who until recently I had assumed was Peter Edmunds. "Your father and my brother are one in the same."

Somewhere in the distance, a pine bough gave up its burden of snow with a muffled thud.

"Get away from me, or I'll kill you!" I shouted.

"If you need more identification, I'll gladly provide it," he said, taking a step toward me. He wiped the air in front of his face, as if he were removing the dust from a very old memory. "Picture a foggy day on a parade field . . . a sixteen-year-old boy and his uncle deep in discussion over an android professor in Social Reasoning 102 . . . a tragic disappointment . . . a nephew wounded . . . a temporary end to a wonderful relationship."

"I said get away from me!"

"Perhaps it would help if I reminded you that it was I who pressed those few, grimy pages of wisdom into your hand."

I stared at him, astonished. "Uncle Ames," I whispered.

"At your service," he said with a smile.

Suddenly I recognized him. Beneath the wonder of plastic surgery, there was a mannerism about him that only a relative would know. So overwhelmed was I, that I hardly noticed my arms reaching out for him.

"May I—"

"Hug me? Well, I would certainly hope for more than a handshake after all these years."

For a few moments, the two of us clung to each other and forgot about the wolves.

"My dear nephew, John," said Ames, his arms like iron bands around me. "I'm sorry I didn't tell you earlier, but I had to know that you were for real. You have no idea how hard it was to keep the secret."

"You have no idea how much I've missed you," I breathed into his gray hair. "Thank you for coming back to me. Thank you for keeping your promise."

"My generation's not so bad after all, are we?" said Uncle Ames.

Suddenly, a thought dawned on me and I jerked back to have another look at him. "But if you're not Peter Edmunds, then who is?"

"The man who wore this face before me," replied Uncle Ames nonchalantly. He laughed when he saw my confusion. "It has been the way of Tonsus since the abbey's conception. No one knows for sure how many men have played the part of Peter. I'd sure like to meet the original one someday. I'll forever be indebted to the Peter Edmunds who returned to VC Midwest in my place and took my termination, so that I might become the head of the Shadow Train."

Instantly, I remembered the portrait. "You mean—"

Uncle Ames nodded. "When you discovered the laboratory and made the wrong conclusion, there was nothing we could do but abort the mission."

The sodium pentothal . . . the body bags . . . the doctor. I looked at my uncle in disbelief. "You were going to switch places with him?"

Peter nodded. "Not that he was in any shape to head the Shadow Train, but at least I could have given him a chance at happiness again."

"You were going to die for him," I murmured, incredulous.

"What more can a brother do?" said Uncle Ames.

"But I thought you hated him."

"All that was changed when I found out what real love is," said Uncle Ames. "It doesn't always come to us in neat packages. Sometimes it's a pretty bloody affair. My Lord could attest to that."

I looked at Uncle Ames's stump and a wave of remorse swept over me when I realized I had prevented my father's rescue. "I didn't know," I cried.

"No use being hard on yourself," said Ames. "The way your mother saw it, August would never be fit for freedom anyway. I was with her at Rivendale the day she came to that realization. I assure you, she wept bitterly."

"Then why all the effort along the way?" I asked. "Why the dance in the wheat field? Why the hugs and the tender words?"

Uncle Ames gave a shrug. "I've never been married. I suppose true love has a way of hoping for the best. The only thing I know for sure is that my feet are frozen."

We both looked down at our shivering legs and began to laugh heartily.

"Come on," I said. "There's a pot of coffee inside."

Deep into the night we talked, then back up the purple slope of dawn. By the time Sarah awakened, Uncle Ames was ready to leave, and in our hearts there was such a terrible sense of pending loss, that we stalled our farewells as long as possible. When at last I saw that his departure was inevitable, I threw my arms around him and hugged him like a child.

"Which way are you going?" I asked, choking back my emotions.

"I've never met a man who went wrong going due north," Uncle Ames replied. "As a matter of fact, I'll be traveling that direction for the rest of my life if no brave soul comes along to spell me."

Uncle Ames eyed Sarah and me gravely, as if to extract our decision about the Shadow Train. I looked away to the north.

"Well, if there's nothing left to say," said Uncle Ames, bending down to pick up his pack.

Suddenly, I sprang forward. "I'll take the Shadow Train," I blurted. "That is if Sarah will take it with me."

For half a minute there wasn't a sound. Then from the bottom of Sarah's throat I heard a sort of choking murmur followed by her voice on a clear, exhilarating note.

"What are we waiting for?" she cried happily.

"I never doubted it for a minute," said Uncle Ames, smiling. "I saw the way you handled yourself on the farm that night, with all the craziness of the gliders crashing in on us! It takes a steady hand to lead the Shadow Train. I can think of no one better for the job than you."

"Thank you," I said, somewhat embarrassed.

Uncle Ames crossed his arms, stood back and surveyed me. "So you'll take the Shadow Train," he said with a smile.

"*We'll* take the Shadow Train," corrected Sarah.

Uncle Ames nodded satisfactorily. "Well, then I should warn you both that more often than not the Shadow Train will take *you* to places you hadn't counted on going; cold swamps where cypress grow and water moccasins wait on logs for no one in particular; bogs bordered by grass so old and thick that it cuts you when you wade through it. At times, you will take your meals in stagnant creek beds, rank with moss and mud, all under gray, weeping skies with a wind blowing. But there will be fair times, too; January nights in woods of jack pine where the snow lies purple and deep, a perfect spot for a rendezvous of squirrels. You will sit at leisure on plateaus along the Floyd River, in the morning hours with the morning smells. On days like these, you will think that Canada is just around the corner and the life of a conductor is the only life for you. However, you will soon find that Canada is *always* around the corner and the rest is *always* miles away—never forget these things, for your sake or the Long Shadows who are traveling with you."

"I won't. I promise."

Uncle Ames's eyes twinkled. "Your father was like that. Same spark, same tenacity. It couldn't help being passed to you."

With that, Uncle Ames hoisted his pack and set off in the direction of Hudson Bay. Whatever his mission was, he seemed determined to make good time, though his legs appeared less eager than the rest of him. He was nearly a hundred yards away when I remembered something and called to him.

"What about the ashes?"

Uncle Ames turned slowly, and even though he cupped his hands to his mouth, I could barely make out what he was saying.

"I put them on my tulips," he shouted.

"You what?"

Ames tried again. "My *tulips*. I put them on my *tulips*. It didn't seem right to put them on the wheat fields."

Suddenly, the mystery of the ashes unraveled for me. Ames's garden bloomed in my mind. And then I imagined a fleet of gaily painted bakery trucks, crisscrossing the free world, shuttling nourishment to a billion beguiled savages.

The ashes. The fertilizer. The wheat.

"They make bread out of *us*," I uttered into the wind.

"What's that?" asked Sarah.

The concept of a government making food out of its citizens made me gag, and all I could think about was a very old movie I had seen as a child called, *Soylent Green,* and I realized that life had finally imitated art. "The bread is us," I repeated. "We . . . we've got to tell. We've got to tell someone."

"I have no idea what you're talking about," said Sarah. She slid her slender arms around my waist and I turned to her with a rush of emotion. Her eyes held me most with their feverish spark, for they were the one feature about her that did not change whenever I awoke from my dreams—her eyes were an unquenchable light.

"Oh, Sarah," I whispered. And then, not wanting to burden my wife with the horror of it all, I said, "Never mind."

Looking back at that moment, I think I half expected Sarah to press me for an explanation, but she didn't say a word.

Instead, she drew me tightly to her. And forever after that when I found cause to be afraid, Sarah Tolles wrapped her arms around me and the dread of tomorrow dissolved with the pressure of her cheek against my chest.

At night the wind howls cold over Basswood Lake and the hail beats against the Canadian landscape with the sound of a thousand ancient gongs. Behind the old ranger station, a mound of earth is blanketed in crystalline baubles. I am an old man now, alone since Sarah's death. My skin no longer stretches tightly across chiseled cheekbones. Like my chest, it has capitulated to the dull tug of dust, as have my biceps, calves, and abdomen. I am a shell of what I used to be, but infinitely glad to be alive on King's Point.

My cabin has become a pilgrimage of sorts for Long Shadows who make it this far above the border. Over the water they come, their paddles flashing up and down like silver bird wings. They are Israel in the wilderness, fleeing the hated known for vaporous unknown, praising, grumbling, thanking, murmuring, all the while looking over their shoulders. As it was with their forefathers, there are signs to guide and comfort them; aurora borealis in exchange for fiery pillar, loons for quail, berries for manna, water and sap for milk and honey. From the south window I study these sojourners, noting occasionally that the hand of God reaches down to part the wind and urge them to my door. I welcome them with hot soup and bread. Some stay for a day or two. Most leave hastily in the direction of Yellow Knife. As always, I pray for the slow, trickling exodus until they disappear around the bend.

Once every few months, I meet secretly with fellow conductors and have my face reworked by a doctor to add appropriate antiquity. After all, Tiller Tolles at 65 must not look like Tiller Tolles at 20. It has been a chore returning to VC Midwest as my former partner. Such masquerading has disallowed the wounds of broken friendship to scab over and finally fade from my memory. Nevertheless, assuming the identity of a tag man does have its advantages. I cannot begin to convey to you how convenient it is to be trusted by Vivi-Centerre. And my clients who are now Canadians cannot begin to convey how glorious it is to grow old. They fairly dance for joy each time their arthritis flares up.

I come now to the end of my story. No doubt some readers have hovered over these words like sparrows in winter, looking for crumbs to sustain themselves. Others have flown away chapters ago. As for me, I will be conducting the Shadow Train until the day I die, because I steadfastly believe that a human life should never be cut shorter than its Maker intended.

Perhaps your own approaching T-date causes you to share my viewpoint. Impending death has a funny way of making pro-lifers of us all. Keep an ear to the wire and an eye out for me. I will be the man on your street corner with my hat pulled conspicuously low, or the passerby whose eye contact lingers slightly longer than necessary. In such moments, you will know that I have come for you, for your heart will run ahead of the greatest good and you will hear something deep within your soul shouting, "All aboard! All aboard! It's a great day for traveling. All aboard!"